Where Have all the Cowboys Gone?

A eep feeling of warmth settled low in Lauren's
st nach. She'd heard of love at first sight, was
th lust at first sight? She wanted to rip off his
sh t, pull down his jeans and discover whether
he eally was as well endowed as the bulge in his
gr n indicated. What was that song her best
fri d Ella loved so much? Something about forget
th horse, ride the cowboy? Suddenly, it made
p ct sense.

e gulped down some more champagne. Was
th illicit excitement of Vegas getting to her?
She never reacted so strongly to a man before
an it wasn't just alcohol coursing through her
ve s. It was pure unadulterated lust. She wanted
to an forwards and touch his full lower lip with
th ip of her tongue just to see how he tasted.

Where Have all the Cowboys Gone?

Kate Pearce

In real life, always practise safe sex.

First published in 2007 by
Cheek
Thames Wharf Studios
Rainville Road
London W6 9HA

Typeset by SetSystems Ltd, Saffron Walden, Essex

Printed and bound by Mackays of Chatham PLC

ISBN 978 0 352 34100 6

Prologue

Las Vegas

'Yee-ha!'

Lauren Redstone punched the air and smiled at her refection in the luxurious restroom of the Mandalay Bay hotel. She'd done it. She'd actually done it. Her company, Retro Girl, was going to provide the styling and props for a series of Professional Bull Rider commercials.

It was her first big break. Her first mini-roar of independence. Lauren unpinned her brown hair and let it fall around her shoulders. She'd come to Vegas to meet the PBR executives who were there for World Finals weekend. She'd travelled alone but she could still celebrate, right? She picked up her purse and headed for the noisy comfort of the bar on the far side of the casino.

It was a relief to kick off her high-heeled shoes and relax. How long was it since she'd sat back and really had fun? All she'd done for the last two years was work her ass off to make her business viable. She toasted herself with her glass.

Her third glass of champagne seemed to contain more bubbles than the others. She squinted at the glass. Exactly how many bubbles were there? She'd not touched a drink for months and the alcohol had gone straight to her head.

Lauren grabbed her champagne, slipped into her shoes and got unsteadily to her feet. She was starving. But this was Las Vegas. There had to be a buffet around somewhere. She was so engrossed in the loud swirling pattern of the carpet that she tripped over the outstretched toe of a black cowboy boot.

And collided with a large warm object. Before she hit the floor, a strong arm wrapped around her waist and pulled her close. Lauren stared into the amused face of a man she'd never seen before. Thanks to her, he wore the rest of his beer on his shirt.

'Are you OK, ma'am?'

Lauren simply gaped at him. He wore a brown cowboy hat and a checked denim shirt. His slow drawling speech made her feel warm and soft like toffee. She focused on his eyes which were the same blue-grey colour as his jeans.

'I'm not a ma'am.'

He grinned. 'Well, lucky old me.'

A drop of beer rolled off his chin onto his chest. Lauren caught it on her fingertip just before it disappeared below the first button on his shirt. His skin was rough and warm to the touch.

'I've made you all wet.'

His smile widened. 'There are a few things I'd like to say to that. But I reckon most of them would get my face slapped.' He settled her deeper into his lap as a waitress squeezed past the booth.

Lauren suppressed an uncharacteristic urge to giggle. Either he had a gun in his pocket or he was reacting as fiercely to her as she was to him. She felt breathless, as if all the chatter and clanging slot machines around them had ceased to exist.

'Can I buy you another beer?'

'Only if you tell me your name.'

She was almost disappointed when he moved her off his lap. 'I'm Lauren Redstone.' She held out her hand and realised she still held the empty champagne glass. He carefully removed it.

'Grayson Turner. And, just in case you're interested,

I'm not married either.' He kept hold of her hand and rubbed his calloused thumb along the edge of her palm.

Lauren managed to stop staring long enough to signal a waitress. When the drinks arrived, Grayson grimaced as he pressed a wad of napkins against the front of his beer-soaked shirt.

'Let me help, it was my fault, after all.' Lauren patted a folded napkin against his stomach, noting the flex of hard muscle beneath the shirt and the subtle hitch in his breathing as he reacted to her touch.

A deep feeling of warmth settled low in Lauren's stomach. She'd heard of love at first sight, was this lust at first sight? She wanted to rip off his shirt, pull down his jeans and discover whether he really was as well endowed as the bulge in his groin indicated. What was that song her best friend Ella loved so much? Something about forget the horse, ride the cowboy? Suddenly, it made perfect sense.

She gulped down some more champagne. Was the illicit excitement of Vegas getting to her? She'd never reacted so strongly to a man before and it wasn't just alcohol coursing through her veins. It was pure una-dulterated lust. She wanted to lean forwards and touch his full lower lip with the tip of her tongue just to see how he tasted.

'Lauren? Are you OK?'

'I'm fine. It's just that –' she waved helplessly in his direction '– I'm not in the habit of pouring beer over guys and it seems I've forgotten how to flirt.'

Grayson took a swig of beer and then focused his attention on her. 'You're doing fine from where I'm sitting.'

'I've just been too occupied with my business to do much socialising.' She gave him a brief airy overview of her deal with the PBR and was impressed by his intelligent remarks and obvious approval. In a few minutes of conversation he understood more about her struggle to succeed than her father ever would.

When she'd finished, he clinked his beer bottle against her glass. 'That takes guts, going into business alone. I've done it a couple of times and it isn't easy.'

His gaze remained direct, his focus entirely on her. She got her second pleasant surprise when he didn't immediately launch into a recital of his own achievements. While she smiled into his eyes her stomach rumbled. She pressed her hand to it.

'Hungry?' Grayson asked.

'I haven't eaten since lunch. That's where I was headed when I bumped into you.'

Grayson put down his beer. 'Would you like to have dinner with me?'

The bar seemed to get quieter as if everyone were holding their breath. Grayson held her gaze, his eyes steady, his demeanour relaxed. Something about his quiet patience resonated deep in Lauren's soul.

Grayson took out his wallet and left a tip for the waitress wedged under his empty beer bottle. He grinned at Lauren. 'I'd give you a business card but I don't carry them any more since horses can't read.'

Lauren choked back a smile. 'You really are a cowboy?'

He tipped back his hat. 'Hell, yes, ma'am.' He glanced around the crowded bar. 'Did you think I was one of those dime-store cowboys who never get their boots dirty?'

To cover her confusion, Lauren took out her business card and slipped it into his wallet. 'From what I've seen, most cowboys are great with animals and not so good at stringing a sentence together.'

Grayson got to his feet. 'There are always exceptions to every rule.' He tucked his wallet in the back pocket of his Wranglers and then held out his hand. 'Are you willing to risk it?'

Lauren studied his face. Part of her wanted to check for hidden cameras. The rest of her wanted a shot at experiencing her number-one fantasy – a night of passion with a real cowboy. Darn it, she was in Las Vegas. Nobody knew who she was. What better way to celebrate her independence than by living out a dream?

When they reached the bank of elevators, Grayson stopped. 'I'm going to have to change this shirt. I smell like a cheap bar.' He indicated a group of chairs in the centre of the lobby. 'Do you want to wait for me here?'

'It's OK. I'll come up and wait in your room.' Lauren couldn't believe she'd said that. She tensed and waited for his reaction. Her strange desire to stay close to him waged war with her deeply ingrained sense of caution.

He reclaimed her hand and punched a button on the elevator. By the time they reached the second level, the elevator was full. Lauren found herself backed up against the wall. Grayson shielded her with his body. Canned music burbled away and the press of bodies increased. He braced one hand above her head.

Lauren closed her eyes and inhaled his citrus after-shave. She shuddered as his lips brushed her hair. God, she wanted to lift her head and kiss him. His warm mouth grazed her temple releasing a rush of lust straight to her pussy. He moved again and the front of his damp shirt brushed her tight nipples.

She looked up, saw his intent expression and allowed his lips to meet hers. She forgot about the elevator and the crush of people as he slid his tongue inside her mouth and gently kissed her. With a sigh, she went on tiptoe to mould her body more intimately into his.

When Lauren opened her eyes, the elevator was empty. Grayson straightened and guided her into the corridor. At the door to his room, he hesitated.

'Just for the record, I don't usually invite women I've just met into my bedroom.'

'You didn't; I invited myself.'

Grayson smiled down at her. 'Well, as long as we're clear on that. Come on in.'

His suite smelt faintly of lemon and leather and was remarkably tidy. He took off his hat and ran his hand through his crow-black hair.

'Make yourself comfortable, I'll just be a minute.'

He disappeared into the bathroom. Lauren contemplated the flashy view of The Strip below. She was trembling. For the first time in her life she wanted to be reckless. Grayson seemed like a nice guy. He was obviously attracted to her. Why not take advantage of her anonymity and have the ride of her life?

Lauren took a deep breath and walked into the bathroom. The faucets were running and Grayson had finished unbuttoning his shirt. She paused to take in the glory of his muscled chest and flat stomach. He went still as she took the wet washcloth from his unresisting hand and rubbed it over his chest.

'Lauren . . .'

She followed the droplets of water down his belly and traced the snap of his jeans with her fingertip. Grayson's hands closed around her waist and he lifted her onto the edge of the vanity unit. His chest rose and fell with each laboured breath.

'Are you sure this is what you want?'

'Yes, aren't you?'

Grayson moved forwards, spreading her knees with his hips, hitching her skirt up to her waist. 'Honey, I'm more sure about this than of anything I've ever done before. God help me, it just feels right.'

Lauren wrapped her arms around his neck. The harsh fabric of his well-filled jeans against the silk of her panties only increased her desire for him. He bent his head, his blue eyes locked on hers. She tensed as his mouth descended and then relaxed into the kiss. He kissed with a restraint she knew he was far from feeling judging by the urgent pressure of his cock against her pussy. The sharp edge of his belt buckle jammed into her stomach. She struggled to insert her hand between their bodies to release it.

He groaned deep in his throat as her fingers worked on his belt and the button of his jeans. She stroked his shaft through the denim, amazed at her boldness, enthralled by his response to it. He tilted his hips, allowing her a glimpse of the crown of his huge cock as it fought its way out of his jeans.

She slid her hand inside and slowly lowered the zipper. His kisses became more urgent as she cradled his shaft. Turned on by the thickness and length, her body softened in anticipation.

'Wait.' He closed his hand over hers and drew back. 'Let me see you.'

Grayson ripped off her pantyhose and stared at the thin black scrap of satin between her legs. He licked his lips as he drew the panties down her legs. He licked her with a voracious need that soon had her pushing her pussy into his face and grabbing his hair to keep his inventive mouth locked onto her.

The slick wet sound of his lapping and the suck of his fingers as he slid them in and out echoed through the bathroom. Lauren didn't care, her attention focused on her fast-approaching orgasm. Grayson continued to circle her sex with his tongue as he searched blindly through his washbag.

Lauren took the condom out of his hand and covered his straining shaft. Without further urging, he wrapped one hand around the base of his cock and positioned it between her legs.

'Tell me you want me. Tell me it's still OK.'

His terse words almost destroyed Lauren's sexual high. He was being way too considerate for a man she never expected to see again. Dammit, but she wanted him. In answer, she pulled him close, driving his cock deep inside her wet entrance. She came almost immediately, clenching around his thick shaft with all her strength. He kept thrusting, making her peak again. His hands were busy pushing her blouse out of his way. His hot mouth latched onto a taut nipple.

Lauren edged closer until her butt almost slid off the counter top. She wrapped her legs around his pumping hips and surrendered to the surge of his cock inside her. As her climax built for the third time she wrenched her mouth away from his, afraid she'd bite right through his luscious lower lip. She screamed her pleasure as Grayson came, his last urgent thrust made her spasm around him again.

When she could finally breathe, Lauren just stared at Grayson. She'd never come three times before in one night in her life. He smiled and tucked a strand of her hair behind her ear. He slowly eased out of her but held her close. She realised she liked the way he smelt. She wanted to nuzzle his skin, lick off the combination of sex and sweat until he was ready for her again.

'Do you still want to get dinner?'

She pointed at the phone. 'Does this hotel have room service?'

Laughing, he picked her up and headed for the bedroom.

An hour later, Lauren sat up and straddled his chest. 'We'll have to go down.'

He smiled up at her, his eyes lazy with lust, his whole body relaxed beneath hers. 'Why's that?'

'Because we have no more condoms.'

He groaned and rubbed at his eyes. 'Damn it, you're right. I wasn't expecting to meet a beautiful demanding woman like you. I only came to Vegas to watch the bull riding and do a little gambling.'

Lauren stroked his nipple. 'I could just go.' She shrieked as he sat up and dragged her hands behind her back.

He glanced down at his cock which now nestled between her breasts. 'I don't think so.' His erection grew as they stared at it. 'We're not finished yet.'

Lauren attempted to climb off him but he pushed her down into the tangled bedclothes.

'How about I make sure you want to come back upstairs with me?' He lowered his head and kissed his way down her stomach. Her hips jerked forwards as he traced her swollen sex with his tongue. She closed her eyes as he lapped at her, his strokes sure and powerful, his finger sliding inside to complete her pleasure. She grabbed the bedcovers as her tension mounted and she anticipated the flood of desire.

He raised his head and grinned at her. 'I think that will do nicely.'

She gaped at him. 'Aren't you going to finish?'

'Nope. If you want more, you'll have to stay the night with me.' He rolled off the bed and hunted for his jeans.

Lauren squeezed her thighs together in a desperate bid for release. How did he know that she craved him enough to put up with being left high and dry? She wandered into the bathroom and picked up her skirt and blouse.

Grayson glanced over at her as she located her bra. 'I ripped your hose and your panties. I'll buy you some new ones.'

It felt strange walking down the corridor with no panties on. Lauren wondered if anyone apart from Grayson could tell. He stood behind her in the elevator, one arm wrapped around her waist. For the first time in her life she allowed herself to lean back into a man's strength. Their lovemaking had only confirmed the depth of the attraction between them. She sensed she could spend a lifetime exploring Grayson's sensual potential.

Lauren waited while Grayson visited the small general store tucked away in the corner of the lobby. An elderly lady and her husband parked themselves on the seat next to Lauren's. As soon as the lady smiled at her, Lauren knew she was going to be dragged into a conversation whether she liked it or not.

'Hi, I'm Peggy. Are you here with someone special, dear?'

Lauren smiled back. 'Yes, I am thank you.'

Peggy kissed her husband's gnarled cheek. 'This is Doug. We come here every year to celebrate our wedding anniversary. We ran away together fifty years ago.'

'That's amazing. Congratulations!' Lauren studied their blissful faces and then turned towards the lobby. Grayson walked across to her with his easy long stride. Peggy followed her gaze.

'Is that your young man, dear? He looks like the steady reliable type. Are you married then?'

'Not yet,' Lauren said with a laugh. 'He hasn't asked me.'

Lauren became engrossed in studying Grayson as he approached her. What would it be like to take a chance and marry a stranger just because you thought you'd connected at a soul-deep level? Was it possible that she and Grayson would be coming back to Vegas in fifty years to celebrate their own special anniversary?

'Lauren, are you OK?' Grayson tipped his hat at the elderly couple and then crouched in front of her. She met his searching blue gaze as best she could. Peggy poked Grayson in the ribs with her walking stick.

'She'd probably feel a lot better if you made an honest woman out of her, young man. I don't hold with all this living together nonsense,' Peggy said.

Grayson took Lauren's cold hands in his. 'Are you planning a wedding, Lauren, honey?'

She waited for the masculine reaction of caged terror which usually accompanied the use of the word wedding. Grayson didn't move and his expression remained as intense as ever.

'If I was going to get married, I'd need a bridegroom wouldn't I?'

His smile died. 'You wouldn't have to look far. I'd marry you in a heartbeat.'

She stared at him intently. What if he was the one? What if he offered her a new start in life and the opportunity to leave her troubled past behind? She needed to move on. She needed to be brave. His gaze narrowed and he brought her hand to his lips.

'Marry me, Lauren, and I swear I'll be the best darned husband in the universe.'

She touched his cheek, felt the roughness of his stubble and the strength inherent in his jawline. If she could trust him with her body shouldn't she be able to trust him with her heart?

'All right then, I will.'

Lauren woke with a start as the never-ending rumble of traffic penetrated the silence in the room. With great care, she removed Grayson's arm from around her waist and scurried into the bathroom. She checked her watch. It was five in the morning. Her gaze remained riveted on the cheap gold wedding band Grayson had placed on her finger not two hours earlier.

She buried her throbbing head in her hands and silently screamed. Two hours ago she'd thought she'd found the perfect man, a man who didn't know who her father was or care less. A man who liked her for herself, not for her connections or for what she could do for him. They'd connected on a level so deep that it stunned her. Marrying Grayson had seemed the perfect opportunity to move beyond her father's reach and declare her independence.

After a deep breath, Lauren raised her head and looked in the mirror. She had to leave. She had no right to involve a good and decent man in the complicated relationship between herself and her father. Las Vegas wasn't big enough for her to hide in. And she was done with that anyway. She had a business to run, a new life to lead.

Slipping into her clothes, she took off the wedding ring and laid it carefully on the countertop. She'd left her business card in Grayson's wallet. She swallowed a sob. When he woke up and discovered she'd gone would he be secretly relieved or mad as hell? If she was lucky, perhaps he would call her and they could begin the messy business of the divorce proceedings.

Chapter One

With a murmured excuse, Lauren squeezed past the passenger on her left and headed for the bathroom. In the enclosed space, the hum of the aircraft increased to a dull roar. She peered into the mirror and, despite the yellowish tinge the lights cast on her skin, she still looked much calmer than she felt. Her light-brown hair remained secure in its sophisticated knot. Only her hazel-green eyes held a hint of apprehension.

What on earth was she doing? When she'd fallen into the arms of the tall, drawling cowboy in the bar of her Las Vegas hotel, she'd never imagined that six months later she'd be on a plane heading towards his ranch in Oregon.

Lauren washed her hands with the sliver of airline soap and inhaled the citrus fragrance. She closed her eyes and recalled the breathless moment when she had landed in Grayson Turner's lap. The scent of his aftershave, even when combined with the smell of the beer she accidentally tossed over him, had intoxicated her. He had held her like a precious object; his touch was at once familiar and so reassuring that she'd felt completely safe.

Lauren winced as the soap slipped through her fingers.

Their marriage in a tacky wedding chapel decorated with white plastic flowers, flooded with piped music and officiated over by a pastor dressed in drag still seemed surreal. But she'd kissed Grayson and promised to love him forever. That was all too real.

Lauren's eyes snapped open. After six months of

furtive emails, she'd agreed to meet him. She wanted a divorce but Grayson obviously wasn't prepared to go without a fight. Wearily she wondered if he'd found out her family had money. Her father always maintained that everyone had a price.

Lauren propped open her old leather purse and withdrew the file of printed emails. Grayson's instructions were simple. She was to meet him at the airport and he'd take her back to his ranch for the weekend. Lauren swallowed hard. A weekend in which she'd promised to allow him to convince her to remain married.

She pictured Grayson Turner. Six foot two in his bare feet, short black hair, faded-blue-jean-coloured eyes. A 35-year-old graduate of agricultural college and a rancher by trade. He was a formidable sight to a five-foot six-inch female even if she did run her own business.

And he wanted her badly. His emails made that clear. So clear that Lauren stopped reading them at work and kept them to drool over in the quiet of her big lonely bed.

A cabin assistant knocked on the door and reminded Lauren they were about to land. She made her way back to her seat and gathered her belongings. She hadn't brought much with her, only an overnight bag.

Her throat tightened and she fingered the long strand of pearls around her neck. Her pale-pink blouse and short black A-line skirt had withstood the journey well. Both came from a garage sale and had been made fifty years ago. Would she stand out as a city girl amongst the more rural citizens of Oregon or would her retro-look make her the height of fashion? Lauren suppressed a choke of laughter. Would Grayson even recognise her after six months apart?

She fastened her seat belt and tried to relax as the plane bumped down onto the runway. Still unable to stop thinking of the man who'd made her break all her rules, she lingered until the other passengers disembarked. Momentarily blinded by the bright glare of the Friday afternoon sunlight, she stepped onto the busy concourse.

At the rear of the arrival hall, Grayson Turner leant against a wall, his brown Stetson tipped slightly forwards, concealing his expression and his vivid eyes. He wore blue jeans and a rust-coloured shirt, his jacket hung over his shoulder. After a deep breath, Lauren took a firm grip on her bag and walked across to him. In his tan cowboy boots he seemed at least seven-foot tall. She had to crane her neck to see him properly.

He straightened up. 'You came then.' To her dismay, he sounded almost disappointed.

'I said I would.' Lauren kept her answer short. She'd learnt the benefits of brevity at her father's knee in a male-orientated business world, which expected females to gush. At 29 she considered herself a fitting adversary for most men.

He smiled and picked up her carpet bag. 'I was getting worried. I thought you'd run out on me.' He held out his hand and she took it, relishing his firm grasp, aware of how insubstantial her fingers looked wrapped in his. The remembered scent of his aftershave wound around her.

'I wouldn't do that to you.'

He glanced down, his eyes considering. 'No, I didn't think you were the type to turn tail.' He steered her away from the exit doors and towards a small coffee shop. Before she could protest, he said, 'I thought we should straighten a few things out before we go. If things don't work out, it's a hell of a long drive back from the ranch.'

Lauren allowed herself to be ushered into the shop. She sat down at a vacant table and waited until Grayson returned with two plastic cups. He held one out to her. 'I got you green tea. I seem to remember you said that was all you ever normally drank.'

Lauren smiled her thanks, surprised he'd remembered. If only she'd kept to tea in Las Vegas, she thought glumly, and not started on champagne, she wouldn't be in this embarrassing situation now.

'What exactly do you want to discuss, Grayson?'

He angled his hat back so that she could see his face. His skin was tanned, faint laughter lines around his eyes and mouth only added to his allure. 'I want to make sure that we agree on what's going to happen over the next two weekends.'

Lauren sighed. 'We've been over this a thousand times. I've agreed to stay with you for a weekend on your ranch and in return, next weekend, you get to stay with me at my apartment in San Francisco. During this time we will try and see if we can make our so-called marriage work. Do I have this right?'

Grayson smiled into her eyes and she tensed. 'Not bad, darlin' but you've forgotten one thing.'

Lauren concentrated on his long fingers, which were wrapped around his coffee cup. His calloused hands were large, yet capable of being so gentle, especially when he touched a woman's body – her body. 'Are you talking about sex?'

Grayson grinned. 'Yes, ma'am. You agreed to allow me to use all my powers of persuasion on you this weekend.'

Lauren lifted her chin and stared right back at him. 'And you agreed to allow me to persuade you to get a divorce when you come to San Francisco. You don't really know me at all and I just don't want to be married, Grayson, not to you or to anyone.'

He reached out and took her hand. 'I know how I feel. But are you still willing to try?'

Lauren shrugged. 'If it's the only way to get rid of you.'

His fingers tightened over hers. 'I've already told you. I believe in marriage and I want to see if we can make this one work.'

Lauren laughed. 'Really? And when did you come up with that old-fashioned notion? After you found out that my family is wealthy?'

She tried to pull away but he was too strong. He slowly relaxed his grip and shook his head, his smile lingering on his lips. 'You city folks are all the same. Greedy, greedy, greedy. I'm not asking for much, just a chance to get to know you. The only mistake you make is in thinking the rest of us are just like you.'

He sat back and took a slug of coffee. 'If you recall, Lauren, I was ready to jump into bed with you five seconds after you landed in my lap. Hell, what did you think you were sitting on? A baseball bat?'

Lauren knew what he'd wanted. She'd been shocked and aroused to discover she wanted the same thing. He seemed to have reached inside her and flicked on a switch of intense sexual awareness she hadn't known she possessed.

'I don't want your money, Lauren. I want you,' Grayson said. 'And if I'm the first man who's ever seen you that way, you should be praying I'll hang around, not trying to kick me in the teeth. This weekend is not just about sex. It's a chance for us to get to know each other better.'

He slipped his hand inside his denim jacket and brought out an envelope. 'I reckoned you'd kick up a fuss so I went to see my lawyer and got him to draw up some papers.'

He spread them out on the table in front of her. 'If things don't work out, we take out of the marriage what we brought into it. I'll keep my ranch and business and you'll keep what's yours. Unless we have a child of course.' He forestalled her interruption with a wave of his hand. 'Not that that's likely, but you never know. If it does happen, all bets are off and we renegotiate, agreed?'

He pulled out a pen, signed his name and handed the pen and paper to Lauren. She read through the document with a practised eye and signed at the bottom below Grayson's flashy signature. Her relief at his businesslike manner began to relax her. So what if she wasted two weekends of her life indulging in an orgy of sex and pretending to be married? She'd never get the opportunity again and it would be something to look back on when her world returned to its hectic pace.

'There's one more thing, thinking of children,' Grayson said.

This time Lauren managed to interrupt him. 'It's all right. I'm on the pill.'

He picked up her hand and kissed her palm, the hard tip of his tongue made her shiver. 'Good,' he said, 'because I'd like to come inside you without any barriers this time. I sent you a copy of my medical records and I've seen yours. Despite my behaviour with you, I don't sleep around. I'm a prime healthy specimen.'

She nodded, her mind too caught up in his softly spoken words and the touch of his tongue to answer properly. He sucked one of her fingers into his mouth and she crossed her legs to subdue the fierce rush of warmth pooling there.

'Are you ready to go?'

Lauren opened her eyes to find his face close to hers. She hesitated for a second and his eyes narrowed. Refusing to be flustered, she got to her feet and allowed him to pick up her bag. As they moved towards the short-term parking lot, he caught her elbow. The hint of command in his blue eyes made her nervous and excited at the same time.

'As your body officially belongs to me now, there's something I'd like you to do. Go into the ladies' restroom and take off any underwear that might get in my way.'

When Lauren emerged from the restroom, after mentally cataloguing the many ways she intended to embarrass him on his return visit to San Francisco, Grayson strolled towards her. His eyes fixed on the gentle sway of her freed breasts beneath her long-sleeved blouse.

Could he see her hardened nipples through the thin fabric? She slowed her walk and let her hips swing with each step. She glanced at his jeans where a huge bulge was clearly visible. He followed her gaze and slowly ran his thumb down the straining zipper.

Grayson swore quietly and held out his hand. 'We've got almost a hundred miles to drive, Lauren. I'm not sure if we'll make it before I have to pull over and bury myself inside you, but I'll sure as hell try.'

To Lauren's surprise, Grayson's black pick-up truck had big comfortable leather seats. She relaxed as he stowed her bag and walked around to the driver's side. He was silent as he manoeuvred the big vehicle through the maze of the airport and out onto the freeway. Lauren let her head fall back and closed her eyes.

Gray let out his breath and stole a glance at the woman beside him. When he'd thought she wasn't on the plane, he'd felt like a horse had kicked him in the gut. It had taken him six months to lure her back and he'd thought he'd blown it. She'd looked so calm and in control in her high-heeled black shoes and slicked-back hair. He'd wanted to feed her champagne until she turned into the relaxed laughing woman he'd met in Las Vegas.

He'd gone to Vegas to watch the Professional Bull Rider finals. He hadn't expected to fall in love. Who did? Especially not with a woman who epitomised everything he'd come to despise in life, everything he'd rejected. Living in the city and climbing the slippery corporate ladder was no longer his idea of fun. But something about Lauren captured his attention from the moment she landed in his lap. When his arms tightened around her, he'd not wanted to let go.

She'd told him about her retro design company with such pride he'd been charmed. She'd even bought him a drink to make up for the one she'd spilled all over his chest. After a drink and some intense conversation, he'd invited her out to dinner and she accepted.

Gray smiled as he remembered what happened next. Lauren followed him into the bathroom and watched him strip off his beer-stained shirt. He'd hardly dared breathe as she'd taken the wet washcloth from his unresisting hand and rubbed it over his chest.

Gray licked his lips. Keeping one eye on the road, he reached across and slid his hand up over Lauren's knee. He knew she was naked under her tight little skirt. She'd done it for him. He sighed as his fingers encountered her moist heat and she slightly opened her legs. As the tip of his finger brushed her sex, he shifted in his seat, aware of his erection pressing hard against the restraint of his jeans.

On that never-to-be-forgotten Las Vegas night, he'd barely managed to find and pull on a condom after ripping off her panties and then plunging inside her. And that hadn't been the end of it. They'd never made it out of the hotel room for dinner, preferring to feast on each other and the odd mini-bar snack. When they finally made it down to the lobby and he suggested getting married, Lauren seemed as eager as him.

Gray still couldn't believe how fast he'd fallen for her. She'd certainly ruined his tough-guy image. He stole a glance at her serene face and fought down a smile. He believed in marriage and intended to make his work. His father had sailed through six marriages and divorces without a thought for the devastating consequences. Gray couldn't imagine doing the same.

If he had to play into Lauren's cowboy fantasy to lure her back, he was quite happy to do so. She'd get to know the real him soon enough and then, hopefully, he could tone down the hokey Marlboro Man image.

When he'd woken up alone in his Las Vegas hotel room he'd realised Lauren had taken fright and left. Luckily he'd kept her business card and had bombarded her with emails ever since. He flexed his fingers against her soft skin and watched the quick rise and fall of her breasts.

She'd come back to him. Sometimes, despite what his father said, being as stubborn as a mule definitely had its advantages.

Chapter Two

Lauren stirred as the truck slowed and turned off the freeway. When she looked out of the window she saw immeasurable fields of golden crops dotted with small buildings, framed against an endless azure sky. She felt like Alice in Wonderland waking up in a whole new world. It was liberating. For the second time in her life she intended to do as she pleased without a thought for the consequences.

She'd tried to analyse her reasons for marrying Grayson in Las Vegas when marriage just wasn't on her agenda a thousand times. It wasn't as if she could blame Grayson. He'd asked and she'd enthusiastically accepted. It had seemed the ultimate declaration of her independence from her father and her old life. At the time, she'd even meant the words of the ceremony. Grayson had an aura of quiet strength and sincerity, qualities she'd begun to believe didn't exist in real men any more.

Waking up beside Grayson and realising what she'd done, sent her scurrying back home like a frightened teenager. Lauren knew she shouldn't have been such a coward. At least she hadn't caved in and asked her father to deal with Grayson for her. God knows what he would've done. Sometimes it was hard for her to remember that she'd decided to run her own life and deal with her own problems.

It took her a moment to notice that Grayson's right hand was buried between her thighs, while he drove with his left. She turned her head and he smiled at her.

'We're almost there, Lauren.'

Grayson slowed even more and headed for a pair of impressive metal gates adorned with the entwined letters G and T. He opened his window, punched in a security code and the gates swung slowly open. Heat poured through the window and Lauren undid the top two buttons of her shirt.

'You can keep going, honey. You're on my land now,' Grayson murmured. 'No one will see you except me. You can pull up your skirt too.'

Lauren thought about pretending she hadn't heard him and then remembered her promise. Sighing, she lifted her butt and allowed her skirt to shift upwards, exposing the back of Gray's hand between her legs. She studied the contrast between his dark suntanned flesh and her pale thighs. His fingers flexed against her and she almost purred.

With slow deliberation, she undid another couple of buttons, displaying the tops of her breasts. Her nipples thrust hard through the cotton. Grayson groaned and slid one long finger inside her.

'How many buttons do you have left?'

Lauren looked down, concentrating on the feel of his probing, callused finger. 'Three.'

Grayson let out a breath. 'That's lucky because I have three fingers left to slide inside you.' He ran the edge of his thumbnail across her clit. 'I need my thumb for this beauty.'

She opened another button as he doubled his presence inside her and she arched her back into his touch. His next question made her open her eyes.

'Have you made love with anyone since Las Vegas?'

Lauren wriggled restlessly as his hand went still. 'No, I haven't, have you?'

'I haven't wanted to touch another woman. I had the best sex of my life with you.'

She sighed as he grunted his approval and increased

the tempo of his thrusting fingers. She undid another button. Her blouse was almost undone, the breeze from the windows exposed her breasts in between ripples of butter-soft cotton. His third finger joined the others, widening her even further, making her moan.

Grayson's frank confession made her feel powerfully female. Her body grew warmer, throbbing against his fingers, making her want him, making her remember the wild night she'd spent with him in Las Vegas. She released the last button and deliberately pulled both sides away from her breasts. Grayson made a low sound as he slid his fourth finger inside her. Under the pressure of his thumb, her pussy pulsed a slow sultry dance of need.

Lauren only opened her eyes when she realised Grayson had shut off the idling engine. He leant towards her, his expression intent, and kissed her hard on the mouth. She brought her arms around his neck and kissed him back.

After he pulled away, he brought his fingers to his mouth and slowly sucked them. Lauren watched as he got out of the truck, came around to her side and lifted her into his arms. Half carrying her, half backing her up, he manoeuvred her up the steps, through a screened door and a mud room, into what appeared to be a kitchen.

Her back hit a work surface. Grayson stopped. 'This will have to do. I can't wait any longer.'

He put his hands around her waist and lifted her onto the tiled countertop. Lauren squeaked as her bare skin hit the cold smooth surface. Grayson gave her no time to do anything as he balanced her on the edge of the counter and pushed her knees apart. She tried to remember to breathe as he struggled to pull down his zipper and his cock sprang free.

He splayed his hand over her butt and the tip of his erection pressed insistently against her already aroused flesh. She tried to relax her inner muscles, knowing he was big and wanting him inside her as quickly as possible. The sensation of being stretched and filled was almost unbearable. Looking down, Lauren realised he had a way to go. He pulled back and thrust again.

'You can take it all, darlin', I know you can. Let me inside.'

Lauren let out her breath, kicked off her shoes and walked her feet up his thighs until she reached his hips. With a satisfied grunt, he rocked forwards and filled her completely. Lauren screamed, grabbed at his hair and came so hard that she thought she'd died. Whatever anybody said, she knew that size did matter.

His tongue filled her mouth, jabbing in the same vigorous pattern as his cock. Five hard deep thrusts before he came, and Lauren felt his hot come at her very centre. After a while she opened her eyes to find herself staring up at a painted white ceiling. The back of her head was cradled in one of Grayson's large hands. He lay over her, his face buried in the crook of her neck.

'Does anyone live here with you?' Lauren whispered, suddenly aware that she was half-naked in a very public place.

Gray's chuckle was smothered against her skin. 'I have a housekeeper who comes in most days but I gave her the weekend off. The ranch hands have their own cook and kitchen behind the other barn.'

He placed one hand flat on the counter and levered himself away from her. She bit her lip as his cock shifted inside her.

'This wasn't how I planned it, Lauren. I intended to be the perfect gentleman and wait until you asked me to make love with you.' Grayson grimaced. 'How about we start again? I'll give you a tour of the house and barn, and then we can grab some dinner. I'm sure you're hungry after your early start.'

Reluctantly, she unclasped her leg from around his thigh and allowed him to pull her upright. She wanted him again and all he could talk about was food? Her displeasure must have shown in her expression. He grinned as he lifted her down.

'We haven't finished yet, darlin'. As we go around the house you can pick the next place you want to make love in.'

Lauren attempted to smoothe down her skirt and buttoned her crumpled blouse. 'Don't you mean have sex?'

Grayson's smile died and he stared levelly back at her. He shrugged. 'If that's want you want to call it, go ahead.'

Lauren ignored him, suddenly feeling as if he'd put her in the wrong. She looked around the open-plan kitchen and tried to change the subject to something she understood.

'Your house looks brand new. How long have you lived here?'

Grayson leant against the countertop, his arms folded across his chest, his jeans still unfastened. 'I built this house two years ago, so everything's relatively new.' He raised an eyebrow. 'Were you expecting some run-down old shack or did you think I lived in a trailer surrounded by barbed wire and cows?'

Lauren pretended to laugh. 'Of course not. I just wasn't expecting this.' She gestured vaguely with her hand. The open layout and stark simplicity of the kitchen and family room beyond reminded her of her parents' beach house near Half Moon Bay. She wandered through to study the stone fireplace on the far wall.

The couch was a deep red brown, large enough to

sleep on and accompanied by two matching chairs. Cherry-wood floors complemented the rich colours and large picture windows. A Navajo rug added its glorious patterned design to the sun-burnished effect.

Grayson dropped a hand on her shoulder. 'I reckon the couch would be a good place to "have sex" don't you think? Perhaps I'll shoot me a bear and have a nice rug for you to lie naked on in front of a roaring fire.'

Lauren closed her eyes as his thumb worked on the tangle of muscles in her shoulder. She leant back and came into contact with his hard chest. 'I think I'd like that.'

He kissed her exposed neck. 'Would you care to see the rest of the house or do you want to stop here? I'm a very adaptable host.'

Lauren smiled then and moved out of his range. 'I'd love to see the rest.' She headed back through the pristine kitchen. 'Do you have an office here or is it just bedrooms?'

She paused at the first door and Grayson pushed it open. The hum of a waiting computer, printer and fax machine greeted her and a warm stale blast of machine-heated air. His office was a model of efficiency and incredibly tidy. A variety of books and files ranging from farming to stocks and shares lined the walls. Lauren looked back at Grayson who remained in the doorway.

'Is this all your own work?'

Grayson gave an embarrassed smile. 'I'm a bit of a neat freak. I have to have everything organised or I can't work. It drives everyone nuts.'

Lauren tried to control her surprise. She'd feared that Grayson, like many so-called cowboys, might be living hand to mouth, trying to ignore the demands of the real world. Instead he had an apparently prosperous ranch and the intelligence to realise that technology held the key to his future prosperity.

She stared out of the window at the white picket fence, which unfurled down the driveway like an unending ribbon. It had been a mistake to come here. Before, she'd been able to think of him as just a sex object. Now he was trying to show her the real man and part of her was afraid of that. She didn't want to like him. She didn't want to feel so ... connected.

To cover her confusion, she backed out of the office and rushed to open the next door along the corridor. A plain white bathroom suite confronted her and she hurriedly moved on. She ignored the remaining two doors and headed to the last at the end of the passage-way. Taking a deep breath, she walked into the master bedroom.

The room was a good size. It contained little furni-ture apart from a big old-fashioned four-poster bed and a dressing table. A large antique gilt mirror hung opposite the bed, reflecting a softer image of the impersonal room. The bedlinen was white crisp cotton and so were the drapes.

'If you'd like to get cleaned up, Lauren, there's a bathroom through there and plenty of closet space. My architect insisted on adding large walk-in closets to my design. She said the future Mrs Turner would thank me for it.'

Lauren kept walking through to the bathroom, which was furnished with a cream-coloured hot tub and double shower as well as the usual items. Before she could shut the door, Grayson followed her in, his expression serious.

'Don't you like it?'

She stared at his reflection in the mirror wishing he hadn't mentioned the future Mrs Turner. 'It's lovely. I'm just overtired. It's been hectic at work for the past few weeks. I had to find a whole set of nineteen-fifties kitchen props for a last-minute theatre production.'

He moved across and stood behind her; his fingers sifted through her hair and gently released the pins. 'I know how you feel. We've just finished harvesting and that's a twenty-four-hour-a-day seven-days-a-week job.'

She closed her eyes and allowed his strength to surround her. What was it about Grayson that made her want to surrender her body to him without a quiver of doubt?

'How about we take a nap?'

Grayson's soft suggestion seemed like a wonderful idea. Lauren nodded and started to take off her blouse. By the time she'd undone the cuffs and slid the sleeves down her arms she could feel Grayson's arousal pressing into her back. Smiling, she bent forwards, pushing her butt into his groin, and slithered out of her skirt.

His hands slid to her hips and held her hard against him as she reached up to remove her pearl necklace.

'No,' he said, 'leave it on.'

Chapter Three

Lauren opened her eyes and turned to look at Grayson who lay sprawled on his back. True to his word, they'd actually slept, cocooned together in the big old oak bed. Golden beads of sunlight peeped through the cracks in the drapes like amber teardrops and then disappeared along with the setting sun.

'I know what's been worrying me about your house.'

Grayson cracked open an eye and lazily regarded her, one hand behind his head.

Lauren frowned down at him. 'Apart from the family room, you have nothing personal here. It's as if you don't really consider it your full-time home.'

She thought of her parents' mansion where her father had obsessively documented every minor event in her life with a photograph or framed certificate. Even her own apartment held a few prized possessions and treasured photographs.

Grayson yawned, his shoulder muscles rippled in the golden light. 'I only moved in a couple of years ago. I've got all that frou-frou stuff in boxes in the garage.' He rubbed his hand over his chest. 'One of my old girlfriends decorated the family room for me. I just haven't had time to bother with the rest of it.'

Lauren studied his unconcerned expression. How could he think such things were unimportant? She knelt up to confront him. 'Don't you know that your living space is a reflection of your personality?'

Grayson shrugged. 'Then I guess I lack a personality. I like white. It's easy to keep clean, hides the dust and everything matches.'

Lauren raised her eyebrows. 'Why do men say that? I suppose I should be grateful you didn't go the other way and decide everything should be black. It's a shame you don't live closer. I have so much stuff in storage at work – that is if you like retro.' She dropped a kiss on his lips. 'You know, a woman's touch and all that.'

Grayson grabbed her hand and wrapped it around his shaft. 'Something else would appreciate a woman's touch, if you've got the time.'

Lauren squeezed harder and Grayson groaned. 'If you can put up with my decorating advice, I'm sure I can fit you in.' She knelt between his legs and bent her head, allowing the soft silky strands of her hair to drift over his thighs and groin. A bead of pearly moisture appeared and she flicked out her tongue to catch it.

She loosened her grip as he grew larger. She slowly swirled her tongue over the tip of his erection, breathing in the scent of aroused male and the faint hint of leather. He caught her around the waist.

'Do you want to see the rest of the ranch?'

Lauren regarded him through her tousled hair. Her mouth was just a breath away from his engorged flesh. She pursed her lips and blew. He shivered and rocked his hips until his cock thrust against her mouth. Sitting back, she stretched, knowing his eyes were glued to her naked breasts, and enjoyed the corresponding pooling of heat between her thighs.

'I think I'd like that, Grayson.'

She leant forwards and kissed him, sliding off the bed as he reached for her. When he growled and unfolded his long frame, she made a run for the bathroom. He caught her in front of the mirror, pulled her into his arms and kissed her so thoroughly she had to lean against him for support.

'Do you have a pair of jeans?'

His question surprised her. 'Of course I do, doesn't everyone?'

He smiled then and indicated her small overnight bag. 'I meant in there.'

Lauren bit her lip and attempted a lie. 'I thought I might buy a pair here if I needed them. You do have shops don't you?'

Grayson snorted. 'Well, we have Mrs Maxwell's General Store and Emporium. She pretty much sells everything. We can go down tomorrow and take a look.'

'Why do I need jeans? It's not cold or anything.'

Grayson strolled across to one of the walk-in closets and extracted a clean checked shirt. 'This is a horse ranch, honey. It's covered in horse shit. If you're going to help with the evening chores, you'll need some protection.'

Lauren crossed her arms across her chest. 'I know that! I'm not stupid. I just didn't think you'd expect me to . . .'

'Get your hands dirty?' Grayson shook his head. 'My ranch, my rules, Lauren. Either help me out or go home.'

Lauren grabbed her bag. 'Great, how long will it take me to get to the airport?'

He turned towards her, his shirt in his hand and considered her. 'Walking? Probably a couple of days, cos there's no way I'm going to take you. You promised me a weekend.'

Lauren scowled as he draped the shirt over a chair and sluiced water from the sink over his face and muscular body. She remembered her first sight of him half-naked in Vegas and the mind-blowing sex that followed. She dropped her bag to the floor. Did she really want to leave? Her bag didn't contain much more than soft silky underwear, a couple of blouses, a Chanel skirt suit and an all-purpose shift dress.

Grayson turned back to her and she threw him a towel. 'What do you think I should wear then?' she asked stiffly.

His lazy, satisfied grin warned her he'd anticipated her lack of suitable clothing. 'I have just the thing.'

Lauren waited suspiciously as he disappeared into the second closet and came out with a skirt and blouse draped over a hanger. Her mouth fell open. The short skirt was denim and had a row of metal buttons up the front. The top was white cotton with a band of embroidery around the wide yoke neck.

'I'm not wearing that! Who do you think I am? Daisy Duke?'

Grayson winked suggestively. 'If the bra cup fits . . .' He continued to look hopeful as he waggled the hanger in front of her. 'I got you cowboy boots as well.'

After glaring at his innocent face, Lauren snatched the hanger out of his hand. 'All right, I'll play along. I'll be Western Barbie to your cowboy Ken. Although how this miniscule outfit is supposed to protect me . . .'

His laughter followed her into the shower. 'Ken's got nothing down his pants and you sure as hell know I do.'

Lauren shouted back over the roar of the shower. 'And I don't need silicon implants like Barbie!'

When she came out of the shower, Grayson had disappeared. Picking up the hanger, she studied the intricate blue embroidery on the blouse. Grayson's arrogant assumption that she would dress up for him should have worried her more than it did. Smiling, she smoothed the soft cotton. She loved dressing up. It was her passion. Somehow, he'd known she would enjoy it as much as he did and, despite everything, she trusted him.

She dressed quickly and was unable to resist taking a peek at herself in the mirror. The idea of fulfilling Grayson's fantasies as he fulfilled hers was arousing.

The skirt finished way above her knees and the blouse was so low cut it revealed the tops of her breasts and the long line of her neck. It wasn't dissimilar to a 1950s cowgirl outfit she already owned. She ran her fingers over her tight nipples and felt sexy and sassy and alive.

In a moment of daring, she left off her underwear. Maybe he'd choke on his cowboy hat.

Grayson stood in the kitchen, a mug in his hand. He didn't say anything about her appearance although he gave her a thorough inspection. The alluring aroma of percolating coffee drifted across to Lauren and she breathed in deeply. Although she preferred tea, the scent of coffee always made her wish she could drink it without ending up with a headache.

On the stove top a kettle came to the boil with a piercing gusty whistle. Grayson retrieved another cup from the cupboard over his head. 'There are tea bags and tea leaves in the pantry. Help yourself.'

Lauren took an English breakfast tea bag and Grayson added boiling water to her cup. They sipped in companionable silence until Lauren became aware of a growing crescendo of noise outside.

'I thought you said we were alone here?'

Grayson finished up his coffee and gave her a slow smile. 'You're never alone on a ranch, Lauren. That caterwauling is because the animals know I'm late feeding them.' He put down his cup. 'Are you coming?'

He led Lauren back through to the mud room where a brand new pair of black and white cowboy boots awaited her. Outside, a slight breeze lifted her hair as she stepped into the gathering gloom. Grayson handed her an empty bucket and headed towards the large red-painted barn.

The barn obviously predated the house. Sunlight had faded the scarlet-painted walls to a softer blush and flaked and crackled the surface like old skin. It reminded Lauren of the toy version she'd love to play with as a little girl. She wrinkled her nose as the smell and the noise grew stronger.

'Chickens first.'

Grayson disappeared inside the barn and Lauren followed. Her eyes watered at the strange combination of earthy animal odours and sweet-smelling hay. The last dappled rays of the sun threaded through the old roof illuminating the spiralling dust motes. Huge plastic barrels lined the walls of the sectioned-off part of the main barn. After relieving Lauren of her bucket, Grayson opened one of the barrels and began dumping shovel loads of brown pellets into the two buckets.

He pointed at a rusty water faucet. 'Add a couple of pints of water to each bucket and give it a stir would you? I'll start on the horses.'

Gingerly, Lauren picked up a battered plastic jug from the workbench and approached the faucet. She struggled to turn the handle and then shrieked as a torrent of water missed the jug and soaked her boots. Surreptitiously, she checked her perfectly manicured nails for damage. To her relief, not only were her nails unharmed but Grayson didn't appear to notice; his attention was focused on his work.

After a good deal of quiet swearing and more strength than she knew she possessed, Lauren managed to accomplish her task. She tried to pick up the bucket and hastily put it down again, surprised by the weight. Grayson came up behind her, picked up the two buckets and turned back out of the barn. A fenced-off area on the south side of the barn housed a chicken run and nesting boxes.

As Grayson and Lauren approached, the noise in the pens reached a crescendo as if they were movie stars arriving on the red carpet of an award show.

'I'll spread the mash, Lauren, if you'll go and look for the eggs.'

Lauren nodded, not liking the avaricious gleam in the chickens' eyes or the sharpness of their prominent red beaks and sharp claws. Grayson handed her a tattered pair of leather gloves and a basket lined with soft foam. She climbed into the back of the nesting shed and felt her way along the narrow ledges, snatching her hand back every time she imagined she encountered an irate chicken.

To her secret delight, she managed to collect two dozen warm eggs. The dim light and musty smell of the chicken house reminded her of her grandparents' feather bed. Choking back a sneeze, she backed out, the basket held protectively to her chest.

A feeding frenzy still went on out front. Grayson stood waiting for her, the empty buckets at his side. Lauren held up the basket.

'Two dozen, Grayson. What should I do with them now?'

He smiled as if enjoying her sense of accomplishment. 'Bring them back to the feed store and we'll finish up with the horses.'

Lauren followed him back to the barn, detouring around any suspicious matter, which slowed her progress. By the time she reached Grayson, he'd already begun to refill the two buckets from another barrel.

'Put the eggs on the shelf over there. You'll see each tray is dated. Chuck out any eggs that are cracked and put the rest in today's box. Most of them are used on the ranch. I take any surplus into town and sell them to Mrs Maxwell. There's a dog bowl on the floor for the damaged ones. The barn cat will eat any left out.'

Lauren crossed to the shelf and carefully inspected each egg before putting them in the correct tray. She glanced down at the dog bowl. 'Don't you have a dog?'

He turned then, regret colouring his blue eyes. 'Not any more. I had to have my dog Petty put to sleep last month.'

Lauren resisted the temptation to put her arms around him. She didn't want him to be a good man who loved dogs. She wanted him to be a shallow worthless loser like most of the men she'd dated. He would be so much easier to leave. The egg she held in her hand cracked and she dropped it in the bowl.

'What's next?' she asked brightly.

'Horses.' Grayson seemed to anticipate her next question. 'Not all of them. The ranch hands take care of the stud animals and the horses in training. These three are more like pets.'

Lauren closed her eyes. God, he kept pet horses as well. What would he come up with next? A house full of orphans he financially supported? To cover her deep confusion, she tried to pick up one of the buckets. It was way too heavy for her. She bent lower to try again.

Grayson's hand clamped onto her naked butt. He cleared his throat. 'You've got no underwear on.'

She pressed against his fingers. 'You noticed. I wasn't sure if you were paying attention.'

He chuckled as he turned her to face him. 'I'm paying attention all right.' He picked her up, moulding her against him and kissed her thoroughly. She moaned as he allowed her to slide down his aroused body. 'We'll finish this later. We've got all night.'

He hefted both of the buckets, his biceps bulging, and nodded to Lauren. 'After we've fed the horses we'll eat and then –'

Lauren couldn't resist kissing him, cutting off his words. 'And then, we'll have sex.'

He didn't answer, his long stride eating up the ground, taking him away from her. Biting her lip, Lauren watched his retreat. She shivered, aware of the cold wind sweeping down the shadowed valley. This wasn't going to be as easy as she'd hoped. Not only did she desire him, she was beginning to like him.

The thought of what her father would do if she tried to introduce Grayson into her world made her pause. She wouldn't expose Grayson to such venom in a million years. He deserved better. With that thought firmly in mind, she followed Grayson to another smaller building tucked behind the barn.

Her booted feet dragged on the muddy ground. Sexual experience was all she could allow herself to gain from this impulsive relationship. Marriage wasn't an option she wanted to consider. However, she was beginning to realise that Grayson wouldn't settle for anything less.

Grayson didn't know it yet, but he should be grateful she didn't expect anything from him. She never wanted to feel that she owed anyone any favours. Her father had taught her the danger of that. She had fought too hard for her independence to give it up without a struggle. Sex with Grayson was easy. Making love or making a commitment was far too dangerous.

Chapter Four

Grayson stood by a gate to an enclosed pasture, which led out from a five-stall horse barn. He patted and stroked the huge animals surrounding him, allowing them to nuzzle his sleeves, chew on his shirt collar and slobber green slime down his back.

Lauren frowned at the pristine field and distant hills. 'Don't you get bored living here?'

Grayson turned to her, pushing away the largest horse who was attempting to stick its tongue in his ear.

'Why should I? It's a beautiful place. I like being on my own land and breathing clean air.'

'But what do you do for fun?' Lauren thought of her hectic lifestyle. The friends she met in the city for lunch, the new bars and clubs they tried out in the evenings.

Grayson chuckled. 'I go to the city, what do you think?' He ducked to avoid the horse licking his face. 'I've lived and worked in cities before, Lauren. I don't choose to do it any more.'

Lauren studied his contented expression. Was it possible to become weary of the life she loved? Would she ever be able to settle down like Grayson had?

Grayson took her hand. 'Let me introduce one lovely lady to three of my oldest friends.' He brought her closer to the fence rail and patted the smallest of the horses on the nose. 'This is Foxy. She's the youngest of the bunch. A couple of years ago she escaped from a neighbour's ranch and got hit by a truck.'

Foxy whickered as Grayson scratched her neck. 'They

were going to put her down. I offered to pay the vet's bills and keep her if she survived.'

Lauren swallowed. 'It wasn't your truck was it?'

He glanced at her, his hand fisting in the horse's mane. 'No, but I knew the bastard who was driving. It was my father and he'd been visiting me. I suppose I felt partially responsible.'

Inwardly Lauren groaned. Another gold star for cowboy Ken. She reached forwards and stroked the silver nose of the second horse. 'Who's this?'

Grayson grinned, the tension left his face as quickly as it had appeared. 'This is Flicka. She belonged to my mom. I offered to take care of her after my mom died.' He frowned. 'I knew my father wouldn't be interested in keeping her and at least I get to ride her occasionally. She's so gentle she'd be great with kids.'

Lauren couldn't help but hear the faint longing in his voice. She could imagine him surrounded by kids, all of them adorable little black-haired scamps, a rosy-cheeked wife in the background . . .

'And this is Robbie, my first horse and still the best. He's a paint.'

Lauren admired the huge white horse with its characteristic swirls of brown markings like swipes of a paintbrush. She rubbed the horse's nose, wishing she'd brought a treat for him.

'My first horse was a paint,' Lauren said. 'They're my favourite breed.'

'You had a horse?'

She grinned, glad to have surprised him for once. 'For most of my childhood I did. I rode English style of course. Since I started work, I haven't had time to ride at all.'

Her smile faded as she buried her face in the horse's mane, inhaling the peppery musty scent. She'd forgotten how much she enjoyed riding before her career overwhelmed her and kept her tied to the city.

Grayson upended the two buckets in the feeding trough and studied her, his expression full of wry understanding. 'When I was a kid, all I wanted was to stay with my mom's folks on their ranch. After the divorce, my dad made it almost impossible for me to get back there. I missed it like hell.' He touched Lauren's cheek. 'I'm going to get some hay. Stay here if you want and get acquainted. I'll be back in a minute.'

By the time Lauren kicked off her boots in the mud room, the outside light had disappeared. She was surprised at how hungry she felt as Grayson guided her into the kitchen and switched on the overhead lights. A worrying thought struck her as she gazed around the welcoming but empty kitchen.

She gave Grayson a cautious smile. 'Are we going out to dinner?'

He leant back against the counter, the mischievous glint back in his eyes. 'Not unless you feel like a long drive. The nearest decent restaurant is thirty miles away.'

Lauren glanced uneasily at the shining cook top and oven. 'You're not expecting me to rustle up a good old country feast are you? Because despite some very expensive cookery lessons, I burn water.'

Gray walked across to the industrial-sized refrigerator. 'Luckily for you, I'm a great cook. When you leave home at eighteen and have to earn your own way in the world, you gather a fine collection of paper hats serving at fast food restaurants and food-packaging plants.'

Lauren tried to imagine a young earnest Grayson in a paper hat instead of a cowboy hat and failed. 'What if I don't like fries?'

He grinned as he flung open the refrigerator door. 'I can do better than that. Tomorrow I'll barbecue but for tonight, my housekeeper left these.'

Lauren took in the stacked plastic containers. Each had a note attached to it detailing a date and brief reheating instructions.

'You could've pretended to cook it all yourself. I'd have been terribly impressed.'

Grayson studied the containers. 'I didn't know you couldn't cook. If I had, I would've tried it for sure.'

Lauren crossed to his side and he put a companionable arm around her shoulders. 'And what would madam like? We have chicken parmesan or beef stew and dumplings.'

'Chicken sounds great.' Lauren didn't care what she ate as long as she didn't have to cook it. 'I'll even volunteer to heat it up if you like.'

Grayson pulled out two of the containers. 'I'll man the microwave. How about you set the table? There's beer in the refrigerator if you like it.'

After discovering an apple pie and a jug of cream as well as the beer, Lauren was well satisfied with her meal. She sat opposite Grayson at the scrubbed pine table and ate ravenously.

Grayson put down his fork. 'So tell me how you ended up running an antiques business?'

'It's not antiques, it's retro, you know, fifties and sixties stuff. When I was a kid, I used to save up my allowance and buy old Barbies and their outfits.'

She smiled as she remembered her closet crammed full of dolls. Her father had never understood why she preferred them to the expensive gifts he gave her. 'I always loved the designs from those decades. As I got older, I spent a lot of my weekends searching for bargains at garage and estate sales.'

She stabbed a piece of lettuce. 'Eventually, my collection grew so large that people started asking me to help out with set design for local theatres and exhibitions. Two years ago, I realised I had an opportunity to develop my own business.'

Grayson smiled. 'What did you do before that?'

'I was a lawyer in my father's accounting firm.'

She caught his look of surprise and grimaced in return. 'I know. I don't know how I stood it either. Don't get me wrong, I know some fine lawyers but I'm definitely not one of them.'

She smoothed her hand over the embroidered white top he'd given her. 'Now I get to wear all my funky clothes to work. No more pant suits and boring black for me.'

Grayson reached forwards and clinked his beer bottle against hers. 'I'm all for people doing what they love.'

Under the guise of drinking her beer, Lauren studied his calm expression. Was he the kind of man who would understand how much her business and her independence meant to her? She'd grown so used to her father belittling her achievements she probably sounded defensive.

Nothing further disturbed the quietness between them except the ticking of the kitchen clock and the gentle hum of the refrigerator. Despite the lack of conversation, Lauren was comfortable with Grayson. She should have felt awkward with a man she barely knew but she didn't.

Grayson seemed to calm her overwrought senses just by sitting there. She'd been drawn to his sense of inner strength and completeness from the moment she'd met him.

When she sat back, she encountered Grayson's amused gaze. He pointed at the microwave. 'You've got a good appetite. I'll show you how to microwave some popcorn later if you behave yourself.'

Lauren groaned. 'Last time I tried that the bag caught fire and I had to buy my friend Ella a new microwave. I'm not risking it again.'

Grayson's eyebrows rose. 'You weren't kidding about

the cooking were you?' He glanced down at the table where a small helping of apple pie remained in the dish. 'How about we share this?'

As Lauren went to dip her spoon in the bowl, Grayson jerked it away to his side of the table. 'If you want some, you have to come and sit on my knee.'

Lauren pretended to sigh. 'I'm not sure if I want it that much. Perhaps I'd better try making some popcorn.' She gasped as Grayson came out of his seat, put his hands around her waist and lifted her clear across the table. She clutched at his shirt as he settled her on his knee.

'After all the food we've just eaten, I'm surprised you didn't rupture something.'

Grayson held his right arm out in a traditional strongman pose and flexed his biceps. 'Honey, I've lifted chickens heavier than you. I didn't feel a thing.' He leant across the table and grabbed her abandoned spoon, presenting it to her with a flourish. 'I bet I can eat faster than you can.'

In her childish desire to beat him, Lauren forgot to care about her manners. It was only when she sat back, her spoon filled with the last piece of apple that she realised she'd spilt dessert all down the front of her blouse. With a shrug, she popped the apple in her mouth and smiled triumphantly at Grayson.

'I win, cowboy. You might be good at lifting heavy things but I'm a lot quicker at eating.'

Grayson grinned, his eyes fastening on the trail of cream down her blouse. 'But as the loser, I get to clean up.' He lowered his head. Lauren tried not to purr as he licked the cream from her lips and slid his mouth down her throat. His hands slid off her shoulders to cup her breasts.

Lauren closed her eyes as Grayson stroked her erect nipples between his fingers and thumbs. He drew them out from her body, tugging gently until she leant away from him, conscious of the mixture of pleasure and pressure. He kissed her deeply, his mouth tasting of apple pie and light beer as he continued to hold her captive.

With a sound of deep approval, he drew her covered nipple into his mouth and began to suckle. The strength of his mouth on her sensitive skin made her press closer. Without releasing her breast, he put his hands on her waist and shifted her until she straddled him. Her short skirt retreated to her hips, uncovering her bare legs and butt.

Without conscious thought, she pressed herself against the zipper of his jeans, enjoying the rough sensation of the cloth against her skin, seeking his hardness, rocking into it. A groan escaped him as he transferred his mouth to her other waiting breast.

'I want this to be slow, Lauren. I want you to enjoy it.'

In answer, she undulated her hips against his in a fast demanding tempo which soon made him thrust back at her. He grabbed her ankles, crossed them at the small of his back and stood up, pushing her down onto the table. One handed, he pulled off her top as she fumbled with the buttons of his shirt. She tried not to laugh as he picked up the cream jug and held it over her head.

'You forgot to finish the cream.'

'You like cream, don't you, Grayson?'

His gaze dropped to her crotch and he fingered her damp panties. 'Yeah, I do, especially when it's on you.'

He angled the jug and poured a thin stream of cream in a figure-eight shape down onto her exposed breasts. The coldness surprised her. Lauren moaned when his mouth and fingers returned to lick and suckle her cream-coated skin.

His weight kept her trapped against the edge of the table and her pussy began to throb with need. He rolled his hips in a steady tempo, mimicking the subtle pull of his mouth and fingers. Lauren came with a shudder that ripped a scream from her mouth.

Before she'd finished, Grayson picked her up and headed for his bedroom. He set her on her feet, one arm around her waist to stop her from falling. She reached for his belt at the same moment he did. His fingers fell away.

'Be my guest, honey, but be careful with that zipper.'

Lauren struggled to undo the top button and then slid her hand inside his jeans as she slowly slid the zipper down. With a delighted sigh, she knelt in front of him. As he stepped out of his jeans, she reached forwards and grasped his heavy shaft at the base. He shuddered, his muscled stomach contracting sharply inwards.

'Lauren . . . I'm real close to coming. If you touch me, I'll . . .' Gray licked his lips as she licked the tip of his cock. His hand threaded through her hair, holding her there as she swirled her tongue over the engorged slick head.

As she toyed with him, Gray closed his eyes and tried to fight against the need to push himself more fully into her soft wet mouth. Her fingers moved from the base of his shaft and caressed his balls, sending shivers of ecstasy up his spine. He couldn't stop the thrust of his hips and surged deeply into her mouth. She sucked him hard, just how he liked it, her teeth grazing his shaft as she worked him. He couldn't quell the raging desire to come, which swiftly consumed and drained him.

When Lauren got to her feet she smiled. Gray waited as she kissed him full on the mouth. He tasted himself, needed her again.

'I've wanted to do that ever since I met you,' Lauren murmured.

Gray caught her hand and laced his fingers through hers. 'Do what?'

She wiggled out of her skirt and faced him. 'That.' She stroked his semi-hard cock, which responded by filling out again. Gray allowed Lauren to pull him over to the bed.

'Most women seem to hate touching a man there.'

Lauren rolled until she was on top of him. Her breasts swung in his face. He licked the tip of her right nipple.

Lauren snorted. 'The way you fill out a pair of jeans, I'm surprised women aren't lining the block to be allowed to touch you.'

Her tart remarks amused him and he kissed her luscious mouth. 'If I'm such a stud, maybe I should start charging. How much are you willing to pay me?'

She bit his shoulder. 'I get you for free this weekend and next and don't you forget it.'

He slid his fingers down past her soft curls and sought her swollen entrance. He couldn't believe how ready she was for him again. She knelt up, grasped his cock and lowered herself down onto him. He held still deep within her, felt the clench and release of her internal muscles around his thick cock.

'Ride me slow, honey. Make me wait.'

Lauren smiled at him as she rose slowly onto her knees. 'Have I worn you out already?'

He swallowed hard as she almost let him come out of her. 'Hell, no, darlin', I was thinking of you.'

He fought a groan as she lowered herself down again and tried to watch his cock disappear inside her. Desperate to see more, he moved up the bed until his back was against the headboard.

Her breasts swung against his face and he rubbed his unshaven cheek on her soft flesh. Mesmerised, he watched the rise and fall of her body over his. His need to come grew. He fought the urge to grab her hips and push the pace.

Her eyes were closed, a small frown on her forehead the only external sign that she was close to coming. He felt it inside her though, the vicelike grip of her sheath around his cock, squeezing him until he wanted to yelp like a puppy. His balls tightened and his come travelled up his shaft.

Gritting his teeth, he held himself deep and tight inside her as her orgasm crashed over them. Only when he felt her relax did he allow his climax to shudder through him. She collapsed onto his chest, her face hidden against his shoulder. He stroked her hair as she burrowed closer and kissed his throat.

Gray stared up at the white ceiling and settled Lauren against his side as she drifted off to sleep. Her comments about his empty house and solitary life kept repeating in his mind. Had he really chosen his own path or was he paralysed, waiting for his father's approval before he could move on again?

Grayson grimaced and glanced down at Lauren's quiet face. Dammit, she was making him think like a woman. He wanted to live here, he believed in his choices. He smiled remembering her comment when he suggested paying him stud fees. Unable to resist touching her, he smoothed his finger over her luscious lower lip. If he had his way, she'd spend the rest of her life getting him for free.

Chapter Five

Lauren opened her eyes and immediately shut them again. It was dark. She couldn't possibly have heard an alarm clock. Beside her, Grayson yawned, stretched out one long arm and silenced the annoying bell. Lauren sighed as he gathered her close and kissed the top of her head.

'It's time to get up, darlin'.'

Lauren burrowed her face against his warm chest and murmured something unintelligible. She squeaked as he gently swatted her backside and lifted her away from him.

'I'll shower first. It'll give you more time to wake up.'

After Grayson rolled out of bed, Lauren squinted at the illuminated clock face. It was 4.30. As far as she was concerned, that was the middle of the night. Where on earth was Grayson going at this time in the morning? She groaned as she remembered the chickens and the other livestock. Perhaps he had a herd of cows to milk as well.

Curiosity propelled her out of bed and she staggered into the bathroom, a sheet clutched to her chest. Grayson was already in the shower, whistling a Johnny Cash song. Lauren cringed at his exuberance and only stopped to admire his muscular body through the clear shower glass. Grayson had the kind of muscles achieved by hard physical labour, not the sculptured perfection of a city gym attendee.

He rinsed off his hair and smiled. Before she could scuttle away, he opened the shower door and pulled her inside, sheet and all. She shrieked as he tried to make her face the spray.

'You're not a morning person, are you?'

He chuckled as he turned her against his broad chest, shielding her from the worst of the lukewarm water. Lauren began to revive as Grayson's large hands smoothed down the length of her spine and back up. Leaning forwards, she licked droplets of water from his chest, enjoying the mixture of scents and tastes.

His fingers strayed lower, sliding down between her buttocks, probing her slick entrance. His tone became caressing. 'Do you think you could manage a little loving before we head out?'

Lauren stood on tiptoe, enjoying the sensation of his cock pressed against her stomach. Grayson put his hands around her waist and lifted her until the tip of his shaft grazed her clit. He leant back against the shower wall, his eyes half-closed as he rocked his hips. Lauren wrapped her arms around his neck and hooked her right foot over his hip, straining to guide him inside.

Grayson's firm grip around Lauren's waist stopped her moving closer. With a helpless sound, she could only watch, mesmerised as he slid in and out of her in a steady, shallow, tantalising rhythm.

When Grayson bent his head and lazily licked her nipple in the same arousing pattern, Lauren closed her eyes. His teeth grazed her skin and she jumped.

'Watch me, Lauren, watch my cock.'

The sliding, gliding pressure began to build as her sex swelled and she grew wet.

'Please, Grayson,' she urged, trying to pull him deeper, 'please . . .'

He slid a little further down the tiled shower wall, bringing her closer to him. 'Are you awake now, darlin'? Can you take a little more or should we be getting along? Those chickens need feeding.'

Lauren dug her nails into his biceps and he winced. 'Don't you dare leave me like this, or I'll be feeding you to the chickens.'

He laughed then and brought her down on top of him in one swift motion. Lauren gulped at the sudden exquisite fullness and came with him as he drove himself inside her.

He held her close, his cock still buried inside her. He allowed the water to drum against his back as he gently soaped her skin and washed her hair. She allowed him to cherish her, amazed at how carefully he touched her despite his strength and superior height. Her eyes closed as she relaxed under his hands.

'What a great way to start the day,' Grayson murmured as he put her down and kissed her mouth. 'Of course, I'll have to set the alarm earlier if it's going to become a habit of yours to seduce me in the shower, Mrs Turner.'

Before Lauren could reply, he helped her out of the shower and dried her briskly, ignoring her attempts to help herself. When he set her free, she stepped into the denim skirt and retrieved a long-sleeved T-shirt from her overnight bag.

Grayson wandered over, in the act of zipping his jeans as she selected a pair of panties. He took them from her and knelt at her feet.

'You don't really need these.'

Lauren stared down at him. 'It's cold out there – I might catch a chill.'

He slid a hand between her legs, his smile intimate, his voice even more so. 'It's as hot as hell in here and twice as inviting. If you get cold, just call me and I'll be happy to warm you up.'

He slid one long finger inside. Lauren tried to mask her instant response but he knew. He brought his mouth closer and bit down on the curve of her hip bone. 'I love it when you're swollen and wet from me.

I love being able to touch you like this whenever I want.'

Lauren tried to keep still as he curled his finger and unerringly located her G-spot. 'Are you sore?' he murmured. She shook her head. 'Well, you will be if I make love to you again.' He pulled her panties up her legs and smoothed them into place. 'Let's wait until after breakfast. We have the whole morning.'

Chasing chickens, cleaning out horse stalls and mixing animal feed before the sun even peeped over the horizon gave a woman an appetite. Lauren almost moaned with greed as Grayson expertly flipped a pancake and added it to the growing stack beside him. Eggs and bacon sizzled in the other pan and coffee bubbled in the percolator.

Lauren took a deep breath and surveyed the homely scene. She could get used to this. A man to make love to her all night and cook her breakfast in the morning. If only he knew how to do the laundry and clean toilets ... With a mental shake, Lauren sipped at her tea. She had no doubt that Grayson could do those things but asking him would indicate an interest she had no desire to encourage.

Grayson brought the warm plates to the table and sat opposite her. His checked blue shirt highlighted the unusual colour of his eyes.

'Eat while it's hot,' he ordered.

Lauren decided not to take offence at his tone seeing as he had done the cooking. The least she could do was show her appreciation. After a substantial silence when all Lauren could think about was food, she glanced across at Grayson.

At home, her father always pestered her with questions as to what she intended to do with her day. Her mother chimed in with gentle criticisms of Lauren's table manners. With previous boyfriends, she'd always felt the need to chat to fill the awkward silences.

Grayson put down his coffee mug. 'You've been staring at me for the last five minutes. Have I got egg on my chin or something?'

'I was just thinking how restful you are.'

Grayson laughed, a deep rumble that started in his chest. 'I've never been told that before.'

'But you are, or at least, that's how you make me feel.' Lauren hastily grabbed her fork and started eating. Yet again, she'd said something stupid. What was it about him that made her relax her barriers?

'It's probably because I'm at peace with myself for the first time in my life. I'm doing something I love,' Grayson said slowly. 'If you can pick that up from me, why can't my father? He still thinks I'm sulking down here.'

Lauren studied her empty plate and fought a losing battle with her curiosity. She understood his desire to find a job he loved, a lifestyle that made him happy. 'Doesn't he approve of your decision to live out here?'

Grayson stood up and began to stack the plates. 'No, he doesn't. Mainly because I didn't choose to do what he did. That's all it took.' He scraped the plates into a bucket and opened the dishwasher.

Lauren scrambled to help. For some reason she wanted to comfort him. 'I know how that feels. My dad still tries to direct my life even though I've started my own business and bought my own apartment. I guess I'll always be his little girl.'

She started loading the dishwasher as Grayson finished cleaning the table.

'My father wants a clone,' Grayson said. 'But I didn't choose to become a lying cheating much-married bastard.'

He dropped the cutlery into the plastic basket with

a crash. Lauren studied his face. Perhaps that explained why he wanted to stay married. She could only applaud him for it, despite the mess it left her in.

In an effort to distract him from a conversation he obviously found painful, Lauren held up the coffee pot. 'Do you want more? I can just about make some.'

'No, I'm fine. I've had more than enough excitement already this morning.' He slammed the dishwasher shut and crossed to the sink to rinse his hands. He glanced at her over his shoulder. 'Talking about my father always makes me unreasonable, don't take it personally.'

Lauren fussed around at the table, lining the place mats up in a precise row. 'That's OK, families can be hell.'

Grayson gave her a reluctant smile. 'Don't I know it. I have five half-brothers and sisters scattered around the country thanks to my father's wildcat ways. As the eldest, I try and keep my eye on them but it's not always easy.' Lauren came towards him and he dried his hands and stepped away from the sink. 'I was thinking we should head into town this morning and get you a pair of jeans. Then after lunch I can take you on a tour of the ranch on horseback. It's the best way to see it.'

Lauren smiled. 'That sounds fine to me. Will you let me keep my panties on?'

Grayson reached forwards and ruffled her hair. 'Of course you can. We couldn't risk you bending over to tie your shoe on Main Street; you'd probably cause a riot.'

Lauren looked around the half-deserted streets of Springtown as Grayson parked his truck in front of the one and only bank. The town looked like a page out of a history book. Wooden sidewalks and stout rails protected pedestrians from the traffic below. Trees offered shade and benches were set out at regular intervals to tempt the weary. The shops had maintained their traditional wood frontings and authentic signs.

Grayson turned the engine off and glanced across at Lauren. 'What do you think?'

'I half expect Billy the Kid to come tearing down the street, shooting his gun.'

Grayson got out of the truck and came around to help Lauren down. 'From you, I'll take that as a compliment. Some of us got together about three years ago and decided to give the town a facelift. We used old photographs, plans and drawings to renovate the buildings in their original style.'

Lauren gazed at the Wells Fargo Bank, with its matching cast-iron boot scrapers outside the ornate double doors. 'I like it,' she said decisively. 'All the modern conveniences within a historical shell.'

Grayson took her hand, his boots thumping on the wooden sidewalk, and led her towards the largest shop. The arched glass windows were painted with the words MRS MAXWELL'S GENERAL STORE AND EMPORIUM.

'You should be able to get some jeans here. Mrs M. swears she has everything a woman wants.'

As they opened the door, a bell tinkled in the dark recesses of the shop. A quarter of the store contained a modern mini supermarket with freezers, chill cabinets and row of groceries. The section in front of Lauren was dedicated to horse paraphernalia. She saw at least forty different types of bits and bridles on the racks and every length of rope imaginable.

Grayson beckoned her towards the back of the store but Lauren just stood and stared. She wondered how old some of the stock was. From her basic survey, it appeared that Mrs Maxwell never returned anything. She could easily spend a day in here buying props for her upcoming project with the PBR.

Moving slowly, Lauren's fascinated gaze skimmed over the shelves of horse remedies for hoof rot, worm and other parasites. A hand-cranked grain mill stood forgotten on a shelf next to a box of candle moulds. She almost tripped over a stack of open boot boxes that littered the floor.

'Careful, there, sweetheart,' Grayson called. 'You don't want to give Mr Givens a heart attack.'

Lauren blinked at the old man sitting in the midst of the boxes trying on cowboy boots. He gave her a wave and muttered something unintelligible into the depths of his white beard.

'Good afternoon, Mr Turner, and what can I do for you on this fine day?'

Lauren could only see the bottom half of the female speaker as she was carrying a four-foot tower of shoe boxes. Grayson relieved the woman of her burden and touched his hat.

'Afternoon, Mrs Maxwell. I've brought my friend Lauren in to buy a pair of jeans.'

A pair of sharp blue eyes behind thin gold-rimmed spectacles focused on Lauren. Mrs Maxwell looked to be in her eighties. 'Welcome, my dear.' She cast a coy glance at Grayson. 'I've never known you to invite anyone to your ranch before.'

Lauren held her breath but Grayson smiled and said nothing. Mrs Maxwell stared expectantly until she seemed to realise she'd get nothing more. Her narrow shoulders sagged in her daisy-print dress and she headed for the furthest corner of the shop.

She switched on the dim lights in the changing rooms, which resembled barn stalls, and waved her hand at a wall of denim. 'Here you go. I'm sure you'll find something you like. Give me a holler if you need any help.'

After Mrs Maxwell returned to Mr Givens, Lauren

walked across to the packed shelves. 'I want size eight, low rise and boot cut. Can you see anything like that?'

Grayson gave a low whistle and took up position at the other end of the unit. 'I'll start looking, but don't get your hopes up.'

After a fruitless fifteen minutes, Lauren went to find Mrs Maxwell. Mr Givens had departed. The shopkeeper muttered to herself as she repacked endless pairs of boots.

'I don't know why I put up with that old man. He never buys anything. I think he just comes in here for the pleasure of watching a woman grovel at his feet.'

Lauren cleared her throat. 'Mrs Maxwell, I'm sorry to bother you but I can't find what I'm looking for. Do you have anything with a low rise or a boot cut?'

Mrs Maxwell pushed her glasses up her thin nose, which looked like an over-sharpened pencil, and studied Lauren suspiciously. 'Do you mean those jeans that the pop stars wear with their belly buttons hanging out?'

Lauren nodded. 'Well, not quite as low as that, but that's the general idea.'

Mrs Maxwell sniffed. 'That Briony Steers. She'll catch her death one of these days.'

Grayson gave a peculiar snort that he turned into a cough and Lauren frantically fought the urge to laugh.

'I did receive a couple of boxes of those kinds of jeans.' Mrs Maxwell pursed her lips. 'I sent them over to Pastor Jenkins for a blessing and then put them in the back of the storeroom. I'll go and see if they are still there.'

When Lauren emerged into the sunlight of Main Street clutching a brown paper bag filled with her new jeans, she hurried towards the truck. When Grayson caught up with her she was still struggling to contain her laughter.

Grayson stored Lauren's bag in the truck. 'How about we get some lunch at the diner and then I'll take you for a ride?' He winked at her. 'You can model your new Briony Steers jeans for me.'

Lauren's eyes filled with tears. 'Stop it, Grayson. I can't laugh any more, my stomach hurts.' She reached out and caught his hand. 'I don't think I've laughed this much since I was a child.'

Grayson brought her hand to his lips and kissed it, enjoying her confession and appreciating her willingness to open up to him. 'Of course, the whole town will know about you by this evening. Mrs Maxwell is a terrible gossip.'

'Really?' Lauren looked uncomfortable and snatched her hand away. 'By the way, thanks for not mentioning the stupid marriage business. It would've made things even more embarrassing.'

Grayson accepted her withdrawal with all the grace he could muster, which he immediately found didn't amount to much. 'Personally I'd be happy to shout it from the roof tops but I know you don't feel that way.'

For the first time that day, Lauren's gaze slid away from his and down the street. She shrugged awkwardly. 'As I said, thanks.'

Grayson ignored his first instinct to let her be and reclaimed her hand. She should have realised by now that he didn't give up easily. 'Come on. Let's get something to eat.'

Chapter Six

Lauren was relieved to see that Alan's Diner was almost empty. She'd braced herself to be the subject of prying eyes, knowing that small towns were notorious for nosiness. How could Grayson bear to live in a place where everyone knew his business? Despite her apprehension, Grayson called out a cheery greeting to the only visible waitress and headed for a booth at the far end of the diner.

After sliding into the crimson leatherette seat, Lauren fiddled with the salt and pepper shakers, arranging them in a neat row alongside the napkins and sauces. The menu was printed on the table top. Lauren pretended to study it. She jumped when Grayson laid his hand over hers.

'If you're not happy to be seen with me, we can leave.'

His terse suggestion made Lauren feel ungrateful. He was doing his best to entertain her and all she could do was study the pristine table top and worry about herself. She forced a smile.

'It's fine, honestly. I keep forgetting...' Her mouth dried as she stared into his intense blue eyes. *I keep forgetting that I'm not supposed to be enjoying myself here. I keep forgetting I'm not supposed to like you.*

She stared helplessly down at the table, unable to say what was on her mind and contemplated their joined hands. If only they could stay in bed for the entire weekend and forget about real life.

'Afternoon, Grayson. Do you want your usual?'

The young waitress wore a white apron and a pale-pink dress, which barely covered her butt. Long thin legs encased in white pantyhose gave her the look of a gangly gosling.

Lauren let out her breath as Grayson turned away to respond to the waitress.

'Hey, Marcie, how's it going? I'll have coffee, a cheeseburger and fries.'

'Do you have any salads?' Lauren asked. For a second she thought Marcie was going to laugh out loud.

'Salads? Like potato salad?' Marcie turned her shoulder on Lauren and spoke to Grayson. 'We don't get much call for salads here, but Daddy could prob'ly strip a few slugs from a lettuce.'

Grayson gave a long slow smile that left Lauren and Marcie staring at his mouth. 'Stop teasing her, Marcie.' He leant towards Lauren. 'They do a Caesar salad with grilled chicken or a good pear and walnut salad.'

Marcie stuck her lip out and gave Lauren another scathing glance. '*She* probably thinks we eat our meat raw out here. She doesn't belong here like you and I do, Grayson.'

Lauren began to relax. It seemed as if the surly waitress had a teenage crush on Grayson and who could blame her? Lauren knew how it felt to dream of the unobtainable. Determined to be charitable, she gave Marcie her warmest smile. 'Do I look so out of place here, then?'

Marcie wrote Grayson's order down on her pad with a much-chewed pencil and stuck it back behind her shell-like ear. She stood on one leg, rubbed her booted foot against the back of her calf and stole a confused glance at Lauren from under her long eyelashes.

'We don't get many visitors around here, especially women like you.'

Lauren kept her voice light. 'I'll have a pear and walnut salad with the dressing on the side and a bottle of water, please.'

Marcie didn't bother to write Lauren's order on her pad. She clumped back towards the kitchen in her Doc Marten boots.

Grayson frowned. 'I wonder what's got in to Marcie? She's normally such a sweet kid.'

'In case you hadn't noticed, Marcie has a horrendous crush on you and my presence was definitely unwelcome,' Lauren said dryly.

Grayson looked horrified. 'Christ – she's only sixteen. I'm more than twice her age! I could've gone to school with her father. Why in the hell would she be interested in me?'

Lauren caught his hand. 'Because you're tall, dark and handsome and you make time for her.' She raised her eyebrows as Grayson continued to shake his head. 'Don't worry. It doesn't take much for a girl that age to fall in love.'

She sensed Marcie's return and swiftly released Grayson's hand. 'Whatever you do, don't let her know you know, just try and treat her the same.'

'What?' Grayson hissed but it was too late for Lauren to elaborate. Marcie arrived at the table, a cup of coffee in one hand and a bottle of water in the other.

'Here you go, the food won't be long.'

She turned to leave and Lauren cleared her throat. 'Could I have a glass for the water and some ice, please?'

Marcie rolled her eyes and cast a martyred look at Grayson who pretended not to notice. After a long while, Marcie returned with the ice-filled glass and thumped it down onto the table. Ignoring Lauren, she leant towards Grayson as if she wanted to tell him a secret.

'Dad says to ask you if you're coming to the Ranchers' Association fund-raiser tonight.'

Grayson looked across at Lauren. 'I forgot about that. I'm not sure . . .'

Marcie's face fell and Lauren said, 'It's all right, Grayson, you can go if you want. I've got masses of work to catch up with.'

Grayson reached across the table, cupped Lauren's chin with his fingers and pulled her close to kiss her mouth. 'You could come with me?'

Lauren lost her bearings as Grayson ran his thumb across her lips. 'OK.'

Marcie made a disgusted noise and retreated to the kitchen banging the door behind her with such force that the silverware on the countertop rattled.

Lauren tucked a strand of her hair behind her ear. 'I sure hope she doesn't poison my salad.'

Grayson grinned. 'I'll taste it for you first to make sure it's OK.'

Batting her eyelashes at him, Lauren cooed, 'No way, cowboy. If I let you near my salad you'd probably eat it all.'

The kitchen door opened again and a large man in a striped apron came towards them bearing two loaded plates. He took a long look at Lauren when he presented her with the salad and then stuck out his hand.

'Now I understand why Marcie's gone home in a huff. Hi, I'm Alan Howard, Marcie's dad.'

Lauren returned the handshake. 'Hi, Alan, I'm Lauren.'

Alan winked at Grayson. 'I think you just broke Marcie's heart.'

Grayson groaned. 'Did everyone know about this but me?'

Lauren hid a smile as Alan nodded. 'Pretty much. In a small town like this we need all the gossip we can get.'

Alan moved back from the table, wiped his hands on his apron and paused. 'Hey, I'm glad you're coming to the fund-raiser tonight,' he said. 'There's been some opposition to your plans for the town's development.

You might want to lay on the charm and put out a few fires.'

When they returned to the truck, Lauren studied Grayson's profile. He hadn't volunteered any further information as to what Alan Howard meant. Lauren was dying to ask even though she knew it was yet another dangerous step towards a more intimate relationship than she wanted.

She sighed and returned her gaze to the open fields. Why should he tell her anything? She was only here for the weekend, not for life.

Grayson gave a low chuckle and put his hand on her knee. 'Go on, spit it out. I know you're burning up with curiosity.'

Lauren continued to look out of the window. 'I don't know what you're talking about. I'm just admiring the view.'

Grayson moved his warm palm further up her thigh and pressed his fingers to the junction of her legs. 'I'll tell you if you promise to make it worth my while.'

Crossing one leg over the other, Lauren trapped Grayson's hand. 'And how might I do that?'

He gave her a sleepy smile which shouted sex. 'You're doing just fine, honey. I like the way you're so quick to take a man up on his suggestions.'

Lauren reached across and ran her fingernail down the length of Grayson's zipper. His hand tightened between her thighs, stimulating her already sensitive flesh. Lauren let out her breath and tapped her index finger against the hard bulge of Grayson's cock.

He kept his gaze on the road but she felt him shudder. 'So what exactly do you want to know?' Grayson said hoarsely.

Lauren allowed herself a triumphant grin. 'What did Alan Howard mean about your plans for the town?'

'I want to build some industrial units on the edge of

town. Apparently, some people aren't thrilled by the suggestion.'

Lauren gazed at the unspoilt farmland. 'Are you sure that's a good idea? It would be a shame to destroy such a beautiful place.'

'I don't want to destroy it.' Grayson slowed and turned into the gates that led to his ranch. 'But there's not a lot to keep people here. Most of the kids like Marcie end up heading for Portland or down into California to find work. The town's going to end up as a retirement community for the rich if we don't manage to kick-start the local economy.'

He manoeuvred the truck through the gates. 'I have a few contacts in the business world who are prepared to start small enterprises here with a view to expanding them if the idea proved profitable.'

Lauren gave him a speculative glance. 'You have contacts?'

Grayson expertly backed the truck in front of the house. 'Just because I choose to live in the sticks doesn't mean I have to lose out. We do have fax machines, telephones and the internet out here you know.'

Lauren felt stupid. Grayson had a high-tech office at his ranch but it hadn't occurred to her that he might be in contact with other business organisations. So much for her fantasy cowboy...

Gathering her resources, Lauren managed a professional smile. 'Which companies have you approached so far? I might be able to help you out.'

Grayson got out of the truck and came around to open her door. He lifted her out of her seat and set her gently on the ground.

'No one you'd know. They're all fairly small fish. I want to attract family-owned businesses who understand how important it is to keep communities together in a changing economy and world.'

Lauren caught Grayson's hand. 'I think that's a great idea.'

Grayson shrugged. 'It wasn't just me. The whole town came together to discuss this. I just happened to miss the meeting when they were electing a president and guess what? I got elected.' He paused to shuck off his boots in the mud room.

Lauren picked one of them up and waved it under Grayson's nose. 'This company, the one who makes these, Prairie Dawg Boots, would be a great place to try. They're a fairly new business and I believe a family-owned company.' She smiled up at Grayson, trying to ignore his puzzling lack of enthusiasm. 'I happen to know about them because I'm using some of their retro boot designs in the commercials I'm working on for the PBR.'

Grayson took the boot out of her hand and dropped it to the floor. He brought Lauren into the circle of his arms and kissed her nose. 'I'll certainly bear them in mind. Now, would you mind getting your hand inside my jeans? I'm so hard after that finger tapping in the truck that I need more petting.'

Lauren dropped to her knees, oblivious to the tiled floor and worked at the straining zipper of Grayson's jeans. He sighed as she took his cock in her hand and then into her mouth. She brought her other hand up to cup his balls as she sucked on him, bringing him deeper and deeper in until she couldn't take any more. His hand fisted in her hair, keeping her where she wanted to be until he came with a knee-buckling shudder.

Grayson helped Lauren to her feet and then into his arms. He carried her the short distance into his bedroom and stripped off her skirt. When his fingers plunged inside her and came out wet, he brought them to his mouth and slowly licked them clean. Heat expanded in Lauren's lower stomach and she moved instinctively towards him.

Grayson shook his head. 'You'll have to wait, honey, until I've time to see to you properly. We're going on a tour of the ranch.'

Lauren hooked her index finger inside her tiny panties and slowly pushed them down her legs. Grayson took a step towards her, his eyes intent as she bent to pick them up. She folded the scrap of lace between her fingers and stuffed it into Grayson's shirt pocket. She imitated his slow drawl.

'I'll hold you to that, cowboy, and it'd better be worth my while.'

Chapter Seven

Grayson saddled two horses while Lauren went to feed the chickens. She seemed to have taken a motherly interest in them, which amused Gray immensely. It was hard not to laugh at her surprise at his ability to conduct business out in the wilds. But, if he wanted her to stay, it was vital she believed it.

His faint smile died. When she'd mentioned Prairie Dawg Boots, he'd almost choked. Of all the companies in the world why had she picked them? Of course, it wasn't that much of a coincidence. When she got back to work and saw his name and his brother Jay's at the top of Prairie Dawg Boots company notepaper she'd be wanting an explanation. He suspected she liked being lied to about as much as he did.

Hell, he hadn't realised Lauren was meeting Barry Levarr, his business manager, in Vegas as well as the PBR guys. He left most of the everyday business to Jay and Barry anyway. By the time he'd worked it out, Lauren had already met, married and left him. What the heck was a guy to do when his life got so complicated?

Past experiences with grasping women who zeroed in on his wealth and connections and not his personality had made Gray cautious. Somehow he knew that presenting himself as both Lauren's new client and her new husband would kill her passion stone dead. As he saw it, he had to make a choice.

His number-one priority was to get Lauren back to see if their marriage stood a chance of success. The business end of the relationship, his involvement with

Prairie Dawg Boots, wasn't important right now and it was only a tiny part of his holdings. Convincing Lauren to stay by buying into her cowboy fantasy was.

Gray slipped the bit into Foxy's mouth. He couldn't imagine Lauren choosing to mix her personal and professional lives; he'd have to persuade her. Foxy butted Gray in the stomach as if in agreement as he tightened the cinch.

He consoled himself with the thought that he hadn't actually lied to Lauren – yet. He wanted Lauren to see beyond the cowboy fantasy and begin to want him for himself. Explaining his business activities would have to come later.

He just didn't see her as a corporate wife, pushing him into expanding the business, using her father's connections to 'help' him along.

Gray didn't want that. He'd tried to please his father by entering the business world and it nearly destroyed him. Yeah, he had all the trappings of wealth and success but at the cost of his soul. Would Lauren understand that life on the ranch and arranging his other business interests around that suited him better?

He reckoned she would if he got up the nerve to be completely honest with her. She'd defied her own father hadn't she? His problem was that she'd probably wish him well and disappear back to San Francisco without a backwards glance. Why was she so set against marriage? Surely he was the one who should be having doubts.

Lauren appeared at the barn door wearing one of his long-sleeved shirts tucked into her new jeans. Her soft brown hair was tied back and she wore no make-up. Gray struggled to remember the poised, fashion-plate of a woman who'd stepped off the plane a day earlier.

He checked Robbie's cinch and watched Lauren pat Foxy's neck. He didn't bother to tell her what to do. Her assured manner around the horses reflected her knowledge and he was content to let her get on with it. He smothered a grin. No doubt she'd snap at him if he offered his help.

'What are you smiling at, Grayson?'

Gray looked up from his task to find Lauren staring at him. 'I was just thinking how nice you look in those jeans and how quickly I'm going to get you out of them.'

Lauren ducked her head to adjust the length of her stirrup but not before Gray saw her mouth curve in an inviting smile. He loved the way her mind worked, he loved the way he just had to look at her and his body hardened. It also confirmed his belief that her hard sheen of city gloss concealed a softer more generous centre.

Lauren squinted up at the cloudless sky as Grayson led the way across a field of uncut hay. In the silence, the swishing of the dry grass against her legs and the creaking of the saddle were the only sounds to mar the perfection of the afternoon. Grayson drew up alongside her and produced something from his saddlebag.

'I got you a present while we were at Mrs Maxwell's.' He held out a dark-brown cowboy hat. 'I think it'll fit.'

Speechless, Lauren took the hat and smoothed her fingers over the soft supple leather.

Grayson gave her an apologetic grin. 'I won't tell you what it's made of. Women tend to get squeamish about such things.'

Lauren recovered her voice and gave Grayson a mock frown. 'That's a very macho thing to say and not appreciated by your average twenty-first century woman.'

Grayson opened his mouth. Lauren set the hat on her head and shook her finger at him. 'That doesn't include me. I will cry if you tell me it's made out of baby bunnies or cute beavers. I can't help it, I grew up on Disney.'

As Grayson's slate-blue eyes narrowed in amusement, Lauren took the opportunity to urge Foxy into a lope. Leaving Grayson behind, she prayed her butt wouldn't be too sore by the end of the ride, but a girl had to make a point. She wasn't surprised when he caught up with her, Robbie's longer stride eating up the ground without effort.

From the slight rise at the edge of the field, he pointed across to the town settled in the river valley. Sunlight glinted off the distant windows and cars like scattered diamonds.

'My land ends five miles from the edge of town. That's where I intend to build the business park.'

Lauren tried to imagine the vast unspoiled expanse of agricultural land interrupted by the presence of functional structures. She turned in the saddle to study Grayson.

'Are you sure you want to do this?'

His face was half-shadowed by the brim of his cowboy hat. His determined nod was answer enough.

Lauren sighed and busied herself patting Foxy's warm neck. It was none of her business whatever Grayson chose to do. If she kept on interfering, he might assume she cared and she wasn't prepared to get into that yet.

Grayson clicked at his horse and turned in a wide circle, then headed for a grove of oak trees. When they reached it, he dismounted and came to lift Lauren down. After hobbling the horses, he turned to her, his expression serious. He wrapped his fingers around her upper arm.

'I know you're not sure I'm doing the right thing, Lauren, but hear me out ...'

Lauren held up her hand. 'It's OK. You have every

right to decide what to do with your own land and community. I'm just a weekend guest. I don't have to live here.'

Even as she said the words, she knew they weren't completely true. Grayson's trust in sharing his plans and seeking her opinion had come as a pleasant surprise. Her father never told her mother anything about his business life. Lauren had worked for his company for years and he'd never included her either. It was one of the reasons it had been so easy for her to walk away.

Grayson let go of her arm. She could've sworn she saw a flash of hurt in his eyes.

'I forgot, Lauren. You're only here for the sex, aren't you?' In swift jerky movements, Grayson pulled off his shirt. 'Where would you like me, ma'am? On my knees or on my back?'

Lauren swallowed hard. 'I didn't mean it like that.' She stepped forwards and placed her palm on his naked chest. His tanned skin was warm and slick with sweat, his heartbeat erratic.

'I don't have a right to make decisions that affect a whole community after a couple of days.' She tried to smile. 'You wouldn't want my advice, anyway. My father always tells me my business decisions are worthless.'

Grayson stayed still under her touch, his breathing slow and steady. He brought his hand up to cover hers.

'Number one, your father's wrong, you're definitely not stupid. Number two, I owe you an apology. I had no right to say that.' He squeezed her fingers, pressing them into his sun-warmed skin. 'Hell, I've got a feeling I'm rushing my fences. I'm not usually like this with women.'

Lauren tried not to smile. She guessed he was usually the one running from commitment not courting it.

'I've got secrets, too, Lauren,' he continued, curving his arm low around her hips, drawing her closer. 'I understand there are things you don't wish to share with me yet, but when I ask for an opinion I want one. I'm not your father.'

Lauren caught a droplet of Grayson's sweat on her fingertip and followed it down his chest. He inhaled sharply as her nail skimmed the waistband of his jeans.

'That's not playing fair,' Grayson murmured. 'I'm trying to have a serious conversation here.'

'So am I.' Lauren eased her finger past the button of his jeans and headed south making his hard flesh grow harder. He caught her wrist but not before she'd skimmed the slick wetness from the tip of his erection. She brought her fingers to her mouth. His pupils dilated until there was almost no blue left, only a bottomless black.

Before she could react, he swung her up into his arms and marched towards the trees. In one deft motion, he set her down on the soft moss and knelt in front of her.

'It's my turn, remember? You've had your fun.'

He pulled off her boots and jeans, leaving her panties. Pressing her knees apart he leant closer, the stubble on his cheek grazing her inner thigh. Lauren tensed as he slowly inhaled the scent of her arousal. All he had to do was touch her and her body yielded.

She sighed as he rubbed his finger against the thin wet silk of her panties.

'You're soaking.' Grayson's soft breath made her soften even more. His finger and thumb sought her clit and moulded it between them. Lauren's hips moved forwards as he lowered his head and sucked on the swollen tip of flesh.

She brought her hand down to the back of his head and pressed him closer, her whole body turning to gooey toffee as his mouth pleasured her. When his fingers slid beneath the silk and dipped inside her, she couldn't repress a moan. His muffled chuckle reverberated against her skin making her tremble as he eased off her panties. She dug her heels into the ground, using all her strength to urge him closer, opening herself wider to his delicious torment.

Her climax crashed over her and he held her on the edge until she built again and exploded into another one. Only then did he soften his stroke, bringing her back down with soothing lapping touches. Blindly, she reached forwards, found the gaping fly of his jeans and his thick cock and wrapped her hand around him. He came almost immediately, stifling his yell against her stomach.

Lauren closed her eyes and let the peace of the countryside envelop her. She'd never considered making love outdoors as being particularly stimulating, but for Grayson, she'd have to make an exception.

He lifted his head and used the tails of his shirt to wipe his wet face. When he bent to kiss her, she could still smell herself on him. The sun had started its slow slide down to the horizon and the shadows were lengthening.

'We'd better get back if we're to make that meeting,' Grayson said.

Lauren allowed him to pull her to her feet. She started rearranging her clothing and watched him zip up his jeans. He caught her watching him and winked. 'Remind me to tell Mrs Maxwell how much I appreciated those jeans you bought.'

Lauren buttoned her borrowed shirt and headed for her horse. 'You do that. She deserves a fright after charging so much for them.'

His warm appreciative laughter followed her as she checked Foxy's cinch and found a convenient place to remount. His ability to see a joke was one of the many reasons she liked him. He never tried to exclude her like some of the men she'd worked with. He treated her like a person with a brain, not as the dumb female who only got a job because of her daddy.

Reluctantly, Lauren thought about her return to San Francisco on the following day. She'd only been with Grayson for a matter of hours and yet she felt she knew him better than any man she'd ever met. A small part of her yearned to curl up in his arms and never let go. The rest of her fought against the sensation with every fibre of her feminist being. She didn't need a man to be happy.

Grayson swept past on Robbie. Heading into the sunset he looked like every woman's fantasy. Lauren couldn't help but smile. OK, she didn't need a man to be happy but it was damned hard to be miserable in Grayson's delectable company.

Chapter Eight

Grayson held the door open and Lauren walked past him into the town assembly hall. Tattered papers tacked to cork notice boards fluttered in the draft. The smell of beer and fruit punch mingled with brownies swamped Lauren's senses. From the look of the empty plates it seemed as if they'd missed the barbecue.

Grayson fitted the palm of his hand into the small of Lauren's back urging her forwards. She caught sight of Marcie by the refreshment table and risked a smile. Marcie scowled, hiked a shoulder and abruptly turned her back. A petite blonde woman put down a pitcher of lemonade and walked across to Grayson.

The woman looked to be about Lauren's age and had an assured fragile elegance that reminded Lauren of Vivien Leigh. She wore a crisp white blouse and a khaki skirt which complemented her tanned legs and flawless skin.

'I'm so glad you could make it, Grayson,' she cooed as she stood on tiptoe to kiss his cheek. 'We have a lot to discuss.' Her gaze flicked over Lauren and instantly dismissed her.

'Mrs Paulson.' Grayson tipped his hat, his smile disappearing. 'Perhaps you'd better thank my friend Lauren. If she'd hadn't agreed to accompany me, I wouldn't have made it.'

As Mrs Paulson studied Lauren, her fingers toyed with the strand of pearls at her throat. 'It's sweet that you recognise Grayson for the important man he is.'

Lauren resisted an urge to twirl her hair around her finger, stand on one leg and chew gum. She knew she should've worn her 1960s shift dress and high heels. In her jeans, she obviously looked about as dynamic and effective as Marcie. Just as she opened her mouth to reply, Grayson curved an arm around her waist and drew her close.

'Lauren's a busy woman. She's got better things to do than worry about me.'

Mrs Paulson patted Grayson's arm, her enormous platinum and diamond wedding band catching the light. 'You're such a gentleman. I'm sure that whatever little job Laurie has she does it real well.'

Lauren stepped away from Grayson and took a moment to rummage in her purse. She handed the obnoxious Mrs Paulson her old business card. It was nice of Grayson to leap to her defence but she was quite capable of handling Mrs P. She hadn't endured a year at a top finishing school without learning how to deal with the princesses of the world.

'My "little job" means that my time is valuable. As is my client's.' Lauren looked around the rapidly filling hall. 'Perhaps we could forgo the social chit-chat and get on with the business at hand?'

After reading the card, Mrs Paulson tucked it in her Gucci purse. 'Are you Grayson's lawyer?' She turned to Grayson, her sapphire eyes wide with alarm. 'Surely it hasn't come to that? We should be able to handle our problems within our own vibrant local community, don't you think?'

Lauren smiled sweetly. 'Do you mean a public trial followed by a good old-fashioned Western hanging?'

Grayson cleared his throat, slipped his arm through Lauren's and steered her away. Mrs Paulson rushed across the room to an older man who immediately put his arm around her.

Lauren fluttered her eyelashes at Grayson in a poor imitation of Mrs Paulson as he smiled down at her. 'I think she meant we should sit down and talk it through, which is exactly what this meeting is all about. Now she'll be complaining to Mr Paulson about you and my goose is cooked.' He led Lauren to a seat. 'As the president, I'll have to sit up front. Wish me luck.'

Lauren watched him exchange greetings with some of the crowd and take his place. He winked at her as he sat down, flanked by Alan Howard and Mrs Paulson.

As the discussion grew heated, it became clear to Lauren where the problem lay. Grayson and most of the older residents wanted the industrial complex. Despite Grayson's pledge to gift the land to the town, the newer, richer folk who'd retired or retreated to Springtown wanted to keep things exactly as they'd found them.

Lauren frowned as the exquisite Mrs Paulson edged her chair closer to Grayson's. If she leant any further over, she'd be sitting in Grayson's lap! Trying to concentrate on the arguments became difficult when all Lauren wanted to do was leap over the table and pull Mrs Paulson's unnaturally blonde hair. Had Grayson slept with her? It seemed likely. They were easily the most beautiful people in town. Lauren pictured them in bed together and mentally set the sheets on fire.

Grayson stood up to speak, drawing Lauren's attention to his long frame and spectacular eyes.

'Perhaps we could hear from some of the younger members of the audience.' His gaze swept the rows of expectant faces. 'How do you feel about having to leave your families to find work?'

A young man wearing a battered cowboy hat and a red shirt got to his feet. 'I work on a ranch in northern California and I'm not complaining.' He winked at the older couple sitting beside him. 'I think my folks were glad to get rid of me. They sure cleaned out my bedroom fast.'

After the laughter subsided the blonde-haired girl on his other side turned on him. 'Well, Scott, it's good to know how much you like being away. If I marry you, I want to live right here near my family. What are you going to do about that?'

Lauren felt a pang of sympathy for Scott as his girlfriend glared at him. He whispered urgently in her ear.

Marcie Howard stood and smiled shyly at Grayson. 'Even if we do want to live here, it's impossible to afford a house.' Marcie's gaze hardened as it swept the Paulsons and Lauren. 'When new folk come in, the prices always rise.'

Grayson nodded and Marcie flushed with pride before sinking down into her seat. 'Marcie's right. One of the projects I hope to start after the small business units get going is a reduced-cost housing programme for original residents and their children.'

A smattering of applause greeted his remarks and Lauren joined in. Mrs Paulson attempted a frown through her smooth Botoxed forehead.

'But that kind of social do-gooding can destroy a community,' Mrs Paulson said. 'It encourages the wrong type of people.' She pretended to ignore Marcie's audible snort. 'This town needs people with money to keep it viable. A town lives or dies by its ability to adapt to market forces.'

'Exactly, Mrs Paulson,' Grayson said. 'That's why we need to move with the times and get those business units in.'

'Hear, hear!' Alan Howard shouted, earning himself a glare from Mrs Paulson.

The hum of conversation grew louder until Grayson banged on the table. 'I think we have enough support to present the issue to the town council. Then everyone will get a chance to have their say.'

Mrs Paulson pursed her lips. 'I'll be starting a petition against this.'

Grayson nodded amiably. 'Go ahead, Mrs P. That's what democracy's all about.' He pushed back his chair. 'Thanks for coming out here tonight, I appreciate it.'

At Grayson's words, the majority of people began to leave. Some loitered in the doorway to talk to their neighbours and keep an eye on their teenagers before they disappeared. Lauren remained in her seat as Grayson finished a leisurely conversation with Alan.

Lauren's view was blocked by the last group of chattering teenagers. By the time they slouched away, Grayson and the table had disappeared. Lauren followed the sound of voices to the back of the hall to a walk-in storage closet.

A weak glow from the overhead light revealed Grayson leaning against the wall. Mrs Paulson stood in front of him, hands on her hips.

'Why are you doing this to me, Grayson?' Mrs Paulson said. 'You know how frail Roger is. All this upheaval could affect his heart. We came out here for peace and quiet and you're proposing to destroy it.'

Grayson sighed. 'Anna, can you get it into your head that it's not about you? You have five hundred acres of land on the opposite side of town. You're not exactly going to be bothered by hoards of people.'

Anna Paulson crossed her arms in a defensive posture. 'You can pretend all you want but I know you're up to something. And I know that your peculiar code of honour means you'd prefer Roger to die before you sleep with me.'

Grayson straightened from the wall. 'What did you say?'

'I know you still want me,' Anna said. 'It wouldn't surprise me if you were prepared to go to any lengths to achieve your aim.'

Grayson laughed. 'Hell, Anna, if this was in one of your lousy movies I might just go along with it. Do you seriously think I proposed the whole business scheme in order to kill off your husband?'

'Well, why not? You were as mad as hell when I married him.'

'No. I wasn't. You'd already done too much damage. By then, I couldn't have cared less.'

'I should never have followed you to Springtown.'

Grayson tipped the brim of his hat. 'That's the first sensible thing you've said so far. Why don't you persuade old Mr Moneybags to take you somewhere nice and expensive to live? I'm sure he'd be happy to.'

Anna slapped him hard on the cheek. 'You're a bastard.'

Grayson caught her wrist before she delivered another blow. 'I only wish that was true then I wouldn't have known my father and neither would you.'

He dropped Anna's hand and turned to the door. He stared straight into Lauren's eyes. 'Are you ready to go, honey? I've just got to put some more chairs away.'

Anna brushed past Lauren without a word and headed for the parking lot, slamming the door behind her. Grayson returned to the hall and brought in a load of stacked chairs. He glanced at Lauren as he passed her.

'Did you get all that?'

Before she could reply, he deposited the chairs in the closet with a resounding crash and went to get more. Lauren waited until he'd finished his third run before following him into the closet where he stood breathing harshly.

'So, it's Anna now is it?'

Grayson didn't reply as she advanced towards him.

'And she thinks you want to kill her husband?'

Grayson brought out a handkerchief and wiped the sweat from his face. 'Anna was an actress before she met Roger Paulson. She's always had a problem distinguishing fact from fiction.'

His flat tone alarmed Lauren. 'You knew her before she moved to Springtown, didn't you?'

Grayson frowned. 'Yeah, and before you ask, I knew her in the biblical sense too.' He thrust his hands into his pockets. 'She's one of those women who look so frail and beautiful that stupid young men like me feel the need to protect them.'

Lauren tried not to react to his even statement, surprised by how much it stung. She knew Grayson must have had other lovers before her. He was hardly lacking in sex appeal.

Grayson smiled. 'That's one of the reasons I'd never get back into a relationship with her. She spent more time in bed worrying about her make-up and how fat she looked than on enjoying the sex.' He shrugged. 'I guess she just can't believe I've moved on.'

Lauren stepped close, brought her hand up and curved it around his jaw, her thumb caressing the hard pulse throbbing in his throat. A surge of possessive pride swirled low in her stomach. 'Did she dump you for Roger Paulson?'

Grayson nuzzled her fingers, bringing them close to his mouth. 'Something like that.'

Surprised at the depth of her anger, Lauren stood on tiptoe, wrapped her arms around Grayson's neck and kissed him on the mouth.

'How could she do that to you?'

Grayson's tongue met hers halfway and the kiss turned from slow and languorous to hot and dangerous. A pulse drummed between her legs, as she pressed herself against his groin and felt his instant response. Her hand was working on the top button of his jeans when Grayson went still. The sound of a key turning in the lock of the outside door and a truck driving away filtered through into the back room.

'Shit,' Grayson breathed. 'I think we're locked in.'

Lauren finally loosened the button and slid her hand inside his jeans. His cock was so huge that there was barely enough room to move her fingers. She squeezed his shaft and he groaned.

'How on earth could any woman let go of this?' Lauren whispered. She encircled the wet tip of his cock with her finger and thumb. 'She must be crazy.'

Grayson picked her up and pressed her against the door, his hands pulled at her jeans, ruthlessly working her left boot off until she was half-undressed and open to him. Resting her left foot on his hip, he slid inside her. Lauren gasped at the sudden blunt heat and hardness as his mouth closed over hers.

The click of an opening lock echoed across the empty hall. Grayson muttered an obscenity, closed his eyes and pulled out. Lauren stifled a moan as he lowered her to the ground. His expression was indescribable. He struggled to zip his jeans over his massive erection.

Lauren stumbled to pull up her jeans and locate her boot as Grayson moved in front of her.

Marcie's hesitant voice floated down the hall. 'Grayson, are you here? My daddy locked up but then I saw your truck in the parking lot so I told him I'd check.'

Grayson took a deep breath, glanced back at Lauren to see if she was decent and opened the door. Marcie's confident smile wavered as her gaze slid past Grayson and fastened accusingly on Lauren.

Grayson grabbed his hat and, holding it in front of him, walked up to Marcie. 'Thanks, sweetheart, Lauren and I were beginning to wonder if we'd have to bed down in the hall for the night.'

Marcie grabbed Grayson's hand, almost dragging him towards the door and away from Lauren. Lauren struggled to keep up, afraid that Marcie might lock the door on her. When they reached the parking lot there was no sign of Alan Howard.

Marcie turned to Grayson, a satisfied smirk on her face. 'Dad must have gone without me. Could you give me a ride home?'

Grayson's frustrated gaze met Lauren's and she shrugged. Giving kudos to Marcie for her excellent planning, Lauren climbed into the back seat allowing the girl to sit up front. In a way, it was a relief not to be too close to Grayson. Her body hummed from their brief coupling, craving more. If she were sitting next to him, her hand would stray to his lap, eager to finish what they'd started.

Marcie talked a lot. Most of what she said seemed deliberately aimed at showing Lauren what an outsider she was and how Marcie would suit Grayson so much better. Lauren let the constant noise wash over her and concentrated on retrieving the sexual thrill of Grayson inside her. There was nothing like a little competition to make a girl realise how hot her man was.

When they reached the Howard house, Grayson left the engine running and got out of the car.

'I'll just check that someone's home, Marcie, or else I'll drop you at the diner.'

Lauren closed her eyes and listened as the thrum of the idling engine vibrated through her skin.

'He won't marry you.'

Lauren opened one eye. If only Marcie knew the truth . . .

'Who won't?'

'Grayson won't. He has loads of girlfriends like you who last about a week and then he dumps them.'

'Really.' Lauren didn't want to fight with Marcie. Being a teenager was hard enough without some adult criticising you or giving you well-meant advice. She tried to ignore Marcie's angry face, inches from her own.

'He needs a woman who understands what it's like to live in a small town and manage a ranch. He needs a wife who'll let him stay here.'

Lauren nodded. 'You're right, Marcie he does. Are you warning me off?'

For a second, Marcie looked unsure and then her face flushed a defiant red. 'Yeah, I am. If you'd just go away, he'd start to realise I'm the one he wants. All I need is a little more time.'

And twenty more years, thought Lauren. Grayson reappeared on Marcie's side of the car and tapped on the window. Lauren leant forwards, grabbed Marcie's hand and shook it. Marcie looked shocked and tried to pull away. 'Good luck, Marcie. Any man should be glad to have you.'

'But you don't think it'll be Grayson do you?' Marcie hissed.

Grayson opened the door and Marcie got out.

Lauren smiled into her eyes. 'As I said, good luck.'

When Grayson returned, Lauren watched him start the engine and reverse out onto the road. He glanced back at her as he drove smoothly out onto the highway.

'Don't you want to sit up front?'

Lauren shook her head. 'I'm too lazy to move and I'm quite happy here.'

Grayson smiled into the mirror; his blue eyes narrowed as he took in Lauren's relaxed body. 'Are you sure you wouldn't be happier up here petting me?'

Lauren unbuttoned her jeans and slid her fingers between her legs. Whatever Marcie and Anna wanted, Grayson was definitely hers, at least for a while. The thrill of arousal shook through her at the possessive thought. She'd never felt quite so carnal about a man before.

The tantalising scent of Grayson's cock lingered between her legs. She gently explored her swollen flesh, noticing how open she was, thanks to Grayson, wide enough to fit three fingers inside without any effort. Her thumb brushed her swollen clit and she gasped.

Grayson's head swivelled back towards her. 'What are you doing back there?'

Lauren repeated the movement of her thumb. 'I don't think you want to know while you're driving.'

Grayson inhaled. 'I can smell you. Are you starting without me?'

Lauren caught her breath as the truck sped up on the deserted highway and fairly flew towards the ranch. Smiling in the darkness, she waited until Grayson came around the car and opened her door, illuminating her.

He went still, his gaze glued to her crotch where her fingers rested. He licked his lips and leant towards her.

'Don't stop on my account.'

She smiled. 'I don't intend to.'

Chapter Nine

Gray drew an unsteady breath. Lauren's jeans were open and her right hand was buried between her legs. His shaft, still hard and unsatisfied from their unfinished coupling, throbbed and pulsed against the zipper of his jeans. Lauren looked dreamy and flushed as she allowed her hips to follow the gentle teasing movement of her fingers.

Without asking for permission, Grayson reached into the car and tugged off Lauren's boots and jeans. She placed her left foot on the back of the seat in front of her, opening her to his heated gaze.

'God, Lauren, show me.'

Her thumb moved, caressing the bud of her sex, as her fingers sunk into her tight sheath. Grayson bit back a groan as she continued to stroke and pleasure herself. Her breathing became more rapid and he recognised the signs of her imminent orgasm. Unable to resist the temptation, he lowered his head and licked her fingers. She gasped as he targeted her with the hard tip of his tongue, moving in time with her, increasing her excitement.

Her hips thrust upwards one last time and he felt the first shudders of her orgasm. He waited until she stopped shivering and added his fingers to hers, widening her even further. She was so wet he could have happily drowned as he sucked and licked and bit at her succulent flesh. Her right foot sat on his shoulder, her toes digging into him with every grinding pulse of her hips.

When he sensed she was ready to come again,

Grayson pulled back. 'I'll give you a choice. Let me inside you now or take my cock in your mouth and finish this. There's no way I can even make it to the kitchen tonight.'

Lauren pushed away from him. He thought he detected a hint of triumph in her eyes. Was she finally realising the power she held over him and, hell, was that a good thing or a bad thing?

'I want you inside me.'

Gray didn't wait for further clarification as she turned her back on him and crawled further along the bench seat. He barely managed to unzip his jeans before he followed her, catching her hips in his hands, driving himself mindlessly forwards into her wet welcoming flesh. She came around him almost instantly, milking his cock with the force of a clenched fist.

The ding-ding sound of the open car door finally penetrated his overloaded senses. He nuzzled Lauren's ear and backed away from her out of the car. After she retrieved her jeans, Lauren jumped down from the truck. Her satisfied smile made him hard again.

'You make me feel like a horny teenager,' Gray murmured. 'I don't think I've gone all the way in a car since I was in high school.'

Lauren pushed her hair behind her ears and turned towards the house. 'I never even got to do that. My father sent me to an all-girls finishing school in Switzerland.'

Grayson grinned as he unlocked the door and followed her inside. 'Damn, that could've been interesting. Did you ever try a little girl-on-girl action?'

Lauren gave him a mock frown. 'Sorry to disappoint you, but nobody there turned me on.'

Grayson laughed out loud. Lauren never failed to surprise him. Beneath her exquisite exterior lurked a fine wit and a voracious sexual appetite which matched his. He couldn't have chosen a better mate if he'd tried. Wrapping his arms around her waist, he dropped a kiss on the top of her head.

'How about I make us some hot chocolate and bring it to bed? You can go ahead and get comfortable.'

Despite looking a little startled by his offer, Lauren agreed and disappeared into his bedroom. Grayson took his time boiling the milk, adding the cocoa and sprinkling cinnamon on the top. Sudden doubt assailed him and he stared down at the homely beverage. He'd never made anyone his favourite bedtime drink before.

Would Lauren think he was boring? Anna Paulson had preferred a slug of gin and a sleeping pill. She'd probably have laughed hysterically if Gray offered her cocoa instead.

By the time Grayson arrived with the drinks, Lauren was in bed. When he put the mug on the nightstand beside her, he realised she was already asleep. In repose, her skin glowed with health and innocence. He stripped, showered and climbed into bed beside her. Rolling onto his side, he loped an arm around her waist and breathed in the floral fragrance of her hair. She smelt of sex and of him. He liked that. He liked it a lot.

Lauren opened her eyes to the discontented screeches of mutinous poultry. The noise seemed to come from right outside the window. Beside her, Grayson began to stir. Lauren got out of bed and visited the bathroom. It took her only a minute to pull on her jeans and one of Grayson's sweatshirts.

Outside, it was still dark. A faint orange glow trimming the hill tops signalled the imminent emergence of the sun. As soon as Lauren stepped out of the mud room, she found herself surrounded by a sea of agitated hens. Grayson followed her out, his shirt half undone, his expression grim.

Lauren turned to him. 'How on earth did the chickens get out?'

Grayson hopped onto one bare foot as a chicken pecked at his toe. 'I'll put my boots on.'

Unable to wait, Lauren began to walk towards the hen house. She'd seen the havoc a predator could cause when she'd stayed on her grandparents' ranch. Mentally she prepared herself for a bloody mess.

When Lauren got closer the reason for the chickens' dawn visit became apparent. Someone had left the gate open. Grayson gave a low whistle as he surveyed the scene.

'Did you shut the gate properly last night after you fed them?'

Lauren remembered how carefully she'd checked the lock. 'Yes, I did.'

Grayson nodded. 'Well then, we'd better try and work out why someone would want to play such a stupid trick on us.'

Lauren couldn't believe his quiet acceptance of her denial. Her father would've kept on about her supposed guilt for hours and then not even bother to apologise when he inevitably found out he was wrong. Grayson believed her.

Still in shock, Lauren followed Grayson around the back of the hen house and they headed for the barn. Obligingly the sun crested the hills and illuminated the way. Grayson pointed at the huge white letters painted on the side of the red barn: OUTSIDERS GO HOME!

Lauren stared up at Grayson. 'Well that must mean me. I'm sorry Grayson. I never meant to bring you trouble.'

Grayson put an arm around her rigid shoulders. 'Don't be too quick to take the blame. I've only lived here for six years. I could have offended a lot of people with my plans for the business park.' He continued to walk, holding Lauren close. 'Hey, it might even have been the chickens.' He squeezed her shoulders. 'I'll check the horses.'

Grayson carried on down the shadowed corridor. Lauren stopped at the first door and stifled a gasp as she peered into the normally pristine tack room. Saddles, bridles and blankets lay in a heap on the wooden floor. The acid smell of spilled cleaning fluids and leather polish caught at Lauren's throat.

'The horses seem fine.' Grayson came up behind her and looked over her shoulder into the trashed tack room. 'Shit, what happened here?'

Lauren went to enter the room but Grayson held her back. 'Let's not touch anything until I've phoned the police.'

In the main yard, the hens continued to tail Lauren like incompetent stalkers. Grayson swore as he narrowly avoided stepping on yet another one. 'Damn, we'll have to put the hens back first. I wish I still had a dog.'

Lauren ran back to the barn and gathered a handful of dried chicken food. Feeling rather like a mother hen, she sprinkled a little grain on the ground and persuaded the hens to follow her back into the pen. After Grayson shut the door on the main bunch, he paused to retrieve three escapees who'd decided to try being free range.

In the kitchen, Lauren put on the kettle and managed to start the coffee as Grayson made his call to the police. She was eyeing the toaster when he hung up. Despite the stresses of their morning, he still looked composed. Her father would be red faced and shouting by now.

'Bob Foster, the chief of police, says he'll be over in about twenty minutes. That should give us time to wash up and have some breakfast.' His gaze fell on the coffee percolator. 'Hey, did you make that for me? Thanks.'

Lauren found him a mug. 'You'd better taste it first.'

She made her tea, followed him to the kitchen table and sat opposite him. After concentrating on his coffee, he lifted his head and smiled at her. 'What?'

Lauren studied him. 'How can you be so calm?'

He shrugged and wrapped his long fingers around his coffee mug. 'What's the point of getting angry over something so minor? Nobody died, nobody got hurt.'

'But someone came onto your property and trashed your barn.'

'Yeah, but possessions can be replaced. People can't.'

Lauren cleared her throat. 'Thanks for believing me about the gate.'

Grayson reached across and took her hand. 'You're a grown woman. I don't imagine you're going to lie to me.' He kissed her fingers and stood up to get another mug of coffee. 'Why don't you go and shower while I put on some breakfast? Bob Foster can put away more than his fair share.'

Bob pushed away his plate and shook his head as Grayson offered him another pancake.

'Thanks, but I couldn't, Gray. How about we take a look around and see the damage?'

Lauren grabbed her jacket and boots and followed the men outside. Grayson explained about the escaped chickens as Bob wrote in his notebook. He paused to study the hostile message painted on the side of the barn. When Lauren reached the barn entrance, the smell of bleach made her gag.

'The tack room's been trashed but the horses are safe,' Grayson said. 'I told Lauren not to touch anything in here.'

'From the smell of it, you're going to have some

damage.' Bob cleared his throat. 'You can go ahead and clean up but write me a list of everything that's beyond saving and include anything that's missing.' He glanced at Lauren, his brown eyes shrewd. 'Anything you'd like to add, Ms Redstone?'

Lauren crossed her arms over her chest. 'Not really, I'm just glad that the animals are OK.'

Back in the kitchen, Bob faced Lauren and Grayson across the kitchen table. 'Have you any idea who might have done this?'

'I've been stirring up the town lately with my ideas for the business park,' Grayson said. 'Someone might've wanted to make a point about that.'

Bob nodded. 'How about any personal grudges? You two been upsetting anyone lately?'

Lauren glanced at Grayson. Would he mention Marcie or Anna? He shook his head. 'I'll have to think about that and let you know. I'll give you a call if anything turns up when we clean up the barn.'

The police chief put his notebook in his pocket and got to his feet. 'You need a dog, Gray. No one would've gotten on the property when old Petty was here.'

Lauren left Grayson in the kitchen and followed the police officer out into the yard. He unlocked the door of his car and paused. 'Is there something else you wanted to tell me, Ms Redstone?'

'I wanted to give you my home number in San Francisco. You might need it to contact me because I probably won't be here after today.' Lauren handed over her business card and scrawled her home number on the back. 'But I was also wondering if you knew anyone who might have some puppies for sale.' Bob's puzzled expression cleared.

'You want to get Gray a new dog? That's a great idea. He looks incomplete without Petty around. I know a couple of people who've got good puppies. I'll find out if they are for sale for you.'

Lauren gave a relieved smile. 'I'll be in town this afternoon. If I pass by the police station, I'll come and see if you've got any information.'

Bob winked and got into his car. 'If you don't mind me saying, Ms Redstone, Gray's a lucky man.'

Lauren watched him drive away and then returned to the kitchen. Grayson had disappeared. She picked up a trail of clothes that led to the bedroom and found him in the shower.

She went into his closet and selected his oldest pair of jeans, a moth-eaten sweatshirt and a faded T-shirt. Brushing her hair into a tight ponytail, she knocked on the door of the steamed-up shower. 'I'll be over at the barn.'

Grayson turned the shower off and stepped outside. 'You don't have to do that. I can take care of it.'

His sudden abruptness surprised her. 'I'll be glad to help, what's the problem?'

Grayson grabbed a towel and wrapped it around his hips. 'I'm just wondering why you wanted to talk to Bob Foster alone.'

'Did you think I was telling tales, Grayson? What happened to the "you're a big girl"?'

He pushed a hand through his wet hair. 'I know I didn't mention Marcie but I wanted to talk to Alan Howard first. If she did this in a fit of jealousy, I'd rather her dad handle it than the police.'

'I didn't say a word about Marcie,' Lauren replied evenly. 'I gave Bob my business card and home phone number so he could contact me in San Francisco. I didn't want him to think I might be here on a regular basis. I'll see you at the barn.'

Lauren stomped down the path towards the barn ignoring the welcoming chorus from the hen house. One minute she was in danger of falling in love with Grayson, the next he behaved as if she was some kind of tattletale.

Lauren stopped walking. What had she just said? She couldn't fall in love with him. How could she even think that? OK, she might've been a little oversensitive to Gray's perfectly reasonable question but it was better if she kept him at a distance. After all – she glanced at her watch – there were only ten hours left until she returned home for good.

Chapter Ten

Grayson swore quietly as Lauren slammed the door behind her. Great job, Gray, he thought, get all macho and suspicious with her. He wasn't surprised she'd walked out on him after his stupid question. Since his recent brush with Anna, he kept expecting Lauren to act the same way and that wasn't fair. Anna wasn't capable of revealing such hurt in her eyes.

After getting dressed, Gray took a moment to call Alan Howard. Alan reported that Marcie was still in bed but that he'd certainly discuss the matter with her when she got up. Wondering if he'd done the right thing, Gray hung up the phone and went in search of Lauren.

He hesitated at the door to the tack room. Lauren kept her back to him as she sifted through the mess on the floor. Her body language screamed at him to leave her alone but he knew that would be a big mistake. Hell, he wasn't going to let one stupid remark ruin the best weekend of his life.

He drew a breath and prepared to eat crow. 'Lauren, I'm sorry. I had no right to question you. You certainly don't have to answer to me.'

He waited until Lauren got to her feet, her expression was wary, her arms were crossed over her chest. A smudge of dirt half covered her cheek. He tipped his hat back so that he could see her face more clearly. 'I carry a lot of scars from women I thought I could trust. But I shouldn't have taken it out on you.'

He shifted his feet as Lauren continued to stare at him, her hazel eyes appraising. Was she the kind of woman who bore a grudge? He hadn't reckoned so but then he hadn't imagined Anna would cheat on him with other men and lie about it to his face.

'Is that it?'

Lauren's quiet question made him straighten up. 'What do you mean is that it? Do you want me to go down on my knees and kiss your feet or something?'

Lauren smiled and he let out a breath he'd been unaware he was holding. 'Usually when a man apologises for something, there's a whole load of additional explanations and justifications attached.'

Grayson immediately thought of Lauren's father. He'd heard about his business methods during his time in New York. He hadn't realised Mr Redstone extended his tough-love approach into his family life as well. Grayson's fingers curled into fists. He'd like to meet the bastard one day. He'd done a fine job of trying to sabotage his daughter's confidence.

It amazed Grayson that Lauren had fought back to become such an outwardly successful and confident person. Was he the only man who could see the vulnerability beneath her strength and did she like him for that or fear him?

Acting on his instincts, Gray crossed the floor and pulled Lauren into his arms. He held her gaze as he looked down at her. 'I was wrong. I acted like an ass. End of story. Do you want it in writing?'

Lauren put her gloved hands on his shoulders and stood on tiptoe to kiss his chin. She smelt of his soap and shampoo. She smelt as if she belonged with him.

'I have baggage too, Grayson, and I probably overreacted. But I'm glad you apologised. I'd hate to leave here on a sour note.'

Gray tightened his hands at her waist. 'You're not leaving till eight are you?'

'That's right, although I do need to run into town to

pick up some more cleaning supplies. You don't need to come with me. Can I borrow your truck?'

Wisely refraining from asking why she wanted to go into town without him, Grayson managed a smile. 'Of course you can. I'll finish up here while you're gone and write up those lists for Bob.'

Lauren parked on Main Street just outside Mrs Maxwell's store and spent a happy hour buying up the place. It seemed she'd been right. Mrs Maxwell had a policy of never sending anything back to her suppliers. After storing Grayson's presents in the truck and avoiding Mrs Maxwell's way too personal questions, she arranged to have the rest of the stuff shipped back to San Francisco.

The town seemed quiet and peaceful on this particular Sunday lunch time. Families returning from church wandered the sidewalks eating ice cream and window shopping. It hardly looked like the kind of place where neighbours fought over land and painted insulting graffiti on barn walls. With a sigh, Lauren rested her forehead on the steering wheel.

Grayson's frank apology had destroyed her feeble hope of building a wall between them to see her through the last few hours of her visit. Somehow she wasn't surprised by his response. Grayson meant what he said. He made it impossible for her to treat him like any other man she'd known. He made it possible for her to trust him and that was a truly rare commodity these days.

Lauren lifted her head as a young mother crossed the road with her toddling son. How would it feel to be able to rely on Grayson's strength and integrity for the rest of her life? She'd have no room for excuses. They might fight but at least she'd know where she stood.

She shook her head. It still wouldn't work. She wondered what he'd do if she suggested they kept their relationship more casual and open. For some reason, she couldn't see Grayson going for it.

And then there was her father. Because of his over-possessive streak, she knew that if she quarrelled with him she'd never get to see her mother again. The idea of Grayson and her father agreeing to tolerate each other also seemed ridiculous. She couldn't stand the thought of having to stand between them. She might as well toss a bone between two ravenous dogs.

Thinking of dogs sent her out of the car and over towards the sheriff's department, one block down. Bob Foster appeared out of his office at the back, a welcoming grin on his face.

'Hi, Lauren. I think I've found some puppies for you.'

Minutes later, Lauren followed Bob's police cruiser down a narrow track to one of the outlying ranches. Dust flew up from the unmade road, drying Lauren's throat and making her reach for a bottle of water. When Lauren stepped down from the truck a chorus of barking greeted her. Bob headed for the barn.

'Beth Sutherland's Australian sheepdog had five puppies a few months ago. They're great dogs. I have one myself.'

Lauren entered the old barn where a makeshift pen had been constructed for the puppies. Three eager faces poked wet noses through the wire, trying to get to Lauren. At least the pups were friendly. She crouched down to study them. With their large feet and mottled brown colouring, they looked like a cross between a collie and an Alsatian.

After a while, the biggest male pup came up on his back legs, put his paws on Lauren's shoulders and licked her face. She laughed at the intelligence shining in his liquid brown eyes.

Lauren scratched the pup's silky ears and looked up at Bob Foster. 'Is this one for sale?'

'They're all for sale.' Mrs Sutherland appeared beside Bob and smiled at Lauren. She wore old jeans and a cherry-red sweater which almost matched her vivid hair. 'I hear this is a present for Grayson. He's a good man. I'd be happy for him to have one of my dogs.'

Lauren pointed to the largest of the three puppies. 'I'll take this one, please. If Grayson wants to change his mind, not that I think he will, I'll send him to see you.' She retrieved her chequebook from her back pocket. 'How much do I owe you?'

Mrs Sutherland named a low figure and Lauren glanced at her, pen poised to write. 'Are you sure that's enough? Bob said these are pure-bred puppies.'

Mrs Sutherland stuck her hands in her pockets. 'Grayson's a friend of mine. He helped me keep this ranch and make it profitable after my pig of a husband ran out on me. I'd give you the pup as a gift but I know he'd be after me for making a bad business deal.'

Lauren wrote the cheque and handed it over. 'Grayson still has a dog carrier in the back of the truck. I can put the puppy in there.'

Beth Sutherland found a leash and collar and handed the puppy over to Lauren. 'He's had his initial set of vaccinations but Grayson might want to take him to the vet anyway.'

The puppy wriggled and licked Lauren's ear. 'Thanks, Mrs Sutherland. I think Gray is going to love him.' She headed for the truck keeping a firm grip on the excited bundle of fur she carried. After stowing the dog safely away, Lauren drove back up the drive away from a waving Mrs Sutherland.

She sure hoped Grayson was going to love him. Her idea of leaving Grayson a companion when she left the ranch had seemed like a good one. Now she wasn't so sure. Would he think her pushy and interfering? Maybe a man liked to choose his own dog.

By the time Grayson buzzed her through the gates, Lauren was riddled with indecision. She parked the truck close to the house just as Grayson came out of the back door. He walked across to her side of the truck and she lowered the window. When she turned the engine off an excited yapping broke the silence.

Grayson frowned. 'What the hell is that?'

Lauren gulped as she got out of the truck and scrambled into the back. 'I got you something as a thank you for having me, I mean, for inviting me to the ranch.' She opened the wire door and the pup exploded out of the kennel straight into Grayson's arms.

For a long moment, he simply stared down at the dog. Lauren held her breath. 'Do you like him?'

Grayson dropped his head and buried his face in the puppy's soft fur allowing the dog to whimper and squirm in his tight grip. When he finally raised his gaze to Lauren, a muscle twitched in his cheek and his eyes blazed blue and clear.

'Don't leave tonight.'

Lauren remained kneeling in the back of the truck, trapped by the intensity of Grayson's stare. Suddenly she found it hard to breathe. 'I have to. I have a business to run.'

The puppy yelped and Grayson's expression changed. 'Hell, he just peed all over me.' He held the dog away from him by the scruff of its neck. 'You need to learn when it's polite to interrupt, buddy.'

Lauren scrambled out of the truck and handed Grayson the dog's leash. 'Do you like him then?' She knew she was babbling but it was all she could manage right now. 'Beth Sutherland said you can come and pick another puppy if this one doesn't suit.'

To her relief, Grayson made no effort to pursue his other line of conversation, his attention all on the puppy.

'Does he have a name?'

Lauren shook her head as she watched the puppy try to negotiate the step up to the back door. 'He has a fancy name for his breeding papers but not a pet name.'

Grayson boosted the dog from behind with the toe of his boot and sent him nose first into the mud room. 'I'll probably call him Petty after my last dog. It's easy to remember.'

Despite Grayson's calm tone, Lauren couldn't forget the startled pleasure in his eyes when she handed him the dog. Had it been so long since anyone had given Grayson a gift? Perhaps because he seemed so good at helping others, nobody thought he had needs of his own.

Grayson caught her hand as she followed the excited puppy into the kitchen. 'I haven't said thank you yet, have I?'

Lauren smiled up at him. 'I think I got that without you needing to say it.' She kissed his warm lips and wrapped her arms around his waist, glad just to hold him for a moment longer, aware of time slipping away.

He raised her chin with one long finger and his mouth descended to cover hers. She joined him in the light gentle kiss wishing it could last forever.

Grayson was the first to draw back. 'Once we've settled Petty, would you like to walk down to the main barn with me? I need to pick up some replacement tack. I can give you a tour around the training and breeding facility if you're interested.'

Lauren gave him her brightest smile. For some reason, he was shutting her out. Perhaps he'd embarrassed himself by asking her to stay with him. A rush of pain centred low in her stomach and she fought to conceal it.

'Sure, that would be great.'

Chapter Eleven

Lauren held Grayson's hand as they walked past the barn and headed up the hill behind the house. She kept quiet, sensing Grayson's abstraction, wondering if she was the cause of it. At the top of the incline, Lauren paused and looked down on a newer set of buildings. A covered arena surrounded by at least forty stalls and three turnouts took up most of the flat space. Two sloping green pastures surrounded by white picket fences completed the compound.

'I talked to Alan,' Grayson said. 'Marcie's denying everything but Alan found paint on her sneakers. He's not too happy with her right now.'

Lauren shuddered to think what her father would have done if she'd gone out and trashed someone else's property. Despite her best efforts, the longer she spent with Grayson, the more she compared him to her father. She stuck her hands in her pockets and stared at Grayson's dusty boots.

'I hope Alan's not too hard on Marcie. At least she didn't hurt the horses.'

Grayson lifted his head and half-smiled into the sun. 'I'm glad she didn't hurt any living thing. That includes you, Lauren, not just the horses.'

Lauren looked back down at his boots. The softening in Grayson's gaze as he studied her was unnerving. He tugged her hand out of her pocket, enfolded it in his and continued walking.

'I'm not sure how Marcie managed to get out to the ranch. She doesn't drive yet and I can't imagine her walking five miles with a can of paint, can you?'

'Maybe she had help. Have you told Bob Foster about this?'

'Not yet, Alan says he'll bring Marcie over to see me later. I'm hoping we'll be able to clear up a few details then.'

Lauren squeezed Grayson's hand. 'Thanks for telling me.'

He gave her an amused glance as they reached the gate leading through into the stable yard. 'Thanks for being so understanding.'

'Marcie's just a kid. If it had been the beautiful Ms Anna Paulson throwing paint around, I might've gotten worried.'

Grayson clamped his fingers onto her elbow. 'Do I detect a hint of jealousy, Mrs Turner?'

Lauren stopped and faced him. 'Yes, you do, although Anna Paulson must be used to that. Most of us are way out of her league.'

'You're worth a thousand of her and don't you forget it.' Grayson flexed his fingers against her skin, drawing her closer.

Lauren studied the grim set of his mouth and whispered, 'What did she do to make you hate her so much?'

'Anna? She agreed to marry me and changed her mind two days before the wedding. She didn't have the nerve to tell me to my face so she arranged for me to catch her in our bed with her lover.'

Lauren stroked Grayson's cheek. 'She was stupid, almost as stupid as I was for running out on you in Las Vegas.'

There, she'd said it. She'd admitted she might've made a mistake. She waited for his response without daring to breathe.

He met her gaze, his blue eyes direct. 'But at least you had the guts to come back here, face me and tell me you don't think it's going to work. You didn't send your father or some employee to pay me off.'

Grayson kissed her hard on the mouth. To her relief, whatever inner conflict he'd been struggling with seemed to have been satisfied. 'Let's make this quick. I'd rather spend our last few hours alone.'

Lauren waited at the deserted end of the indoor arena while Grayson arranged for someone to drop the tack up to the house. Despite it being a Sunday, the immaculately turned out barn was still busy. Behind her, a man drove a small tractor full of manure and soiled straw bedding from the recently cleared stalls along the narrow passage and out into the sunlight.

She jumped when Grayson came up and placed his hands on either side of the rail, trapping her between them. 'Do you mind if we wait a minute? My stallion, Cole is going to cover one of the young mares for the first time. I'm just going to watch from here to see if everything goes OK.'

Lauren glanced down at the other end of the arena where three men waited with a tall black stallion. Even from a distance, Lauren admired the wildness of the stallion's long arched neck and gleaming muscled coat. She wondered how the mare would feel at such an awesome display of masculine power and energy.

'If you want to go down there, I'll wait,' Lauren offered, her gaze fixed on the stallion.

Grayson shook his head. 'I'm supposed to be off work today and my deputy manager is dealing with this. If I go down there, I'll get in the way.' Grayson looked pained. 'I know it's good for me to delegate but I hate doing it.'

Lauren laughed. 'So do I. I always think that no one can do the job as well as I can.'

'We'll just watch from here then and hope they don't

notice us.' He glanced around. 'This end of the barn is deserted. We shouldn't be in anyone's way.'

Lauren's attention returned to the far end of the arena. 'Is that the mare? She looks a little nervous.'

'Yeah, that's Brown Sugar.' Grayson pointed at the stallion. 'See how Cole's ears have come up and he's taking in her scent?'

Lauren leant closer into the fence, one foot on the lower bar and Grayson crowded behind her. She could feel the warm press of his body from shoulder to knee. The stallion neighed and pawed at the ground reminding Lauren of a thousand Western movies. Grayson laid one arm along the top of the fence surrounding Lauren in his embrace.

His soft-voiced comments stirred the hair behind her ear and made her skin tingle. Her breasts pressed into his arm, tightening her nipples. Finding it difficult to breathe, she whispered, 'Why do they have to hobble the mare and cover her face? It looks more like an execution than a mating dance.'

'Because Brown Sugar is new at this we want her to remain as calm as possible. If she panics, she'll do less damage to herself, the stallion and the guys than if she was loose.'

Lauren shivered as Grayson bit down on her neck and then licked the same spot. 'By taking away her sight, she's relying on her other senses and less likely to be distracted. She'll smell and hear the stallion, which is the most important element of a successful mating.'

'I thought all this mating business was done in a test tube these days.'

'Sometimes it is, but Brown Sugar's owners wanted to try it the old-fashioned way. Apparently the mare's dam had problems conceiving artificially and they're concerned Brown Sugar might be the same.'

As the stallion was led closer and closer to the

tethered mare, his vocal challenges became louder, her whickering replies less so. Lauren held her breath as the two handlers lined the stallion up behind Brown Sugar. The mare turned her head, scenting his presence, and swished her tail out of the way.

'She's telling him she's ready for him now,' Gray murmured. 'Cole will be able to mount her.'

Lauren caught a glimpse of the stallion's sexual equipment as he reared on his hind legs and came down over the mare. Dust kicked up by the stallion formed a cloud around the coupling horses. The savagery of the primitive act made Lauren catch her breath. 'Jeez, it's a good job she can't see or else she'd run a mile. He's certainly a big boy.'

Grayson chuckled and the sound vibrated through his chest setting Lauren's senses tingling. She arched her back as the hardness of Grayson's erection settled against her buttocks.

Grayson groaned. 'There's nothing like being around an aroused stallion to make a man feel inadequate.'

'You feel just fine to me,' Lauren whispered.

Grayson's forearm tightened across her breasts as the stallion pushed off from the mare and was led away. As the swirling dust motes and sand resettled over the arena, Grayson turned Lauren to face him within the circle of his arms.

'You enjoyed that, didn't you?'

Lauren nodded as Grayson's fascinated expression became predatory. Without speaking, he took her hand and led her towards one of the empty stalls. He pushed the door shut and circled her. Lauren found it hard to believe how turned on she was and how quickly Grayson had picked up on it.

The sweet smell of hay washed over her as Grayson halted in front of her. He held out his hand, his gaze commanding. 'Take off your boots and jeans.'

Aware of heat and moisture pooling between her

legs, Lauren complied. Grayson's borrowed denim shirt came down to her mid-thigh, leaving her decently covered. He pointed at it. 'Unbutton the shirt.'

Lauren took her time sliding the buttons free, aware of Grayson watching her and the building anticipation of pleasure. He swallowed hard as he took in her tight nipples showing through the sheer silk of her bra. She resisted a brazen urge to touch herself, to bring that wild look into his eyes and make it boil over.

He walked her across to the empty hay manger in the corner of the stall. 'Hold onto this and bend forwards.'

Lauren grasped the wooden structure with both hands, aware of Grayson moving closer. From her position, she had a nice view of his bulging jeans.

'I'm going to cover your eyes, just like the mare's.' A folded blue and white bandana appeared briefly in front of her blocking out the light. Lauren could smell a hint of Grayson's aftershave on the stiff fabric. She drew in a deep breath, trying to adjust to her lack of sight, trying to judge exactly where Grayson was.

The silence stretched. A horse neighed somewhere in the distance followed by a man's faint laughter. Lauren imagined Grayson staring at her half-exposed body and licked her lips as her heart rate increased.

'You're beautiful, Lauren.'

Gray swept his hand up the inside of Lauren's shirt, caressing her naked spine from bottom to top. She shivered at the faint roughness of his palm and the hint of possessiveness in his voice. The soft hiss of his leather belt being drawn out of his jeans made her listen more intently. She sensed him edge closer and held her breath.

'Do you remember how the stallion sensed the mare?' Grayson inhaled, the sound loud in the sultry silence. 'I can smell you, Lauren. I know that when I want to push inside you, you'll be wet and ready for me.'

Lauren bit her lip and pressed her thighs together. Grayson was right. She was more than ready to take him. He snapped the end of his belt out and grazed her butt. The leather felt warm and supple against her skin. He did it again, surprising her with the small sting, and then drew the length of the belt across her back. Her fingers fisted as he wrapped the belt around her wrists and secured her to the hay manger.

Grayson unzipped his jeans; the zipper rasped close to her ear. Lauren tensed as she smelt the familiar scent of his arousal.

His hand clasped her neck and guided her head to one side. She gasped as her lips brushed the crown of his erection. 'Do I taste as good as I smell, Lauren?' His wet fingers returned to her mouth bringing with them the taste of the sea and of new life. She sucked them clean.

He pulled up her shirt and trailed his hand down from her neck to her buttocks making her shudder. His fingers tangled with the lacy string of her thin panties and ripped the side open. They slid to the floor leaving her lower body naked to his gaze. His sinfully sexy voice was more of a lure without the gift of sight than she'd imagined.

'When the mare was ready for the stallion, she moved her tail out of the way for him.'

The rough texture of Grayson's jeans brushed the backs of Lauren's thighs as he moved behind her. 'If you open your legs for me, I'll know you're ready too.'

Lauren parted her legs and Grayson moved up close. His fingers dug into her hips; the soft hair on his belly rubbed her lower back. He groaned low in his throat as his cock probed her slick passage and slid home.

Lauren arched her back, desperate to take him as hard and deep as she could, to feel every pulsing inch.

Gray bit down on Lauren's neck as she clenched around his shaft, leading him in a sharp dance of thrusts and withdrawals. She wouldn't let him slow the frantic pace. She demanded he take her fast, forcing her to a climax and making him want to come too.

Gray's heart pounded against Lauren's skin and his breath shortened as he fought the overwhelming urge to spill inside her. He gripped her hips, allowing her to push back against his mighty thrusts, amazed at her power and voracious appetite for more.

He managed to pull back, holding her still with his superior strength, making her wait. She writhed in his grasp as he brought his right hand in front and settled it between her legs. Crouching over her, he stretched his fingers and circled the place where his cock disappeared into her body.

God, he didn't want to lose her. He wanted the welcome her body provided for him every day of his life. Having this to come home to at night would make his life worth living. He drew his fingers up from the straining flesh until they found her clit.

Lauren moaned and pressed her beautiful butt against him. He resisted the urge to plunge deeper and concentrated on stroking her swollen bud with the lightest of touches. He closed his eyes as she squirmed against him until her inner muscles clenched and reached for his cock. He thrust hard then, sheathing himself in her demanding heat, letting her take his come until he lost touch with anything except her body surrounding and completing him.

He tore off her blindfold as the last pulse almost brought him to his knees. He steadied Lauren around the waist as she sagged against him. He licked the sweat from her neck, continued to stroke her hard nipples, reluctant to stop touching her.

She nestled against him, her body relaxed and pliant. He wanted to bring her down to the hay-covered floor and start all over again. He wanted her sex flooded with his come so that she'd never get rid of the scent of him. When he managed to breathe again, he reluctantly pulled out and zipped up his jeans. He released Lauren's wrists and turned to help her into her clothes.

She avoided his gaze. Grayson caught hold of her chin and made her look at him.

'What's up?'

Lauren grinned. 'God, I can't believe how much I enjoyed that.' She gestured at the empty stall and stooped to pick up her ruined panties.

Grayson smiled slowly. 'Honey, there were two of us here. I behaved just as badly as you did.'

'Yes, but you're a man. You probably felt some macho need to prove yourself after seeing that stallion. I'm supposed to be a little more sophisticated.' Lauren finished buttoning her shirt and wrenched open the stable door. To Grayson's disappointment, there was no one around to see them.

'And did I?'

Grayson waited in the doorway until Lauren turned around and noticed he wasn't following her.

She frowned, wrinkling her elegant nose. 'Did you what?'

'Prove myself.' Grayson arched an eyebrow. 'You wouldn't want me walking around feeling insecure now, would you?'

Lauren opened her mouth as if to reply and seemed to change her mind. The scathing look she gave him was enough. Grayson made a theatrical bow and followed her back up the hill, his laughter warming the air behind them.

Chapter Twelve

'Marcie, just answer the darn question. Did you trash Grayson's barn or not?'

Grayson laid a restraining hand on Alan Howard's arm. 'I think we can take that as a given considering her sneakers and hair are speckled with white paint. What I want to know is why?'

Marcie folded her arms across her narrow chest. Her gaze slid across to Lauren. 'Because you invited her here. Because you like her too much.'

'I've had girlfriends before, Marcie,' Grayson said. 'But I don't recall you letting out my chickens and writing graffiti on my barn because of it.'

'But she's different, isn't she?'

Grayson shot an amused glance at Lauren who sat curled on the couch, her feet tucked underneath. Her skin was flushed, her lips reddened from his kisses. His body ached and hummed with satisfaction from their recent lovemaking. Damn, she'd be leaving him in two hours and here he was chatting to Marcie. 'Yeah, she is, but that's my problem not yours.'

Alan ran a hand through his short greying hair, his expression strained. 'I'll pay for the damage, Grayson. Marcie can work for nothing at the diner and repay me. I'd send her up here to work the debt off but I reckon she'd like that too much.'

Marcie bit her lip, her face reflecting a mixture of emotions as she studied her father. For the first time she seemed to be considering how what she'd done might have affected him.

'How did you get out here, Marcie?'

Grayson waited for an answer but Marcie continued to study her well-chewed fingernails. 'I doubt you walked so someone must have brought you. I'd like to know who it was.'

Marcie glanced at her father who looked right back at her, no help in his stern brown eyes. 'You won't believe me even if I tell you.' She directed a venomous glance at Lauren. 'You think she's perfect.'

Grayson drew in a calming breath. 'Lauren was with me all night. I know for a fact she wasn't driving you around.'

'Marcie . . .' Alan growled.

Marcie looked defiant. 'I didn't say she drove me anywhere. After I got home from the meeting at the community centre I got a phone call.'

Grayson arched an eyebrow. 'From Lauren?'

'I'm not sure, the voice was muffled,' Marcie said. 'The woman said that if I wanted to get back at you, she had the perfect solution.'

'This makes no sense,' Gray muttered. 'What did she do, fly you here on a magic carpet?'

Marcie went red. 'Of course not. She told me a truck complete with supplies would pick me up and take me out to the ranch.'

Alan groaned. 'You got into a truck in the middle of the night with a complete stranger? Haven't I raised you better? What the heck were you thinking?'

Marcie heaved an exaggerated sigh. 'I knew him, Dad. It was Billy Cooper, one of the guys from the rental car company who comes into the diner.'

'You think that makes it better, Marcie? Well, it doesn't.'

Grayson hastened to intervene as father and daughter glared at each other. 'Did Billy stay in the truck or did he come in with you?'

'He stayed in the truck. He told me he'd been paid to drive not to trespass.'

'Billy Cooper's obviously a lot smarter than he looks,' Alan muttered. 'He knew when to stop.'

Grayson shot Alan a warning glance and he went quiet. 'Marcie, I could call Bob Foster right now and he'd have to come and take you down to the jail to make a statement.'

Marcie's gaze widened. 'You wouldn't do that to me would you?'

'Of course he wouldn't,' Lauren said quietly.

'I don't need any help from you, Ms Redstone,' Marcie hissed. 'You're only being nice to me because you're worried Grayson will see through your attempts to make me look bad.'

Grayson leant back against the family-room wall. 'And exactly how did you work that out?'

Marcie pointed a finger at Lauren. 'If she hadn't called me and made it easy for me to damage your property, I wouldn't have done anything. She did it to make sure that you'd hate me.'

'But I didn't call you.'

Lauren's calm tone seemed to make Marcie even more agitated. She spun back towards Grayson, tears falling down her cheeks. 'Can't you see what she's doing to us?'

Marvelling at the way Marcie's mind worked, Grayson shook his head. 'There is no "us". I'm way too old for you. You'll always be special to me but that's because you're my best friend's little girl.'

Marcie continued to stare at him as if willing him to change his mind.

Lauren appeared with a box of tissues and guided the unwilling girl to the couch. Grayson sat opposite Marcie and Lauren. 'I'm not going to call Bob Foster and give him your name. Somebody else has taken advantage of your jealousy and used you to play a cruel trick on me.' Marcie's mouth opened but Grayson continued, 'Think about what you did. You didn't hurt Lauren; you hurt me and my ranch.'

Realisation dawned on Marcie's face and she began to stutter. 'I didn't mean ... I never wanted to ...'

'Hurt me? Maybe not, but the person who set you up did.' Grayson let that sink in for a moment and then asked, 'Do you know who was on the phone, Marcie?'

Marcie dabbed at her eyes with a tissue and glanced at Lauren. 'If it wasn't her, I don't know who it was. Why would someone want to hurt you through me?'

Grayson got to his feet. 'Because you let them, Marcie. Now go home and make it up with your dad. He deserves an apology too.'

Lauren waited until the sound of Alan's truck faded down the drive before she got to her feet and went to find Grayson. He stood by the house, Petty glued to his left leg. Lauren walked up behind him and slid her arms around his waist.

'Marcie will survive this, Grayson.'

His taut stomach muscles flexed beneath his shirt and then relaxed. He sighed. 'I know. It's just that I don't like all the unanswered questions. I don't like the thought of someone using Marcie to get at me.'

Lauren laid her cheek against his cotton shirt. His now familiar scent, a mixture of citrus, leather and pure sex curled around her senses. She'd know him anywhere.

'I have to go soon,' Lauren said softly.

Grayson bowed his head as Lauren released him and stepped back. She headed for the house, wondering if he would follow or leave her to gather her belongings in peace. She wasn't sure which she'd prefer. If he asked her to stay again it might start an argument and that was the last thing she wanted.

In the quietness of the luxurious bathroom, it only took Lauren a few minutes to pack her bag. She hung her Barbie cowgirl outfit back in Grayson's closet and placed the cowboy boots on the carpet below. She smoothed the garish blouse with her fingertip.

The thought that she might not come back here scared her more than she'd believe possible. In only a couple of days the secluded ranch felt like home. It shocked her to realise that she hadn't even missed the city.

Sternly, Lauren reminded herself of all the many reasons why holiday romances didn't work. She and Grayson led different lives and had totally different expectations. Just because they were sexually compatible did not make them fit for the everyday business of a successful, committed relationship.

Lauren put on her pink-checked Chanel skirt suit and a white blouse. She pinned up her hair in front of the mirror. Did she look the same? Would anyone know she'd spent the weekend having the most fantastic sex of her life?

In the bedroom, she paused to leave Grayson her last gifts. She'd taken a digital photo of Robbie and Foxy, his two horses, enlarged it and printed it out in black and white on his computer. The silver frame she'd purchased in Mrs Maxwell's complemented the picture beautifully. She propped the picture up against the wall hoping Grayson would hang it up if he liked it enough.

She also read the note she'd written him. 'I've left you a few decorating items for your bedroom in the box in the mud room. Use what you like and take the rest back to Mrs Maxwell.' She'd chosen reds and browns to warm up his bedroom and Western-themed art to complement his gentleman cowboy nature.

Grayson waited for her in the kitchen. He sat on the edge of the table cradling a mug of coffee in his hands. His gaze swept over her but he made no comment on her altered appearance. He dumped the coffee in the sink and retrieved his car keys.

'Are you ready to go, Lauren?'

Lauren found it surprisingly difficult to speak and nodded instead. Grayson picked up her bag and led the way out to the yard. Lauren took a moment to cuddle Petty who seemed to want to jump into the truck with her.

'Look after Grayson for me, Petty,' Lauren whispered into the puppy's sleek fur. He yelped as she squeezed him hard and then he settled back into his basket.

Lauren took one last look at the whitewashed ranch house before she got into the truck and then shut the window. In the gathering darkness, the house looked welcoming and secure. Grayson reversed the truck and slowly drove down the gravelled track. In the distance, Lauren could make out the faint shapes of the horses in the paddock.

She drew in a breath as a rush of unexpected emotion flooded her. 'Dammit, I forgot to say goodbye to the chickens.'

Grayson didn't reply, his attention on the road as he joined the heavy traffic on the freeway. He didn't know what to say to her. Part of him yearned to tie her to his bed and keep her there forever. The slightly more civilised part wanted to keep arguing with her until she stayed simply to shut him up.

He knew in his soul that neither idea would work. Armoured in her business suit, Lauren would give him a dismissive stare and refuse to allow him to meet her in San Francisco the following weekend. If he wanted to see her again he needed to bite his tongue and at least act like a gentleman.

When they reached the turn-off for the airport, Lauren laid her hand on his knee. Grayson gritted his teeth and willed her to slide her fingers up to his groin and pet him.

'You don't have to park. You can drop me off right in front of the airport.'

Grayson scowled and moved into the left lane making the car driver behind him brake and honk his horn. 'Tough, I'm parking.'

Lauren snatched her hand away as if he'd bitten her. He stole a glance at her averted profile as he hunted down a parking space big enough for his truck. She looked pissed off with him for not doing what he'd been told, her lips were folded into a thin line.

He grabbed her bag from the back of the truck and stalked towards the elevators. Lauren followed him, her high heels tapping on the yellow concrete floor. He didn't need to ask her where the flight left from. He'd used the service so many times he could've piloted the damn plane himself.

Lauren refused to run after Grayson as his long stride ate up the ground leaving her behind. She'd had it with chasing men, period. She checked he was going the right way and then followed at a more leisurely pace. In the last two days he'd developed a bad habit of stalking off and leaving her to follow meekly behind. Why wasn't he talking to her?

She caught up with him just as the flight was announced. He stared down at her, his face a blank, his eyes the hard blue-grey of slate.

A spark of anger awoke deep inside her. 'You don't have to come to San Francisco next week if you don't want to. We can finish this now.'

Grayson dropped her bag onto the floor and gripped her by the shoulders. 'I don't know what kind of men you generally hang out with, Lauren, but I'm coming to San Francisco. We made a deal and I don't break my promises.'

He traced his thumb along her lower lip, his expression softening, his gaze filling with more emotion than she guessed he could handle. Lauren gasped as his mouth descended and he crushed her to his chest. He kissed her until she forgot the people moving past her to the gate. He kissed her until she wanted to wrap herself around him and never let go, until she forgot why she had to leave. When he raised his head she could only stare helplessly into his eyes.

'We haven't finished this game yet, Lauren,' Grayson whispered. 'It's only halfway done. By this time next week we'll see who wants to leave who. I'm betting you'll change your mind.'

Grayson handed Lauren her bag, tipped his hat and strode off into the crowds. Lauren turned to find the cabin crew of the aircraft gawping at her. She patted her hair and wondered if she had any lipstick left on at all.

The oldest of the three women checked her ticket and winked at Lauren, respect colouring her gaze. She lowered her voice. 'Honey, that is one gorgeous hunk of a man. It's a wonder he allowed you out of bed long enough to get on the plane. How can you bear to leave him?'

Lauren cleared her throat and refused to look back for a last glimpse of Grayson striding away from her. She managed a shaky smile for the enthralled cabin attendants. 'I don't know.'

Chapter Thirteen

As soon as Lauren reached her apartment, she dropped her bags on the floor and rushed to the phone. After dialling the number, she kicked off her shoes and curled up on the couch. The phone rang and rang.

'Hello?'

'Ella, it's me.'

Her best friend gave a delighted squeal which made Lauren jerk the phone away from her ear.

'Oh my God, you're back, how did it go?'

'It went well ... way too well, Ella.' Lauren bit her lip and tasted a faint hint of Grayson. Her body relaxed into the soft fabric of the couch. 'I need your advice, girlfriend. I'm in big trouble.'

'I'll be there in twenty minutes.'

Lauren sat up and surveyed her apartment. She always hoped it might be magically transformed in her absence. Despite her insistence that she owned the space, her father had paid for the apartment to be decorated. Six months ago, she'd returned from a business trip to discover a décor that reflected his taste for extravagant decadence not her preference for more funky European design.

She sighed. It was always the same with her father. He presented his attempts to control her in many guises. Refusing his 'gifts' made him sulk and made it hard on her mother. She'd fired the decorator and got rid of the worst of it. But she had to put up with the rest because she couldn't afford to take money out of her business and redo it – yet.

Most people her age went to IKEA. She'd been

landed with French antiques mixed with a touch of Vegas princess. Her bedroom was the worst. It was a little girl's fantasy in shades of pink. Ella reckoned it was Lauren's father's attempt to remind her not to grow up. She couldn't imagine a man feeling comfortable in it.

Lauren switched on the lamp by her silk-swathed four-poster bed and hurried to take off her clothes. Her body ached from the hours of intense lovemaking she'd shared with Grayson. She stretched and imagined his hands moving over her willing flesh.

She shut her eyes against the image and only succeeded in making it more vivid. She slipped into an old T-shirt and faded sweatpants and headed back to the kitchen. By the time she had brewed coffee and put on the kettle, Ella rang her doorbell.

Ella breezed in, her arms full of bags, her face half-hidden behind a soft green knitted hat.

'I brought food. You never have any. Now what's up?'

Lauren had met Ella during her year at finishing school in Switzerland. They bonded within seconds after realising they were the only girls there whose number-one ambition wasn't to marry a prince and become queen of England.

Although Ella was taller and thinner than Lauren and could eat anything she wanted without putting on a pound, Lauren loved her anyway. Apart from Grayson, Ella was the only person who always told Lauren the truth.

Ella grabbed a cup of coffee and set about making a salad before Lauren turned off the kettle. Within five minutes she carried two plates of chicken Caesar salad and a bottle of red wine through into the sitting room.

After their second glass of wine, Ella curled her long legs up on the couch and turned to Lauren. 'So tell me what happened. You sounded panicked on the phone. He couldn't have been that bad.'

Lauren put her wine glass back on the table. 'He wasn't. He was...' Damn, what on earth could she say? She wanted to gush like a besotted teenager. 'He was great.'

'He was great?' Ella's eyebrows rose. 'Is that it? Do you mean he had a great personality or he was great in bed – or what?'

'All of the above and more.' Lauren pressed her hands to her flushed cheeks. 'I ended up making wild passionate love with him in a barn where people might have seen us. He brought out an uninhibited sex goddess inside me that I never realised existed. That's how great he was.'

Ella choked on her wine. 'Then what on earth are you doing here? Why didn't you stay with him?'

'Because it wouldn't work.' Lauren struggled to meet her best friend's incredulous gaze. 'He's too great.'

'You're not going to pull that "I'm not good enough for him" crap on me are you?' Ella frowned. 'I thought we decided you were over that the day you left your daddy's house.'

'It's not just about me,' Lauren said quietly. 'My father would destroy Grayson. I don't want that to happen.'

'How do you know?'

'Because Grayson has made choices that my father would consider weak.'

'Do you think Grayson's weak?'

Lauren pictured Grayson's strong face and found herself smiling. 'No, I don't. But that doesn't mean I want him to have to deal with my father.'

Ella swept her long black hair over her shoulder and got to her feet. 'So what are you going to do? Let your father dictate your love life again? You know he's got that creepy guy Simon Tilney who works for him lined up to marry you.'

'I'm not that stupid. Simon's been hanging around me for months. God knows what he tells people. I'm asked when the wedding's going to be at least twice a week.'

Ella returned from the kitchen with a tub of strawberry ice cream and two long spoons. She sank down on the couch next to Lauren and offered her a spoon. 'Isn't Grayson supposed to be coming to San Francisco next weekend?'

Lauren popped the lid off the ice cream. 'He says he is. I'm not sure if he'll follow through though. He was kind of mad at me at the airport because I wouldn't stay with him.'

'Did he sulk or create a scene?' Ella looked interested as she sucked a chunk of frozen strawberry from the back of her spoon.

Lauren smiled. 'That's not his style. He kissed me until I wondered why the heck I was leaving too.' She grinned inanely at her friend and Ella grinned back.

'I think you like him, Lauren. I think you like him a lot.'

'I do.' Lauren found it a relief to admit it. 'But I'm still not sure whether we could make it work together. We'd fight a lot, that's for sure.'

Ella took Lauren's hand, her brown eyes serious. 'But you could try, right? You've got another weekend to find out.'

Lauren let the last of the ice cream trickle down her throat. 'That's what I'm trying to figure out. Do I start a real relationship with him or do I send him back to Oregon for Anna and Marcie to fight over?'

'You have competition already? You've only been married for six months.'

'Nobody knows we're married apart from you. Grayson swore he hadn't told anyone.' Lauren licked her spoon, her serious gaze fastened on Ella. 'Whether I decide to keep him or not, you're going to have to help me. Grayson seems to think I have a glamorous big-city lifestyle.'

Ella fell back on the couch she was laughing so much. 'You? You used to be wild but you've been so dedicated to building your business this year that I doubt you've been out after seven in the evening. How on earth did he get that idea?'

'I gave it to him. When I first arrived at his ranch, I didn't want him to think I was some kind of pushover.'

Ella wiped a tear from her smooth brown cheek. Lauren had given her the nickname Pocahontas after noticing her striking resemblance to the cartoon figure. Ella called her Laura Ingalls in return.

Lauren wrapped her arms around her knees and hugged them. 'I'm scared, Ella. I think he knows how much I like him. And I'm still not sure whether that makes me want to run away screaming or run straight into his arms. I'm not ready to make a commitment to somebody. I'm not ready to be in love.'

'Well, we can't have that, can we?' Ella said thoughtfully, her gaze locked on Lauren's face. 'We'll have to find out what he's made of.'

'I want to shock him,' Lauren blurted out. 'I want to show him that I'm not going to be easy to win over. If he wants to be with me he's going to have to be tough enough to deal with my father and find a way to make our marriage work.' She dropped the spoon into the empty ice-cream container with a decisive thump. 'There's a possibility that apart from his strong sexual appetite he's a deeply conventional man and I don't want to turn into the little wife at home on the ranch.' She frowned. 'Not that I think that's what he wants, but you never know.'

'So do you want to borrow my social life and make him work his butt off for you?'

Lauren grinned. 'That's exactly what I want. I'll study up on those *Sex and the City* DVDs you got me for Christmas and we can work out a weekend that will decide whether Grayson Turner can take the heat or not.'

Ella knelt up on the couch, her hands clasped together. 'Oh my God, this could be fun, introducing the boy from Hicksville to the city of sin.'

'He's hardly a boy, Ella. But if he runs straight back to Oregon I'll know he was just an overconfident jerk. If he can stand a weekend competing with my work schedule and your hectic lifestyle, he might even be worth keeping.'

Chapter Fourteen

Grayson checked his watch for the third time. His plane had arrived early and there was no sign of Lauren at the San Francisco airport arrivals hall. Damn, she didn't even have her cellphone on. He was almost certain she'd done it deliberately.

Behind him, someone cleared their throat. Grayson turned. A tall black-haired woman wearing a chauffeur's uniform smiled at him.

'Good evening, sir. I'm Ella. Are you waiting for Ms Redstone?'

Grayson tipped his hat. With the advantage of his height he couldn't help but notice that his 'chauffeur' wore nothing under her jacket but a black silk bra. Her tight black skirt barely covered her butt as well.

'Yeah, I'm Grayson Turner. I was expecting Ms Redstone to meet me herself.'

'I apologise, sir. Ms Redstone sends her regrets. She's in the middle of a meeting.' Ella offered him a sympathetic smile. 'I'm to take you to her office in the city.'

Grayson picked up his bag and hoisted it over his shoulder before Ella could make a grab for it. Fine. Lauren was too busy to meet him. He'd imagined wrapping his arms around her as she rushed into his embrace in countless lustful dreams. He stared back at the arrivals gate. Perhaps it would be better if he just went home.

Ella hovered at his elbow, her expression politely puzzled. 'Are you coming, sir?'

'Obviously not as soon as I hoped,' Grayson murmured as he followed her out of the airport into the balmy San Francisco evening. Ella led him to a black Mercedes limo parked just outside. Someone must have clout to get that parking place. What was Lauren trying to do? Scare him off?

Grayson grinned as he got into the back of the limo. Lauren obviously had no idea who she was playing with. It might be amusing to find out what else she planned for his so-called entertainment. His smile died as the purring limo engine increased its speed and left the airport complex behind. Had Lauren regretted the intensely sexual nature of their weekend together? He couldn't allow himself to forget that she'd run away from him once before.

After they exited the crowded freeway he watched the familiar shadowed streets of the city as they were swallowed up by the limo. The view of San Francisco coming in from the airport wasn't one to sing about. Whoever his driver was, she sure knew her way around the congested traffic. He glanced at the back of her head. Her long black hair hung like a heavy curtain down to her waist. She caught his eye in the mirror and gave him an assessing smile.

Grayson winked and she flicked her gaze away. The limo stopped in front of one of the high-rise buildings on Montgomery Street and he unbuckled his seat belt. He waited until the chauffeur came around and opened his door before collecting his bag and stepping out.

It was quiet in the dead way office space gets on a late Friday afternoon. He knew the area well. His old company had held office space in the building across the street. The height of the tan-coloured buildings blocked the sunlight leaving the sidewalks in perpetual gloom. It was no wonder people wanted to escape to their homes for the weekend.

'I'll take you up, sir,' Ella said. 'Ms Redstone's office is on the twelfth floor.'

'My lucky number,' replied Grayson as they crossed

the deserted marbled hall and arrived at a bank of elevators. Ella glanced at him and moved to press the button to summon the elevator.

'It's not that high, sir. You'll be fine.'

Grayson struggled to repress a smile as the elevator doors opened. Did she think he hadn't been in a city before? And should he play it up or tell her the truth?

'I hate to burst your bubble, Ella, but I have been in an elevator. I live in Oregon not Amish country.'

Ella laughed and turned it into a cough when he tried to get her to look at him. She was out of the elevator as soon as the doors slid open. Grayson followed more slowly down the lushly carpeted hallway.

To his surprise, Ella knocked and then stood aside for him to enter. 'Ms Redstone's in here. I'll see you later, sir.'

Grayson dug into his jeans pocket and pulled out a five-dollar bill. 'Thanks for the ride, Ella. I'll be sure to mention you to the boss lady.' He winked as he tucked the five dollars into her hand.

She retrieved the bill and looked at it as if he'd handed her his dirty laundry. 'Five dollars? That's very kind of you, sir. I'll let Ms Redstone know what a generous man you are.'

Grayson left her at the door and made his way into the reception area. There was no one behind the orange plastic oval desk. The back wall was painted red with the company's logo RETRO GIRL splashed in large white letters across the centre.

The whole office radiated a sense of style and individuality Gray already associated with Lauren. He knew she'd picked out every detail of her workspace, he could feel it in his bones. All the stuff she'd left for him in Oregon had appealed to his taste, especially the portrait of his horses. He nodded in silent approval. No out-of-date magazines or aquariums for Lauren, just bright colours and great modern art.

Four closed doors fanned out beyond the seating area. Gray pondered which one was Lauren's. She would take the office with the view. He headed for the door on the far left and knocked.

'Come in.'

Grayson smiled and congratulated himself on his choice. Lauren sat behind a large white desk. Her light-brown hair was twisted into a sophisticated knot on the top of her head and she wore reading glasses. Bathed in the soft glow of an overhead desk lamp, Lauren looked as serene and elegant as a statue.

His body tightened as his gaze slid over her black-and-white shift dress and knee-high black boots. He imagined suckling her through the stiff fabric, how long it would take him to make her nipples hard and sensitive. As if she'd read his mind, she crossed her arms over her breasts.

Grayson touched his hat. 'Lauren.'

He fought a smile as Lauren whipped off her glasses and sat up straight. 'Grayson. I'm sorry I couldn't meet you at the airport.' She fumbled to put away her glasses. 'I landed three new clients this week and I've been trying to free up some time for the weekend.'

Grayson dropped his bag to the floor and sat in one of the brown leather chairs in front of Lauren's desk.

'We all get busy sometimes.'

She gave him her professional smile and it riled him. He hadn't come to be patronised and ignored. He'd come to see his wife. Abruptly he stood up and stalked over to the window. Through the smoke-glass windows, he could just make out a chain of lights leading down towards the Embarcadero and the bay.

'You have great office space.'

He thought he heard Lauren sigh. 'My father offered it to me. Unfortunately, I'm not in a position to refuse his help until I can start drawing more income out of the business.'

Done with pleasantries, Grayson studied her reflection in the glass. 'Are you ready to go?'

'I have to attend a cocktail party at one of my client's homes.'

Grayson resisted the urge to grind his teeth together. 'Fine, remind me where the nearest BART station is and I'll get back to the airport.'

Lauren put down her pen and had the nerve to smile at him. 'Are you leaving so soon? I never thought you a coward.'

Grayson sat back down in his chair with a thump. Dammit, the woman was right. Just because he'd expected instant sex didn't mean he had to get it. It made him remember all the women he'd kept waiting over the years while he'd been too busy to attend to them. Perhaps there was such a thing as karma.

He guessed Lauren was trying to make a point. Grayson forced himself to relax. Lauren was in charge now.

'I'm not going anywhere. What can I do to please you, oh mistress? And how long will it be before I can get you into bed?'

Lauren pointed to a door set in the back wall of her office. 'I was hoping you'd accompany me to the cocktail party. I've got some clothes for you in there, if you'd like to change.'

Grayson narrowed his eyes. 'You aren't trying to get back at me are you?'

Lauren tried to look innocent and failed miserably. 'Why on earth would I do that? I loved dressing like cowgirl trash.'

Picking up his bag, Grayson headed for the bathroom. He could only hope she hadn't chosen see-through plastic pants and a black garbage-bag vest for him. To his surprise, he found a charcoal-grey Armani suit, a blue shirt and a silver tie. There was no underwear.

He washed up, shaved and put on the clothes. Everything fitted to perfection, reminding him of his days in the city. He folded his jeans and shirt and returned them to his bag. At least his black cowboy boots could stay on his feet. It was good to have something to remind him that at least the shit he waded through these days was of his own choosing.

Grayson straightened his tie one last time and sauntered back into the office. Lauren wasn't there. He turned a slow circle. The outside door opened and he composed his features as Lauren came in.

She wore high sandals with diamanté straps and a long black coat which covered her from ankle to neck. He straightened as she walked towards him. The whisper of silk beneath her coat and the warmth of her body beckoned to his senses.

'Grayson, you look ... wonderful.' Lauren's open admiration made Grayson feel sexy as hell. She walked around him as if he were on display at a museum.

'You can touch me if you like, I'm real.'

Lauren laughed, her soft amusement dissolving the lines of strain on her face. 'I know you are. I'm just amazed at how well you ...'

'Scrub up?' He bowed. 'I feel kind of naked without my Stetson, but I'll have to deal with it.'

Lauren stroked his arm, as if admiring the fit of the jacket. 'You look as if you were born to wear this suit.'

Gray wanted to laugh. She was way too close to the truth. He'd started his first business at the age of five buying cheap candy at the local store and selling it at a profit door to door to local teenagers who were too lazy to go into town.

He took her hand and kissed her fingers. A surge of lust shook through him and he mentally sized up her desk. If he 'cleared some space', he could lay her down and make love to her before they went. Lauren pulled her hand away.

'We really need to get going, Grayson. The party is in Pacific Heights and we're already late.'

Gray looked around for his hat and then remembered he couldn't wear it. He picked up his bag instead. 'I hope this party isn't going to last too long. I was kind of hoping we'd get to spend some time alone together.'

'Welcome to my life, Grayson.' She sighed extravagantly. 'Business always comes before pleasure.'

Lauren waited in the corridor until he came past her and then locked the door. He followed her down to the front of the building where Ella waited in the car.

After Lauren settled herself in the seat, Grayson gestured at Ella. 'How come you have a female chauffeur?'

Lauren looked surprised. 'Why should it be a problem? She's just as capable of driving around the city as a man.'

Grayson settled back against the leather seat. 'I'm not trying to be sexist but wouldn't you prefer to have a big guy behind the wheel in case you run into any trouble?'

Lauren's face cleared. 'I see what you mean, but I've never had a problem and Ella, well, Ella provides me with companionship and privacy when I need it.'

Grayson reached forwards and took Lauren's hand. Soft-pink nail polish glinted on her perfectly manicured fingernails. 'So she's like the three wise monkeys?'

'I suppose she is.' Lauren's smile turned inwards. 'I trust her Grayson. She's my best friend. She would never betray me.'

He licked her fingertips and she shivered. 'So if I pulled you onto my lap and started making out with you, she'd turn a blind eye?' His shaft swelled, brushing against the soft fabric of his pants, as he imagined driving himself into her tight wet heat.

Lauren licked her lips and he followed the motion of the delicate tip of her tongue. She disengaged her hand and sat back. 'Perhaps we'll find out on the way home.'

Grayson smoothed his hand over his bulging groin and watched Lauren check him out. 'How about now?'

She smiled then. 'Oh no you don't. We have a cocktail party to attend.' The car turned a sharp corner and climbed another monstrous hill, the engine straining against the gradient. Lauren glanced out of the window. 'We're almost there anyway.'

Grayson pretended to frown. 'How do you want me to behave, Lauren? Like a business associate, a boyfriend, a lover or a husband?'

The car stopped at the kerb and Ella got out. Lauren drew her coat around her as she prepared to open the door. She looked uncomfortable. 'I want you to behave like yourself.'

Grayson followed her up the steps of the magnificent Victorian mansion. He'd owned a similar house not far from here and knew how expensive they were to buy and maintain. A butler awaited them in the hall. Grayson waited while Lauren unbuttoned her coat and then eased it from her shoulders.

It took him a few seconds to comprehend what the coat had covered. Lauren's back was bare from the nape of her neck to the swell of her buttocks. A thin circle of black silk encircled her neck anchoring the front of her dress. He wanted to lick his way down the swanlike curve of her spine, to feel the soft flesh against his mouth, to make her his again.

'Grayson?' Lauren turned towards him, an enquiring look on her face.

If the back view made him speechless, the front view made thousands of lights explode throughout his brain. Her black silk halter-neck dress was held together between her breasts with a silver brooch and then flowed down over her hips to just below her knees.

Grayson struggled to swallow. 'You look great.'

Lauren smoothed her hands over the front of the dress emphasising her curves. 'Do you like it? It's nineteen-fifties Dior couture.'

He nodded wisely as if what she said made a lick of sense. He briefly wondered whether she'd mind if he ripped the dress off her writhing body.

She gave him a concerned glance and touched his arm. 'Grayson, are you ready to go in?'

Grayson tugged her closer until he could whisper in her ear. 'Anytime. I'm ready whenever you are.'

Lauren ran her finger along his jawline making his toes curl. 'You'll have to catch me first.'

'Is that a dare?' Grayson asked as they mounted the ornate staircase to the second-floor reception rooms.

Lauren paused outside the main door and bit her luscious lower lip. Grayson's cock threatened to drill a hole through his zipper.

'I suppose it is,' Lauren whispered. 'But only if you can seduce me without destroying my reputation.'

Grayson tipped an imaginary hat at her. 'Lady, I love a challenge, you're on.'

Chapter Fifteen

As they waited in line to meet their host, Grayson idled away the time stroking his fingers up and down Lauren's exposed spine. Every time he reached the lower curve of her back, she shivered and moved closer. Grayson's confident smile widened. If he had his way, she'd be naked and straddling him very shortly.

He'd expected to see a different side of Lauren in her work environment, in fact, he'd looked forward to it, but she was definitely on edge. She was presenting a more sophisticated, harder image. It was like watching a little girl play dress-up in her big bad sister's clothes. All Grayson had to work out was which sister Lauren really wanted to be.

He placed his palm in the centre of Lauren's back as they were introduced to the owner of the house and his wife. From Lauren's relaxed conversation, Grayson gathered that the Cooks were old friends of Lauren's father. When Lauren introduced him, Grayson stepped forwards to shake Mr Cook's hand.

The older man gave him a thorough inspection before relaxing his grip. Grayson wondered how long it would take for the news of his appearance at Lauren's side to get back to her father. He knew, even if she didn't, how business really operated – through old friendships, over a round of golf, in a men's club. He realised Mr Cook was speaking.

'Your name sounds familiar. What do you do, Mr Turner?'

Grayson smiled. 'I'm a rancher, Mr Cook.'

Lauren pressed his arm. 'Grayson runs a horse-breeding and training programme in South Oregon.'

Mr Cook's gaze lingered on Grayson's jacket. 'It was good of your employer to let you out for the weekend.' He smiled revealing over-whitened teeth. 'Judging by that suit, he must pay you real well.'

Forgetting his party manners, Grayson winked. 'Hell, no, Lauren bought me this. She didn't want me to feel out of place amongst all you city folk.'

Lauren drilled her heel into his foot. He tried not to wince.

'Grayson's just kidding. He's actually his own boss.'

Grayson held Mr Cook's derisive stare and allowed the anger he felt to spill over into his gaze. He despised men like Mr Cook and his own father who judged everyone by the size of their bank account. He already regretted his promise not to spoil Lauren's evening.

'As the lady said, I was kidding. I wouldn't want you getting the wrong idea about me being Lauren's boy toy or something.'

Mr Cook remained silent and lowered his eyes first, leaving Grayson feeling victorious. Lauren grabbed his arm and smiled warmly at Mrs Cook. 'Thanks for inviting us and give my regards to Amy. I heard she's getting married in the fall?'

Lauren dragged Grayson as far away from their host as she could in the limited space available. Grayson steeled himself for her anger. In attempt to delay his fate, he plucked two glasses of champagne from a passing waiter and handed one to her.

'I should imagine that's one wedding I'm not going to be invited to and thank goodness,' Lauren said. 'His daughter is the biggest bitch going.'

Grayson touched his glass to hers. 'Aren't you going to scream at me for my appalling behaviour?'

To his surprise, Lauren smiled. 'I've never seen anyone reduce Mr Cook to silence before except my father.'

Grayson wasn't sure why, but that appeared to be a point in his favour. He wasn't inclined to question it.

'He's been known to make his staff cry.' Lauren toasted him with her champagne glass. 'You made him look vulgar and prying.'

Grayson smiled into her eyes. 'My pleasure, ma'am.' He looked around the crowded room. 'Is there anyone else here you'd like me to insult for you?'

Lauren raised her eyebrows. 'I thought you were trying to seduce me, not make me laugh.'

Grayson brought his hand up between their bodies and stroked her breast through the black silk of her dress. His breath caught as he grazed her tightened nipple with his fingertips. He trapped the tip between his finger and thumb and squeezed. Lauren made a soft sound and closed her eyes.

He leant into her, rolling her hardened flesh between his fingers, urging her closer. 'When I get my mouth around this, I'm going to suck for hours until you beg me to stop.'

He watched her lick her lips and wished he could drag her down to her knees and push his cock into her luscious, willing mouth. The butler announced another guest. Grayson reluctantly pulled away but not before he'd inhaled the wondrous scent of her arousal mixed with champagne.

Lauren turned to the window and Grayson followed. Looking down at her, he could see her nipples straining against the silk. He wanted to be inside her with all the urgent lust of a sixteen-year-old kid. He kissed her shoulder and then smiled at their reflection in the old Victorian window glass.

'How long do we have to stay at this party?'

Lauren let out her breath. 'Not for too long. Mr Cook likes to give a tour of his house, which usually starts in the wine cellar. He's an avid wine collector and likes to show off his knowledge to his guests.'

Grayson considered the advantages of a wine cellar. Most were badly lit, had barrels to hide behind and secluded dark corners. It could suit his plans for seduction very well.

'I say we do the tour and then get out of here.'

Lauren gave him a relieved smile. 'You don't have to worry about all that "seduction" business. I was only teasing you.'

Grayson didn't bother to answer, his attention on their host who had come forwards to invite his guests on a tour of his historic house. He took Lauren's hand and walked back into the centre of the room.

'Let's go and enjoy the tour, honey. I love a good wine buff.'

As he'd hoped, Mr Cook's wine cellar was shadowed, badly lit and quite extensive. Grayson held Lauren back as the other twenty guests gathered around their host. Casually leaning against one of the oak supports, Grayson turned Lauren towards him.

While Mr Cook extolled the virtues of a Californian Chardonnay, Grayson edged his hand beneath Lauren's black skirt. Her stockings ended halfway up her thigh leaving plenty of warm bare flesh exposed to his touch. He slid his fingers higher, searching for the soft curve between her buttocks. She shivered and pressed against him.

His fingertips brushed a soft dense fabric which felt like velvet. He ran a finger down the soft scrap of material until it became something else. A soft silk ribbon barely concealed the female delights between Lauren's thighs before joining again with the velvet just past her sex.

Grayson exhaled, wondering what colour the tiny G-string was and how it would feel against his mouth and his cock. The sleekness of the satin and the softness of the velvet made his fingers itch to pull up her skirt and take a closer look.

He winced as his shaft jammed against the zipper of his suddenly tight-fitting pants. Decorum and his promise to seduce Lauren with discretion made his first choice of action impossible. But he'd make sure Lauren paid for his reluctant acquiescence somehow.

He withdrew his hand as the guests moved forwards. 'Very nice, Lauren. Silk and velvet, my favourite flavours. I can't wait to taste them.'

Lauren glanced at him over her shoulder, her face flushed from his gentle exploration. 'That's up to you, isn't it?'

He pulled her back against him, letting her feel the size of his erection against the swell of her bottom. 'Don't worry, darlin'. I'm working on it. You'll come around and I'll be tasting you very soon.'

Lauren stiffened as Gray slid his hand inside the back of her dress and over her buttocks once again. He opened his fingers wide, his long middle finger settling over the central silk section of Lauren's panties. Gray began to rub the tip of his finger over the satin, smiling as Lauren's breath hitched. The slight delineation of her clit swelled under his careful ministrations.

Soon the ribbon was wet. After another stealthy glance around and then at their oblivious host, Gray brought his other hand up to Lauren's breast. Her nipple was already hard for him. He squeezed firmly through the fabric of her dress and whispered, 'I thought you were supposed to be making this difficult for me? You're already wet and wanting aren't you?'

Lauren didn't reply and Gray stroked her nipple in time to his questing, stroking finger below. 'I remember you letting me make love to you in my barn, where anyone could've come in and seen us.' He paused and pressed the pad of his finger directly onto Lauren's sex. 'Do you like the thought of getting caught, Lauren? Does it turn you on?'

'Grayson...' Lauren's whisper was so faint, he had

to bend his head to hear her. He ran the tip of his tongue around her ear and bit gently on the lobe. Just like that, he felt her come, without him even getting a fingertip inside her. He smiled into her neck, supporting her weight as she shuddered and shook beneath his hands.

'That's right, honey, come for me. You'll be doing it again soon when I get my mouth on you.'

Lauren looked around to see if anyone had noticed what she and Grayson were doing. To her relief, everyone seemed unaware, their attention respectfully fixed on Mr Cook just as hers should be. Unable to resist reminding Grayson that he was vulnerable too, she leant her hip against his groin and made a slow circle around his huge erection. His breath hissed out and she smiled in the darkness.

She inhaled the oaky smell of wine barrels and the slight hint of decaying fruit and hoped it masked the scent of her arousal. As the group moved into another section of the cellar, Grayson took her hand and ducked into one of the narrow passageways stacked with wine bottles. He pinned her to the brick wall and slid his hand between her legs.

Lauren tried not to gasp as he inserted one long finger inside her tight welcoming sheath. His mouth descended over hers, blocking any sounds, moving in the same unhurried pattern as his finger. Her excitement began to build again and she tried to bring him closer.

To her annoyance, he shook his head and withdrew from her. With a wicked grin he licked his finger clean and held out his hand. Lauren was suddenly aware of the low sound of Mr Cook's voice not five feet away and the coldness of the wall at her back.

She ignored his hand and walked back out into the main cellar just in time to pick up a glass of wine from the barrel in front of Mr Cook. The wine tasted of the sharpness of fresh apples and a hint of honey. She picked up another glass and handed it to Grayson who had appeared at her shoulder.

'You'll like this. It tastes like you.'

Grayson made a face and then tasted the wine. 'I taste like apples?' He lowered his voice. 'If that's the case, you'd think that more women would enjoy going down on a man.'

Lauren tried not to laugh. Grayson's ability to joke about anything was one of the things she treasured about him. Her father only saw a joke when it was at someone else's expense.

'We'll move on to the red wines now.' Mr Cook favoured his guests with a gracious smile. 'If anyone needs to visit the restrooms on the first floor, this would be a good time to go.'

Grayson took Lauren's hand and set off back up the cellar stairs. 'Grayson, I don't need to go to the bathroom.'

'Neither do I, darlin'.'

He nodded at the butler who had remained stationed in the hall and set off down a long carpeted corridor. Lauren blinked as he turned under the stairs and switched on the light in a small but elaborately decorated Victorian bathroom.

'How did you know where to find this place?'

Grayson locked the door and leant against it. 'I've been in a few of these houses before. There's only a certain number of places you can fit bathrooms in these old floor plans.'

The room shrank with Grayson in it. Lauren took an uncertain step back and bumped against the vanity unit. Grayson gave her a predatory smile that set her pulses racing.

'That's perfect, Lauren.' He put his hands around her waist and lifted her off the floor. She found herself sitting on the edge of the narrow marble countertop, clutching at Grayson for support. He knelt between her legs and pushed them wide with his broad shoulders.

'Thank you, God. How did you know that I love black velvet and black ribbon?' He sat back on his heels and looked up at Lauren. 'I know we can't be away for too long, but I'm sure as hell going to get a taste of you before we have to go back.'

The first gliding pass of his tongue over the narrow wet silk of her inadequate panties made her clutch at his hair. He growled deep in his throat and sucked on her through the fabric. Closing her eyes, Lauren rested her feet on his broad shoulders and opened herself wide to his questing tongue.

His roughened cheek grazed her inner thigh. 'I've missed touching you. I've woken up hard every night thinking of you in my bed.'

Lauren tugged at his hair, willing him to stop talking and finish touching her. She was close to coming again. He used a finger to drag the scrap of silk to one side and then his mouth descended on her unprotected flesh. She fought a scream as his tongue drove inside her. The cream and gold of the bathroom wallpaper began to swirl and dance in front of her heated gaze as Grayson's teeth grazed her clit, pushing her over into orgasm.

He waited until she stopped pulsing against his mouth and then slowly got to his feet. With a flick of his finger, he set her panties straight. He placed his hands on either side of the wall behind her and leant in to kiss her. She could taste herself on his tongue.

He brushed his lower lip against hers. 'Don't pretend you don't want me, Lauren. We're not finished yet. Before this evening's out you're going to beg me to push my cock into your mouth. You're going to beg me to make love to you.'

Lauren brought both her hands up and pushed hard on Grayson's chest. Dammit, Ella would be furious with her for giving in so easily. She was supposed to be showing Grayson how sophisticated and unimpressed she was. Unfortunately, whenever she tried to pick up the pace he seemed quite happy to speed up along with her. She had to do something.

She reached behind her back and turned on the faucet. Cupping her hand, she allowed the water to fill it. With a sweet smile she flung the cold water in Grayson's face. 'Perhaps you're the one who needs to cool down. I don't beg for anything.'

Grayson straightened until he seemed to fill the room. Droplets of water hung from his long eyelashes and settled like dew on his lips. His tongue came out and licked some of the moisture away. He studied her for a long while before wiping his face with a towel.

'There's a first time for everything, Lauren.'

Trying to ignore him, Lauren slid down from the vanity unit and pretended to be busy straightening her dress. She tried to step aside as Grayson moved forwards to wash his hands. He trapped her against the wall, his slate-blue eyes narrowed and considering.

'Perhaps I'll be the first to beg. You'd like that, Lauren. Imagine. Me on my knees, my cock wet and hard begging for you.'

Lauren swallowed hard and dredged up a cool smile. 'Perhaps I would.'

Chapter Sixteen

Lauren waited in the hallway until Grayson retrieved her coat and helped her into it. His fingers brushed her bare skin and she fought to control an urge to turn into his arms and simply breathe him in. The lights on her father's borrowed limo flashed outside and Lauren remembered Ella's instructions.

She couldn't take Grayson home yet. She was supposed to pretend that her average Friday night extended into the small hours. Lauren smothered a yawn. These days she was often in bed by eleven. What was odd was that she didn't even miss the clubs and the bars any more. She wasn't worried about Grayson holding up. He looked as if he could keep going all night. She was worried about herself.

Ella appeared at the bottom of the tiled steps that led up to the massive glass front door. Lauren buttoned her coat and went down to greet her.

'How did it go?' Ella hissed as she opened the door of the limo.

'Grayson seems to be enjoying everything I do. The more outrageous I become, the more he seems to like it.'

Ella looked thoughtful. 'He seems to be quite a nice guy and he's definitely not stupid.'

Lauren bit her lip. 'Are you sure we should go through with this? Perhaps he really is unshockable.'

Ella made a face. 'We'll see about that. I'm taking you to Caspar's next. Then we'll know for sure.'

Lauren didn't have time to reply as Grayson sauntered down the steps, hands in his pockets. 'Evening, Ella.'

Ella smiled and stepped away from the car. 'Good evening, Mr Turner.'

He got into the car and took the seat opposite Lauren. Ella shut the door behind him, leaving them enclosed in luxurious silence. Lauren watched him sprawl against the leather seat. He looked far more at ease than she did. For a wild moment she contemplated crawling across the space that separated them, burying her head in his lap and begging him to take her back to the ranch.

She'd been shocked by the wave of pure lust that had shaken her when he'd arrived in her office. It had taken all her resolve not to strip naked and wrap herself around him. He was even more handsome than she remembered and nicer too. His concern for her a living breathing thing that made her feel encircled with love. How could she throw that unique sensation away just because she was afraid of repeating her mother's mistakes?

Dismayed at her own thoughts, Lauren simply stared. Grayson stared back. One eyebrow rose as he contemplated her rigid stance.

'How far is it to your apartment?'

Lauren cleared her throat. 'We're not going to my apartment yet.'

Grayson went still. 'I thought you said . . .'

'But it's only ten thirty. I never go home this early on a Friday night.' Lauren pretended to pout as Grayson's expression hardened. 'Are you too tired to join me? I could always drop you off at a hotel and meet you in the morning.'

Grayson rubbed a hand along the line of his jaw and sat back. He stretched his long legs out until his booted foot brushed the tips of her open-toed sandals. 'That's OK. I'll come with you. I can always sleep in tomorrow.'

Lauren struggled to look enthusiastic. She almost

wished he'd disagreed with her and demanded to be taken to a convenient hotel. At least then she could've gone home and crawled into bed.

Lauren knocked on the glass panel that separated her from Ella. 'Can you take us to Caspar's?'

Ella looked delighted. 'Yes, ma'am, Caspar's it is.'

Grayson studied Lauren through half-closed eyes. What the hell was going on? Had he missed something? Admittedly, he didn't know Lauren well, but this new incarnation puzzled him. He hadn't reckoned her for an all-night-party kind of girl. Running a business was hard work. If she was as successful as she claimed, he couldn't imagine where she got all her energy from.

Perhaps she had a personality disorder and he was finally getting to see her dark side. The thought made him smile. He looked out of the window to avoid Lauren seeing it. If she was some kind of crazy lady, better to find out now rather than six months down the line. And what kind of relationship did she have with her female chauffeur? They seemed rather too close in Grayson's opinion.

He nudged Lauren's toe with his boot but she refused to look at him, her attention fixed on the streets slipping by outside. Perhaps she took drugs and this was how she was when she got high. Grayson sniggered at where his imagination had taken him. He'd seen Lauren naked and she didn't have the look of a woman being consumed from the inside like one of his old girlfriends in LA.

When the car stopped, he waited for Lauren to get out ahead of him. The red-brick building they stood beside was dark and windowless. Steam rose from a manhole cover in the centre of the street giving the place an other-worldly feel. Lauren pointed to a set of rickety steps leading down to a basement.

'Caspar's is down there.' She gave him a defiant look. 'You don't mind if Ella comes with us, do you?'

Grayson shrugged, took her hand and headed for the stairs. He wasn't prepared to get into an argument about Ella, yet. A wise man waited until he could see the extent of the trap before he blundered right through it.

At the bottom of the stairs a flashing fluorescent light spelt out the name of the club. A guy of linebacker proportions stood by the single entry door in a traditional bodyguard stance, hands clasped in front of him. He smiled as Ella approached him.

'Hey, baby cakes, how're you doing?'

Ella kissed the guy on the cheek. 'I'm good, Jack. I've brought Lauren and her cowboy to sample the evening's entertainment.' Grayson strained to hear as Ella whispered something in Jack's ear.

After opening the door and ushering Ella in, Jack turned to Lauren. 'Nice to see you again too, babe!' He nudged Lauren in the ribs. 'I'm surprised you decided to show your face after what you did last time you were here.'

For a second, Lauren looked startled and then she blushed and pushed past Jack. Grayson followed more slowly and allowed his eyes to adjust to the dim lighting. The overpowering rumble of house music vibrated through the floor making his feet ache.

His smile widened as he realised that ninety per cent of the occupants in the bar were women. Either, he was about to find out that Lauren and Ella had a very special relationship indeed or be a very popular man.

He took his time finding his way through the small tables to where Lauren and Ella stood at the bar. By the time he reached them he'd had five phone numbers stuffed in his pants pocket, two requests for a dance and the dubious pleasure of being groped by a woman old enough to be his mother. Just to add to his secret amusement, Lauren was frowning at Ella.

He tipped an imaginary hat. 'You were right, Lauren. This sure looks like a great place to spend a few hours. Can I buy you both a drink?'

Lauren couldn't believe she'd allowed Ella to bring Grayson here. She'd never really thought about the predatory females who prowled the room on the look-out for anything remotely male. Grayson seemed to be enjoying himself. Lauren glared at three women who were attempting to get up close and personal with Grayson's unprotected left side.

She smiled sweetly at Ella. 'How about we let Grayson sit in between us?'

Grayson shot her an enquiring glance. 'I'm quite comfortable here.' He winked at the three women to his left. Lauren could almost smell the waves of lust mingled with cheap perfume that drifted towards him. 'Don't move on my account.'

She grabbed Grayson's arm and he let her pull him off the bar stool. 'That's OK. We're already moving.' Damn, she hated having to shout every word.

Grayson clinked his beer against her Cosmo, a satisfied smirk on his face. 'So what did you do to make Jack the bouncer remember you so well?'

Ella laughed as she took off her black jacket and revealed her black lace bra. 'She got drunk and tried to strip off whilst doing a karaoke version of Madonna's "Express Yourself".'

Grayson spluttered into his beer. Lauren wasn't sure if it was because of Ella's scanty attire or the old story about her.

'Damn, I wish I'd seen that.' He grinned at Lauren, his slate-blue eyes full of heat. 'Maybe you'll do a private performance for me later?'

Lauren sipped at her drink and tried to ignore the ever-growing circle of women around Grayson. She knew from personal experience how hard it was to get a date after the age of 25 but surely some of them could show a little more restraint?

Ella tugged at her hand. 'Come on, I need to use the restroom.'

Lauren glanced at her hardly touched drink. 'I'm OK, Ella. I'll wait here with Grayson.'

Ella tugged harder, her expression so threatening that Lauren allowed herself to be marched off to the ladies'. Her view of Grayson was instantly blocked by an indiscreet tidal wave of women surrounding him.

The restroom was full to bursting. Ella pushed Lauren into the only empty stall. Lauren slammed the door behind her and confronted Ella, hands on hips.

'Are you crazy or something? He'll be eaten alive.'

Ella opened Lauren's purse and took out a colourless lip gloss. 'We already discussed this. It's a great opportunity for you to see how honourable Grayson is. If we go back out there and he's making out with someone else, you'll know he's not to be trusted.'

Lauren snatched her purse back. 'Ella, some of those girls are really hot. He'd have to be dead from the waist down not to notice how many of them are better looking and younger than me.'

Ella pressed her lips together, and walked out of the stall. She gazed at her reflection in the mirror and smiled at Lauren. 'Sweetie, I didn't say he has to stop looking but he's married to you. If he wants to remain married to you he needs to show you that you're the only woman in his life.'

Lauren felt a childish desire to stamp her feet. 'But I don't want to be married to him. I don't want to be married, period!'

Ella raised her eyebrows. 'Then why are you getting

so upset? You can't have it both ways. If you don't want the guy, give someone else a chance.'

Lauren didn't even attempt to answer Ella. She made an ineffectual attempt to smoothe down her hair. In the harsh overhead light, she looked tired and drained. How much longer would Ella expect them to remain at the club? When could she take Grayson home and have him all to herself?

They exited the restroom and headed back to the club. Lauren's stomach dropped as she realised Grayson was no longer sitting at the bar.

'I don't see him, Ella. And I don't like it at all.'

Ella had the gall to laugh. 'Take that grim expression off your face and try to look glad to see him. Grayson's coming straight for us.'

Lauren tried to smile as Grayson reached her side. He curved an arm around her shoulders. 'Thanks for abandoning me, ladies. I felt like fresh meat at a piranha convention.'

Ella led them towards a table on the edge of the miniscule dance floor. 'Most men enjoy the attention.' She sat opposite Grayson and continued talking. 'In fact, most of the men I meet seem to think they can just sit back and wait for me to do all the work.' She made a face. 'Sometimes I think equality sucks.'

Grayson left his arm around Lauren's shoulders. 'At the risk of being called sexist, I agree. I have friends who think that. They reckon the girls crawling all over them should put out on a first date. They claim to love equality.' He smiled softly at Lauren. 'Trouble is, I think it scares most guys when a woman comes on to him. I hate to sound old-fashioned, but men need the thrill of the chase to really appreciate a good woman. You can make it too easy for some guys.'

Lauren sighed. 'You have no idea how hard it is to get a date in a city this size when you're over twenty-five. When a half-decent guy turns up, he can pick and choose and nobody faults him for it.'

'Women can't win can they?' Ella sneered. 'If they go after a man like a man would a woman, they're considered easy. Women aren't supposed to just "want sex". If they don't go after a man, someone else will, and they'll remain single and lonely.'

Grayson shrugged. 'As you said, equality sucks.'

Ella poked a finger in Grayson's face. 'Yeah, well, that's men and their double standards. Nothing's really changed, has it?'

She got to her feet and headed for the bar leaving Lauren alone with Grayson for the first time. The music increased in volume until their small table vibrated. He gave her a long slow smile and took off his jacket and tie. Unable to resist the temptation, she leant forwards and undid the top two buttons of his shirt. He caught her fingers and brought them to his mouth.

'I don't treat women like that.'

Lauren tried not to meet his amused gaze. 'I never said that you did.'

'But you thought it. I can see it in your eyes.' As he spoke, Grayson dug his other hand in his pocket and began to pull out pieces of paper, ripped bar mats and business cards. All of them had phone numbers and girls names scrawled on them.

Lauren jerked her fingers from his strong grasp as he emptied his other pocket and added more from his jacket. He frowned as he finally removed two business cards jammed in the waistband of his pants.

He studied the mound of paper in front of him before compressing it in his fist. He darted a glance at Lauren. 'Damn, I wish I was single. I could've got laid from here till Christmas with that little collection.'

'Don't let me stop you,' Lauren huffed as she folded her arms in front of her. Grayson started to laugh.

'Hey, Lauren, are you jealous or something?'

Lauren got to her feet, swept the crushed mass of paper to the floor and ground her heel into it. 'Now why would you think that?'

Grayson rose in one fluid motion and encircled her in his arms. He nuzzled her neck and instantly re-ignited the passions Lauren hadn't yet had a chance to satisfy. She sighed and allowed her body to lean into his strength. When she opened her eyes, Ella was glaring and gesticulating at her. Lauren knew she was supposed to be playing it cool but she didn't feel like testing Grayson any more. After seeing the competition, she wanted to take him home and let him make love to her.

Ella pointed at the restroom sign and Lauren gathered herself to leave the security of Grayson's arms. She pushed at his chest. His head came up, his eyes full of thwarted lust.

'I'm off to the powder room. I'll be back in a minute.'

A muscle flexed in Grayson's jaw as he stepped away, his hands on his hips. 'Again?'

Ella gave him a sweet smile as she swept Lauren along with her. 'It's a girl thing, you wouldn't understand.'

'We're leaving, Ella. I mean it.' Lauren strode into the restroom and turned to confront Ella.

'Not yet, sweetie, calm down. He's doing real good but we've got to ask the one-million-dollar question.' Ella struck a provocative pose. 'Will he hit on your best friend?'

Lauren studied Ella for a long moment. 'If I agree to this, will you let us go home?'

Ella grinned. 'Of course I will – that is, if you still want him by then.' She winked seductively at Lauren. 'Hey, he might prefer me after all.'

Chapter Seventeen

Grayson sipped his second beer as he waited at the bar for Lauren and Ella to return. He glanced around the small packed club and wished he was back in Oregon watching the sun set behind his ranch. Damn it – he was definitely getting old.

He couldn't decide what Lauren was up to. His instincts told him that he'd met the real woman at his ranch. A woman sympathetic enough to find him a new dog and to photograph his horses in an attempt to make his house feel more like a home.

Grayson scowled into his beer, scaring off yet another woman who'd begun to approach him. Hell, she'd been different in Vegas too. Which was the real Lauren and what did she want from him?

Ella appeared on his left and linked her arm through his. He gave her a polite smile and pointedly looked over the top of her head for Lauren. Ella put her hand on his arm and stood on tiptoe to shout in his ear. 'She'll be back in a minute. She's just gone to make a phone call.'

Grayson nodded. It was all he could manage over the noise. Ella grinned and dragged him towards the miniscule dance floor. He only just managed to put his beer down on the bar without spilling it.

In the press of gyrating bodies, Grayson tried to keep his distance as Ella began to dance. After she rubbed her lace-covered breasts against his chest for the third time, he locked gazes with her. She ran her tongue over her lips and blew him a kiss.

Grayson looked around again for Lauren but couldn't

see her anywhere. Had she called a cab and left him to the tender mercies of her chauffeur? God he hoped not. To add to his discomfort, the music slowed and Ella wrapped her arms around his neck and pressed against him.

Already half-aroused from his unfinished encounter with Lauren, Gray tried to avoid the insistent pressure of her hips against his hardening cock. He made the mistake of looking down and saw her triumphant smile.

Grabbing her elbows, he held Ella away from him. 'Whatever you're thinking, that's not for you. You're just stoking the coals.'

She reached between them and scraped her long fingernails down the zipper of his pants. She whistled her approval. 'Are you sure about that, cowboy? You seem pretty damn fired up to me.'

Grayson abandoned Ella on the dance floor and spotted Lauren hovering by the exit. He took her hand and marched outside.

'Did you tell her to do that?' Beyond angry now, Grayson faced Lauren, his hands fisted at his sides. 'Does your best friend and some-time chauffeur always get to make out with your boyfriends or am I a special case?'

Lauren opened and shut her mouth, a blush rising on her cheeks.

'Is this some kind of weird test? Does Ella get to sleep with us or something?' Grayson demanded. 'Hell, why not? It wouldn't be the first time I've satisfied two women.'

'You've had sex with two women at the same time?'

Grayson squared up to her. 'Yeah, I have. Why? Are you interested? Shall I go back inside and tell Ella to come and join us?'

Lauren lifted her chin. 'No. I don't want to share you with anyone. I'll tell Ella to behave herself.'

She turned to the door but not before Grayson caught a glimpse of her satisfied expression. He let her go, giving himself time to calm down and to contemplate his next move. Staring at the flashing neon sign, he grinned. He'd been set up. She'd had no intention of allowing Ella to join them. It had been a test all along.

Had she expected him to back off and leave her with Ella? Unfortunately, he wasn't a gentleman cowboy and she hadn't shocked him. He'd lived in San Francisco for a few years, some of his best friends were gay. He began to smile. Now what could he do for payback?

Lauren watched Grayson as the limo pulled away from the kerb. He sat opposite her, one arm along the back of the seat, his long legs crossed at the ankle and stretched out in front of him. At least he'd refused Ella's outrageous attempts to flirt with him. Lauren admitted to a few anxious moments when she'd seen Ella lay all her best moves on him on the dance floor.

Damn, it was getting harder and harder to ignore her possessive feelings for this man. She wasn't sure she wanted to expose him to her other female friends. They might expect her to share.

Ella had suggested going on to another club. Lauren couldn't face it. She preferred to go home and face the storm brewing in Grayson's slate-blue eyes. The limo drew to a stop outside her apartment and Ella came around to open the door.

Quick as a snake, Grayson reached out and yanked Ella into the interior of the car. He deposited her in the seat beside Lauren and shut the door. Lauren tried to smile at him in the brittle silence.

'Ladies, I think I've done you an injustice,' Grayson said.

Ella and Lauren exchanged a mystified glance.

Grayson nodded at Ella. 'Lauren told me that she had a "special relationship" with you.' He made quotes with his fingers. 'I didn't understand exactly what she meant until now.'

He leant forwards and took Ella's hand. 'It must have been very difficult for you to watch me with Lauren tonight. You must have felt jealous. That's why I'll forgive your attempts to come on to me.'

Lauren stared at Grayson but he looked perfectly sincere. Did he really think that she and Ella were a couple?

'I don't think you quite understand –'

Lauren was interrupted by a wave of Grayson's hand. 'It's OK, if you prefer to spend your evenings with Ella. You should have told me about this before.'

He'd gone too far. Lauren regained her composure as it occurred to her that there was no way a macho guy like Grayson Turner would allow her to continue in a lesbian relationship without trying his hardest to convince her out of it.

She smiled back at him and slipped an arm around Ella's neck. 'Oh, I'm so glad you feel that way, Grayson,' she cooed. 'Ella was feeling so left out.' To punish him further, she decided to try out most men's number-one fantasy and brought her mouth into contact with Ella's.

It was surprisingly easy to kiss her best friend. Ella, of course, responded with gusto, sticking her tongue down Lauren's throat as if she was really into it.

When Lauren came up for air and disentangled herself from Ella's embrace she couldn't help but notice that Grayson's cock was clearly outlined against the confines of his pants. He swallowed twice as Lauren licked Ella's lipstick from her lips.

Lauren held his heated gaze as he cupped his erection.

'Could you do that again?'

His quiet question and the hint of command in his voice made all her senses come to life.

Gray waited to see what Lauren would do. To his delight, she turned back to Ella and resumed the kiss. Gray sat back and watched as Ella stroked Lauren's hair and they turned their bodies into each other. Lauren brought her knee up on the seat as she ran her hand down Ella's back, bringing them even closer. Ella's fingers closed around Lauren's breast.

Gray unzipped his pants before he embarrassed himself and stroked his aroused cock. The top of Lauren's black stocking showed beneath her rucked-up dress as she moved with Ella. Damn, he'd never liked to watch, he always wanted to play. Gray fell to his knees in front of the two women. His shaft pressed against the edge of the leather seat and sent stabs of pure lust straight to his brain.

He manoeuvred his shoulders between Lauren's thighs and bent his head to lick and suck at her pussy. Ella grabbed his left wrist and brought it between her legs. Gray pushed aside her lace panties and shoved three fingers deep inside her, moving them in the same rhythm as his hips and his mouth.

His dripping cock slid against the leather as he pumped his hips, driven crazy by the women's sensuality, desperate to make them both come. He felt Lauren tense and redoubled his efforts with Ella. She gripped his wrist and rode his hand, grinding her mound against his palm.

Lauren came hard. He kept his mouth on her to enjoy every ripple of pleasure. Ella soon followed, clenching around his fingers like a vice. He allowed his hips to slam into the seat once more and came, struggling to breathe, his face still buried deep in Lauren's pussy.

When he regained his breath he managed to drag

himself back into the seat opposite. He pulled out a handkerchief and mopped his face. Lauren and Ella were still curled up together, their faces hidden on each other's shoulders.

Lauren was the first to look up. She smoothed down her dress and simply stared at him. He handed her the handkerchief, indicated the wetness on the seat. In silence she cleaned up, her dishevelled hair covered the expression on her face.

Grayson smiled. 'Shall we take this upstairs?'

Ella righted her clothes and leapt out of the car, her shoulders shaking with laughter. Lauren followed her out trying desperately not to laugh as well. Grayson took his bag from the trunk and came to stand behind her.

'I think I'll pass,' Ella choked, her hand covering her mouth. 'I need to get the car back and I'm not sure I'm ready to watch Lauren having full-blown sex with you yet.'

Before Lauren could say a word, Ella bolted for the limo and drove off with a squeal of tyres.

Lauren studied Grayson's black cowboy boots and cleared her throat. 'Would you like to come upstairs?'

'I'm not sure,' Grayson said gravely. 'Do you want me to?'

Lauren forced her gaze up to his face. His eyes brimmed with suppressed laughter tinged with desire. It was a lethal combination.

'Yes, I do.' She gave him an innocent stare. 'Perhaps Ella could join us another night.'

Grayson reached out one long arm and pulled her hard against him. 'No. She couldn't. You'll be far too busy satisfying me to worry about Ella.'

'Are you sure about that?'

Grayson's mouth descended and cut off her attempt

to continue. He kissed her so thoroughly that her knees threatened to give way.

'Yeah, I am.' He studied her swollen mouth and stroked his thumb over her lower lip. 'You'll be so full of the taste and feel of me that you'll forget what it's like not to have me inside of you.' He kissed her again, his arms tightening around her back. 'And you'll want that as much as I do.'

After the shock he'd given her, Lauren couldn't resist teasing him a little. 'And if I don't, you'll let me go back to Ella?'

She shrieked as he picked her up and slung her over his shoulder. He grabbed his bag and headed up the steps.

'Not a chance, lady.'

The doorman of her apartment building tipped his hat, accepted the twenty-dollar bill Grayson handed him and obligingly punched the elevator button for Lauren's floor.

In her awkward position, Lauren had a fine view of Grayson's butt. She shuddered as his hand slid under her dress. He spread his fingers out across her bottom.

'Would you really prefer Ella to have this rather than me?' His middle finger slid between her cheeks to rest on her already-aroused sex. 'Perhaps it's time to remind you that you belong to me this weekend.'

When the elevator doors opened, he shifted her weight until she had to cling to his belt as he lowered her to the floor. She managed to find her key and let them into her apartment. When the door shut behind Grayson, he leant against it and folded his arms.

'Take off your dress, Lauren.'

She allowed her purse to drop onto the carpet and held his gaze as she unzipped her dress. It fell to the floor and she stepped out of it. He studied her breasts, his eyes lingering on her tight nipples.

Without asking, he collected one of the high-backed chairs from her dining table and put it behind her. 'Sit down.'

Lauren settled herself on the edge of the seat as he resumed his position against the door. Her heart rate slowed to match the insistent pulse between her legs.

'I think you've teased me enough tonight, don't you?'

She couldn't risk answering him, her body was too near the edge and too needy to spoil the moment. He hooked a leg of the chair with his boot and brought her closer.

'I think it's time I teased you.' His voice became compelling. 'Open your legs wide and clasp your hands behind the back of the chair.'

Lauren slowly complied, taking her time to expose the soaking wet strip of her panties, inhaling her own scent. Would he tie her hands to enforce her obedience or trust her to leave them where he'd told her to?

He stepped closer, flicked the tip of her breast and then the other. 'We'll start here. By the time I've finished suckling you, you'll be so sensitive you'll still think my mouth is on you in the morning or whenever you take a breath.'

Lauren bit her lip as he sucked her satin-clad nipple into his mouth and pulled strongly. He didn't touch her anywhere else although she was aware of the heat and strength of his body towering over her. By the time he'd finished his thorough investigation of her second nipple, she wasn't sure whether she wanted to beg him to stop or to continue for ever.

He reached behind her and unhooked her bra. She couldn't hide a flinch as the wet fabric dragged over her sensitised nipples. Her breasts felt cold without his mouth on them. Grayson knelt in front of her and stared at her tight hard nipples. When he touched her with the tip of his tongue, Lauren fought back a moan.

He took her chin in his fingers. 'Did you think I'd finished with them? Darlin', I've only just started. I want to hear you crying out before I've finished. I want you coming from just the touch of my mouth.'

Lauren stared down at his bent head as he resumed his suckling, watched his cheeks hollow as he drew her flesh into his mouth, felt the ache build until it was almost pain. A trickle of moisture slid down her thigh, reminding her of how much she'd missed Grayson. She wanted to wrap her legs around his hips and rub herself against him until she gained her release.

She guessed that if she tried anything, he'd simply stop and she wasn't prepared to risk it. She came after he bit gently down on her hardened nipple, the slight graze of his teeth enough to send her spiralling into release.

Grayson drew back to watch her face as she shuddered in pleasure. Before she'd composed herself, he slid one finger through the narrow strip at the front of her panties. 'Do you think I've teased you enough, Lauren?'

She studied his finger, aware how close he was to her clit and how much she wanted him there. 'Yes.'

'Hell, no. I had to relieve myself in the bathroom on the plane I got so hard thinking about you meeting me at the airport.' He smoothed a hand over the front of his tented pants and got to his feet. 'I reckon you should take me in your mouth and suck me dry before I even take a good look at your pussy.'

He unzipped his pants and grasped his shaft around the base. His cock was already wet. Lauren opened her mouth as he guided the thick crown towards her. She'd forgotten how big he was. He held her head as he pushed steadily into her. She ignored the instinct to gag and took him deep, enjoying the thrust of his shaft and the thick fullness in her mouth.

She was able to concentrate completely on him. He

didn't touch her with any other part of his body, just his cock, and her hands were safely behind her back. He surged deeper, groaning as she steadily sucked. She enjoyed the textures of his slippery shaft and his gathering tension.

He came in thick pulsing waves and she swallowed as fast as she could. As he withdrew, she couldn't resist a last swirl of her tongue around the tip of his shaft. Lauren always enjoyed the feel of him coming in her mouth. He definitely tasted as good as he looked.

She licked her lips as he stepped back. 'That was nice, Lauren. I'm definitely feeling a little better now.'

He dragged his finger along the line of her panties and knelt in front of her. Lauren shivered as he gently explored her. He pressed the strip of ribbon until it disappeared inside her, adding to the friction on her clit.

He kissed his way up her thigh from her knee and then down the other side. Lauren started to shake with the strength of her repressed desire. Grayson paused to study her. His expression was pure alpha male, possessive and demanding. She stared back at him. What could she say to make him make her come?

'I wanted you as soon as you walked into my office.'

Grayson raised an eyebrow.

Lauren continued to talk as his fingers made small circles on her knee. 'I've wanted you all week. I tried to convince myself that when I saw you again all the heat would be gone and that I'd be able to treat you just like any other guy I've slept with.'

His hand closed around her bent knee. 'You see, that was your first mistake. I'm not like any other guy you've slept with.' He slid his hand along her thigh and touched her panties. 'Have you ever let a guy treat you like this before?'

Lauren held his gaze. 'Of course not.'

He smiled then. 'But you don't seem to be complaining, honey.' He circled her swollen sex with his fingertip. 'Perhaps I'm the first man to see that you like to give up control occasionally. A fine businesswoman like yourself must get tired of being the boss all the time.'

He slid his finger beneath the satin and probed her sheath. Lauren wanted to clench down on his finger and never let it go. He knelt up and gripped the back of the chair on either side of her head. 'I'm going to fuck you now. And it will be hard and fast and furious, cos that's what I need and you'll like it too.'

She let him pull her panties down and felt the first brush of his cock against her wetness. He resumed his grip on the back of the chair and entered her in one long thrust. Lauren was pushed back into the seat with the strength of his body moving against hers. His arms trapped hers behind her back. She grabbed the rungs of the chair and held on tight as the chair rocked backwards onto two legs.

She screamed as she spasmed around him, her body determined to milk every drop of pleasure he could give her. He kept pumping and made her come again and again until she couldn't stop moaning his name. His final thrust pushed them and the chair over the edge.

Grayson wrapped his arms around her, protecting her from the fall, taking their combined weight on his forearms. Lauren lay still for a moment until Grayson rolled to one side and helped her up.

He smiled down at her and took her hand. 'How about we try and have sex in a bed for a change?'

Lauren reached out and touched his cock. 'Don't you mean make love?' She circled her thumb in the slick wetness as his cock began to fill out again.

'Yeah,' he said hoarsely. 'Making love sounds good too.'

She led him into her bedroom. He stopped at the

door and looked around. 'Holy cow, have I died and ended up locked in a fairy tale?'

Lauren removed his suit jacket and started work on his cuffs. 'I'll explain later.' She pinched his nipple to force his fascinated gaze away from the frothy pink drapes. Grayson stepped out of his boots and pants. He ran a hand over his erection as Lauren bent to unroll her stocking and then kicked off her shoes.

'Let me do that.' Grayson moved up behind her, the heat of her body driving him wild. She arched her back and pushed against him as her stockings pooled on the carpet. When she tried to turn in Grayson's arms he held her fast, his hands on her waist.

'Christ. You look beautiful.'

Lauren was framed in the mirror above her vanity unit. Grayson's hands looked large spanning her narrow waist and hips. He rested his chin on her shoulder.

'When I saw you sitting at your desk in your office, I wanted to spread your legs wide and push inside you.' His left hand came up to cup her breast while his right travelled lower and rested over the triangle of dark hair at her crotch. Lauren relaxed her thighs and allowed his fingers to slide downwards.

'I was praying you'd wrap those long legs around my waist and let me come inside you.' He slid his long middle finger inside her. She bit back a moan as he used his thumb to caress her with slow even strokes.

'I even hoped one of your employees would come into your office and you wouldn't even notice because you'd be so caught up in taking your pleasure from me.'

Lauren shuddered as he slid two more fingers inside her. She rocked into his hand as he increased the tempo.

'I don't think that would be a very good image for the director of a business to portray to her staff, would it?' Lauren managed to gasp as Grayson bit down hard on her shoulder. He licked the sensitive spot his teeth made and smiled at Lauren in the mirror.

'If you were my boss, I would have enjoyed it. I would've been praying you'd try it on with me next.' He guided her forwards until her hands clasped the high back of the wrought-iron chair in front of her vanity unit. With easy strength, he turned the chair at an angle to the mirror so that she could see both of their bodies.

Lauren couldn't stop staring at herself. She looked wild and aroused. Grayson worked his fingers back inside her and she put her left foot up on the chair seat. She could see how deep his fingers were going inside her now. His cock pressed against her buttocks, a hot hard presence which made her whole body throb with need. She knew what he wanted her to say.

'Grayson, will you make love to me please?'

He smiled then and allowed his erection to probe the slick entrance of her sheath. He barely entered her and yet she climaxed again almost immediately, clenching around him with a week's worth of pent-up need. He kept his stroke shallow until she almost begged him to let her climax.

When he pulled out, she wanted to howl. He led her to the bed, pressed her down on the covers and crawled between her legs. He held his shaft around the base and positioned it against her. 'It's your turn now, Lauren. Tell me how you want it, slow or fast?'

She reached up and grabbed him around the back of the neck. 'Just do it, Grayson.'

He chuckled against her mouth as he slid inside her. 'Do you still want to call Ella, then?'

Lauren aimed a weak punch at his muscled bicep. 'Grayson ... just finish making love to me and then I want to go to sleep in your arms. Does that sound OK?'

Grayson picked up the pace and grinned down at her. As she opened her eyes after yet another exquisite orgasm she felt his hot come right at her centre. He kissed her mouth with infinite care. 'Honey, that's the second best thing you've said to me all night.'

'What was the first?' Lauren whispered as he settled her in the crook of his arm. A rumbling snore was her only answer.

Chapter Eighteen

Lauren woke up to the persistent sound of the phone ringing in the kitchen. She stumbled out of bed, grabbed Grayson's shirt and tiptoed out. Bright sunlight hit her eyes as she made her way across to the phone. Last night she'd been so preoccupied she'd forgotten to close the drapes. She wondered if her neighbours had enjoyed the show

She squinted at the miniscule phone display which revealed her father's private cellphone number.

'Daddy, it's eight in the morning and it's Saturday. Why are you calling me?'

His trademark hearty laugh boomed down the line. 'You should be up and about making your fortune, sweetie, not lounging in bed.'

Lauren flopped onto the couch and pulled one of the large cushions against her stomach. 'Don't tell me, you've already made yours and you're moving on up to world domination.'

'You're too funny, darling.'

He laughed again. Lauren squeezed the cushion hard. Why was he being so nice? He rarely called her sweetie any more, only when he wanted something.

'I had a call from my old friend, James Cook, last night. He says you have an interesting new boyfriend. Some kind of cowboy.'

Lauren clutched the phone hard in her fist. She should have realised Mr Cook would call her father.

'He's not really a boyfriend. He's more of a client.'

A slight movement to her right made her look up. Grayson stood framed in the bedroom doorway, his expression chilly. Had he heard her? From the hard set of his mouth, she guessed he had. She tore her eyes away from his as she realised her father was still speaking.

'... So bring him by for dinner this evening will you? Your mother would like to meet him.'

'Daddy, we're busy, I've already made plans –' She gasped as Grayson snatched the phone out of her hand.

'Mr Redstone? Yeah, that's correct. I'll bring Lauren over at seven.' He tossed the phone back to Lauren, a challenge in his eyes.

Lauren nodded, forgetting her father couldn't see her as he said goodbye and hung up. She glared at Grayson.

'Don't you ever do that to me again.' She dropped the phone on the couch. 'It's my phone and I was having a private conversation.'

Grayson towered over her, his hands on his hips. 'What's the problem? I'm going to have to meet the in-laws some time. What's wrong with tonight?' He scowled at the cushion she had pressed to her breasts. 'Don't you think I'm good enough to meet your folks?'

Lauren drew a deep calming breath. 'That's not what this is about. I'm not that much of a snob.'

Grayson backed up a couple of steps and sat on the arm of one of the paisley-patterned chairs. 'You could've fooled me.'

'I was trying to protect you, dammit!' Lauren knelt up on the couch and launched her cushion at him. 'The last person I want you to meet is my father. He's like a piranha. He'll strip away everything you value about yourself and then serve you up for dinner with a smile.'

Grayson crossed his arms across his bare chest and studied her. A slow smile crept over his face. 'You were trying to protect little ol' me?'

Lauren gathered his shirt to her breasts and got up. 'I don't know why I bothered. You're just going to tell me that you can handle him fine by yourself, aren't you?'

'Hell, no, I'm not that stupid,' Grayson said quietly. 'I was hoping we could handle him together. And I shouldn't have taken your phone.'

Lauren walked into the bedroom and sat on the side of her bed. She pressed her hands to her flushed cheeks. Grayson came in and sat beside her. The mattress gave under his weight.

'I'm not going to let your father destroy me, Lauren.'

'You don't know him,' Lauren whispered. 'He's ruined every real relationship I've ever had. He only tolerates Ella because her father is as rich as he is.'

Grayson took her hand and squeezed her fingers. 'Perhaps he thinks he's protecting you. Any man who truly wants you will have to prove to your father that he's tough. I reckon I can do that.' He kissed her fingertips and Lauren tried to relax. Perhaps Grayson was right. She should've known she could never hide him from her father.

In an effort to change the subject, she pushed him backwards until he sprawled on the bed, arms spread wide. She shook her head as he looked hopeful and his cock rose to brush her stomach.

'We have a busy day ahead. I thought we'd do touristy things this morning and then I've arranged a business lunch. I'd like you to come with me.'

Grayson reached up and stroked her arm. 'It's OK about your dad. We'll deal with him together.'

Lauren winced and wished she could just crawl back under the covers and pretend she was five again. Except with Grayson there with her, the games she got to play might be a lot more exciting. So much for her attempts to change the subject. She rolled off the bed and headed for the bathroom. 'Seeing as we're up so early, we might as well make a start.'

Grayson stayed where he was and contemplated the pink gauze bed curtains sewn with tiny rosebuds. He felt like an awkward Prince Charming. Despite Lauren's fears, he looked forward to meeting her father and setting him straight about a few things. He knew all about fathers who used the ties of love to make their kids behave.

His own father, Beau Turner, a legendary football player turned oilman, was an expert in manipulation. As a boy Grayson had idolised him. As an adult, he'd come to despise him and ultimately turn his back on everything his father held dear. It looked as if Lauren might need some help to get out from under her father's long shadow.

After a quick shower, Grayson headed into the kitchen. Lauren sat perched on a stool nursing a glass of orange juice. Her soft brown hair was tied back in a ponytail. She wore a pink leather miniskirt, a white crocheted top and white platform boots. Pale-pink lipstick and thick black eyeliner completed her city look.

'I'm taking you out for breakfast,' Lauren said. 'We'll go to Kate's Kitchen in Lower Haight. Is that OK?'

She looked too tense for his liking but he decided to give her some space. According to the tattered magazines he was forced to read at the dentist's, women were big on personal space.

Grayson took her orange juice out of her hand and swallowed the rest in one gulp. He opened the refrigerator to get more and pretended to blink at the startling expanse of white emptiness. The orange juice sat next to a carton of fat-free milk and that was it.

'You weren't kidding about the cooking were you?' He refilled her glass and handed it back to her. The kitchen walls had been stencilled to death to resemble a magical woodland scene. He pointed at an elf peering through the foliage. 'Do fairies appear when you're at work, clean up the place and leave you delicious meals?'

Lauren's answering smile was more genuine this time. 'I didn't choose the décor, all right? It was my father's idea.'

Grayson grinned. 'He probably thought it would scare all your boyfriends away. Personally, I quite like it. I feel like a horny prince awakening a virgin princess.'

Lauren gave him a wry smile. 'You would.' She sipped at her orange juice and then passed him the glass. 'My father makes it difficult to refuse his gifts. He came in here while I was away on business and had the place redecorated without consulting me. When I complained, he acted as if I'd hurt his feelings.'

Grayson grimaced. 'My father preferred to let his fists do the talking, and do the hurting for real, but the results are the same. Some fathers just don't know how to keep out of their kids' lives.' Grayson put down the orange juice on the countertop and wiped his mouth. Where the hell had that come from? He didn't usually share his feelings about his father with anyone.

He stole a glance at Lauren's face. She didn't seem surprised, she just looked interested. Her lack of reaction helped him relax and finish off the juice.

'I'm not trying to say that makes your father any better than mine, Lauren. I'm just saying that parents can sure as hell mess up their kids.'

Lauren slid down from the stool and took the empty glass across to the dishwasher. She looked at him over her shoulder. 'Sometimes I think it would've been better if I'd had siblings. I didn't really start to grow up until I realised I would never please my father and that it was stupid to keep trying. To him, I'll always be a second-rate boy.'

Grayson walked up behind Lauren and wrapped his arms around her waist. 'I'm sure glad you're not a boy.'

She looked up at him and they shared a moment of deep understanding that startled him.

'I'm beginning to be glad about that too,' Lauren whispered.

After a morning spent revisiting all the tourist spots of San Francisco – something she hadn't done in years – Lauren glanced up at Grayson as they crossed the road. He'd reclaimed his Stetson and jeans and yet still managed to look at home in the busy crowded streets.

'How come you know the city so well?' Lauren asked.

Grayson looked down at her. 'I lived and worked here for a while during the nineties.'

'Doing what?'

His gaze slipped away. 'This and that. Nothing I'm particularly proud of.'

Lauren waited, but he didn't add anything to his comments. She checked her cellphone messages and then pointed to a restaurant along the street.

'We're going to meet our clients at Lulu's. Barry left me a message earlier. He should be there by now.'

Grayson shot her an amused glance. 'Our clients? Am I on your payroll now?'

Grayson didn't know it yet, but Lauren hoped he'd be interested in helping her clients as well. He held the door of the restaurant open for her. She walked in to the warm hum of conversation and the smell of hot coffee.

In the far corner of the room she spotted another cowboy hat. 'I think we're sitting over there.' She took Grayson's hand and threaded through the packed tables. She felt him baulk behind her and come to a sudden halt as the two men at the table got to their feet.

She recognised Barry Levarr, who started to say something. He was interrupted by the man beside him.

To her dismay, the tall blond cowboy ignored her and scowled at Grayson. 'What the hell are you doing here?'

Grayson spread his hands wide and glanced at Lauren. 'I was just about to ask you the same question, but without the profanity.'

Two pieces of information clicked into place in Lauren's brain. One, that despite their different colouring, the two cowboys looked disturbingly alike. And two, she made a wild guess that both of them bore the same surname.

She held out her hand to the blond-haired guy. 'You must be Mr Turner, the designer of Prairie Dawg Boots?'

He shook her hand, his grip as firm as Grayson's. 'That's right, call me Jay.' He frowned over her shoulder at Grayson. 'I didn't expect you to bring my big brother with you. I thought you said we were meeting a potential business-site developer.'

Grayson shot her an accusing look and Lauren sighed. 'If I told you guys that I didn't know there was a connection between you, would you believe me?' Two pairs of equally unimpressed blue eyes met hers.

'Don't you read your clients' letterheads?' Jay said. 'Grayson's listed just below me.'

Lauren rallied at the implication that she hadn't acted professionally. 'Of course I did. Turner is quite a common name.'

'Guys?' Grayson cleared his throat. 'Perhaps we could sit down. People are starting to stare.'

Lauren took the seat next to Barry Levarr, the business manager she'd met in Vegas. At least he'd had the sense to keep out of their discussion. He smiled and shook her hand as the two brothers settled themselves on the other side of the table. Both wore blue shirts and identical frowns. Their wide shoulders competed for room in the narrow space across the table.

She smiled at Grayson who didn't smile back. Why hadn't he mentioned his connection with Prairie Dawg Boots when she'd discussed them with him last weekend? Didn't he trust her? Perhaps he was more like her father than she realised, keeping business secrets because she was only a female.

If he expected her to get flustered and forget why she'd arranged the meeting, he didn't know her at all. She opened her purse and brought out a folder.

'Despite the fact that you two are related, I don't see why we can't continue with this discussion in a businesslike manner.'

Jay looked mutinous. 'Did he get to tag along so that he could keep tabs on me?' He glared at his brother. 'Don't you think I'm capable of running this company on my own?'

Grayson picked up his water glass and drank deep. 'Miss Redstone's right. I had no idea this meeting would involve you. I promised to be a silent partner in this venture of yours and I intend to remain one.'

Lauren decided it was time to intervene. 'Grayson's only here because he's developing a small business park on part of his ranch in Oregon. I thought that as Prairie Dawg was looking to expand their business operation they might consider moving there.'

Jay sat back and looked sceptical. 'Why didn't you just offer the site to me?'

Lauren wondered the same thing.

'Because I promised not to interfere.' Grayson sighed. 'I wasn't sure you'd want your company to be situated a stone's throw from my ranch.'

Lauren studied the two brothers. They seemed ill at

ease with each other. What had happened between them to make their relationship so tense? She slid the folder across to Jay.

'I've gathered some information for you. I know this is not exactly my area of expertise but it used to be when I practised law. I believe your relocation will improve all areas of your company. I've included comparative business and property values across several states. I think you'll find that Grayson's proposed site stands up very well in terms of cost and position.'

A waiter appeared and Lauren spent the next few minutes ordering food and sipping iced tea. Barry Levarr made small talk with her but the brothers remained silent, both staring into their coffee as if it might be poisoned.

Lauren waited until the food arrived and then launched her second attack. 'Jay, Barry says that you are looking for a new advertising angle for your boots. Now that you're going to be involved with my commercials promoting the PBR, have you considered investing in the PRCA or the PBR?'

Barry spoke through a mouthful of spaghetti Alfredo. 'What are they? Basketball teams?'

Grayson and Jay exchanged guarded smiles as Lauren hastened to explain. 'No, they are professional organisations for the rodeo circuit and the bull riders.' She nodded at Jay. 'Just the kind of people who'd love the rugged design of your boots.'

Jay nodded. 'That's not a bad idea. My only worry is how much it would cost. We have a limited marketing and promotional budget.'

'I know, but if we worked together we could look for someone young and up and coming who'd be glad of a little money and free pairs of boots.'

Grayson put down his glass. 'I might be able to help with this.' Lauren stared at him, a question in her gaze. 'Dakota's a bull rider.'

Jay made a disgusted sound. 'Don't tell me you've discovered another one of Dad's cast-offs?'

Grayson didn't smile. 'Yeah, Dakota's a couple of years younger than you. I went to Las Vegas to watch him in the PBR finals. He's pretty good. It took some persuading that we were family but he relented in the end.'

Jay caught Lauren's eye. 'My big brother considers it his mission in life to gather up all my father's by-blows and make us into some kind of family.' He poked Grayson in the ribs. 'So how come I haven't met this Dakota yet?'

'Because last time we talked you told me to stay the fuck out of your life.'

Jay hunched his shoulder and sipped at his coffee. Lauren retrieved a second file from her case and leafed through the contents.

'I have a Dakota Scott on my list of potential riders to approach.' She glanced up at the brothers. 'Perhaps one of you would like to call him and ask if he'd be interested? And if he's a good-looking as you two are, he might even be able to work as our advertising model.'

Two identical expressions of revulsion crossed Grayson and Jay's faces. Lauren wasn't sure if it was her reference to their looks or the thought of a modelling assignment which offended them more.

Barry Levarr glanced at his watch. 'I'm sorry, Lauren but I need to be out of here by one. I left my wife shopping at Saks.'

Jay laughed. Lauren couldn't believe the difference it made to his face. 'Are you afraid she'll wear out your credit card?'

Barry got to his feet and searched his pockets for his cellphone. 'She used that up years ago. I'm down to protecting the kids' college funds.' He grinned at Lauren as if to make sure she knew it was a joke.

Lauren moved out of his way. 'Give me a call when you and Jay have gone over the information I've provided. I'll let you know when I have more definite dates for the filming of the first commercial.'

Barry shook her hand. 'I sure will and thanks for your input. Jay and I have a lot to talk about.'

Barry left. Lauren was left with the check for lunch and, more worryingly, with the Turner brothers. Grayson seemed to be avoiding her gaze. She couldn't work out whether he was annoyed with her for duping him into a meeting with his brother or worried about her reaction to his lies.

Jay cleared his throat. 'So how do you two know each other then?'

Lauren opened her mouth and couldn't think of a single thing to say.

'We met through mutual business acquaintances,' Grayson said smoothly. 'Lauren's also been helping me out with the new plans for my ranch land.'

Lauren studied Grayson. He sounded so sincere. Perhaps he was a better liar than she realised. Jake finished up his coffee and liberated the remains of the apple pie from Grayson's plate.

'I need to get going myself.' He grimaced as he stood and rubbed his right thigh.

Grayson took a breath and very carefully didn't look at his brother. 'Is your leg still hurting you? If you need the money for the surgery . . .'

'Don't try to buy me, Grayson,' Jay snapped. 'You sound just like Dad.' Jay's expression darkened and he turned his back on his brother. 'Nice to finally meet you in the flesh, Lauren. I'll call you when we've made some decisions.'

Without a backwards glance he strode out of the restaurant. He slammed the door so hard that he caused a mini tornado among the closest tables. Lauren called for the check as Grayson rubbed his forehead.

'And it was going so well,' Grayson muttered. 'Why does Jay have to be so touchy?'

Lauren shot him a straight glance as she scribbled her name on the bill. 'Perhaps it runs in the family.'

He stared right back at her. 'Perhaps we'd better talk.'

Chapter Nineteen

When they left the restaurant, Lauren headed back towards the Embarcadero. Grayson kept pace beside her, his hands in his jeans pockets, his hat tipped low over his eyes. The sun had defeated the morning fog and blazed high in a cloudless blue sky.

'When did you realise I was connected to the Prairie Dawg Boot company?' Grayson's terse question shattered the uneasy silence between them.

'I didn't. It never occurred to me that you were.' Lauren kept her answer short. Men always expected women to jump in and justify themselves. She wasn't prepared to do that just yet.

Grayson moved closer to avoid a collision with a UPS guy struggling to carry a large package. 'Then why did you set me up for this lunch? Were you trying to make me look stupid?'

To Lauren's surprise, he didn't sound too annoyed. 'As I said earlier, I was hoping you could do business together. I had no idea you were already involved with them.'

Grayson sighed so loudly that Lauren heard him above the street noise. 'I'm not really "involved" with them. I lent Jay the money to start the business and put him in touch with Barry who used to work for me. I knew they'd be successful without me sticking my nose in.'

Oblivious to the glares of her fellow pedestrians, Lauren stopped walking and turned to face Grayson. 'You might have mentioned that "non-involvement" of yours when I mentioned Prairie Dawg last weekend. You made me look unprofessional.'

Grayson took hold of her arm and drew her to one side. 'Dammit, I knew this would happen. That's why, until I met you, I've always made it a rule never to mix business with pleasure.'

Lauren gritted her teeth. 'And what exactly is that old cliché supposed to mean?'

He tipped his hat back so that she could see his slate-blue eyes. 'I didn't mention my connection to Prairie Dawg Boots because it would just have confused things between us.'

'You don't think things are confused enough anyway?'

'Well, hell, yes, but how would you have reacted if I'd told you about Prairie Dawg last weekend? You might have had the same rule of no fraternisation that I used to have. I had to make a choice.'

Lauren stared at him. 'You didn't want me to see you as a business client. You wanted me to see you as a lover, is that it?'

Grayson gave a slow nod. 'Yeah, that about sums it up. At the ranch it was more important that you saw me as a man rather than as a potential customer.'

Lauren started walking again. Her instinct was to deny what Grayson said but something stopped her from saying it out loud. Even though his explanation sounded a little contrived, the expression in his eyes was sincere.

'Perhaps I should've told you who we were meeting for lunch,' she reluctantly conceded. 'It would've given you an opportunity to tell me the truth before it got embarrassing for both of us.'

'At least you'll have to agree that I didn't go behind your back and talk to them about you,' Grayson remarked. 'I hadn't spoken to Jay since before I met you in Las Vegas. I was as surprised to see him as you were.' Grayson draped his arm over her shoulders.

Lauren decided it was time to move on. She wasn't

quite sure that the matter was resolved to her complete satisfaction, but she'd worry about that later.

'Don't you and your brother get along?'

'Sometimes,' Grayson said, 'when we're not fighting.' He half-smiled. 'We don't have the same mother but we're still too much alike. Our father brought us up to compete against each other. Jay still can't get it out of his system.'

And you can? Lauren didn't make the mistake of making the comment out loud. 'I noticed that.' She expertly negotiated a pedestrian walkway crowded with dawdling tourists. 'He seems to resent you enormously.'

'While simultaneously borrowing money from me.' Grayson smiled. 'Not that I begrudge him the money. He's a very talented guy. He still feels second rate because he didn't follow Dad's orders and go into the oil business. He used to be a rodeo cowboy before he smashed up his leg. I still think his true talent lies in design though, which is why I persuaded him to start the business.'

Lauren repressed a shiver. 'I don't like the sound of your father.' She glanced back at the city. 'Does he live here?'

'No, he spends most of his time in Texas. Although I believe he owns an apartment in San Francisco.' Grayson gave her an amused sideways glance. 'Are you disappointed? Would you like to meet him?'

Lauren allowed herself to respond to his smile. A knot of tension uncoiled in her stomach. He'd handled the lunch as smoothly as she had, turning a potential disaster into an intriguing set of possibilities. She should be proud of him for reacting so well instead of criticising him for keeping a business secret from her. And he did have a point. She might have baulked at getting involved with someone on her client list.

She grabbed his hand, stood on tiptoe and kissed

him on the mouth. A group of construction workers whistled and bawled out lewd suggestions to Grayson as he kissed her back. He held her close and stared down into her eyes.

'Does this mean you've decided we can be lovers *and* business associates?'

Lauren smiled. 'As long as we keep our priorities in order, I don't see why not.' She gasped as he picked her up and twirled her around in a circle. The construction workers went wild and some tourists paused to watch the show.

When he put her down, she laughed out loud and they walked hand in hand down to sample the delights of Pier 39.

When her alarm clock rang, Lauren allowed Grayson to roll over and switch it off. Evening shadows crept up the pink silk walls of her bedroom enhancing the gilt fixtures and fairy-tale setting. After their exhausting morning, they'd decided to spend a couple of hours in bed before getting ready for dinner with Lauren's parents. To Lauren's amazement, she'd slept, cradled in Grayson's warm embrace.

He set the alarm clock on the bedside table and grinned down at her. Lazily, she raised her hand and rubbed his roughened cheek with her knuckles. He grimaced.

'I know, I need to shave.'

Lauren bit her lip and slid her other hand up his muscled bicep until she reached his neck. 'Could you shave a bit later?'

His blue gaze sharpened and he smiled. 'What do you have in mind, honey?'

In reply, she pushed him down until his face grazed her stomach. He rubbed his cheek against her soft skin and she purred in delight. His fingers slid between her legs and discovered just how wet she was. She gasped as he probed her belly-button ring with his tongue and then moved lower.

'Open your eyes, Lauren. Watch me enjoy you.'

Grayson used his wide shoulders to open her legs. He pulled a pillow down from the head of the bed and slid it under her hips, presenting her woman's softness to his mouth like an appetiser on a plate.

Lauren shivered at the first delicate lap of his tongue against her sex. He licked her again, the tip of his tongue hard against her swelling arousal. As he continued to caress her, his fingers slid in and out of her sheath in a complementary rhythm.

Soon, all she could think about was the slick sound of Grayson's mouth and fingers working her towards a climax. She reached down and grabbed his shoulder. 'I want you inside me when I come, please.'

He chuckled against her thigh and scraped his chin over her most sensitive parts. 'Next time. Come for me now.'

She tried to hold back, to deny herself the gift he offered her, but her body clenched around his thrusting fingers. He took her into his mouth and suckled hard. She bit back a scream as her climax shuddered through her.

He continued to lick and stroke her gently as he changed position. Lauren lay back on her pillows, too exhausted to protest. He crawled towards her, one hand wrapped around the base of his huge erection. Lauren reached out and laced her fingers with his.

'We'd better make this quick. I don't want to be late for dinner.'

Grayson settled himself over her and looked disapproving. She bit her lip as he slid slowly inside her. 'Quick's not a word that works for me right now, Lauren. Let's just agree to take all the time we need.'

He hooked her feet over his shoulders and knelt up,

angling her pussy so that his cock rubbed hard against her sensitive flesh. He withdrew until she tried to follow him with a jerk of her hips. Holding her gaze, he licked his middle finger and probed the tight bud of her back passage.

'Has anyone had you here, Lauren?'

She shook her head, her gaze fixed on his.

'I'm going to.'

He added a second finger. 'I like the thought of you being filled with my come in every possible way.' He pressed his cock fully into her pussy, felt his own fingers through the thin wall as he slid past. 'If I had my way, you'd always have my come somewhere inside you.'

Her pupils widened until there was almost no colour left. He eased another finger in, felt her tight muscles clamp around him. She didn't need to know the full extent of his macho territorial thinking. He wanted his scent on her when they met her father. He wanted the old guy to know that Lauren belonged with him now.

'Would you like that, Lauren?'

She came suddenly, surprising him with the extent of her passion. He held still and gritted his teeth against the desperate urge to spill in her. When she finished shuddering, he withdrew his cock and stared at his fingers still embedded in her.

'You're too tight for me to get into today. But we'll work on it.' He reluctantly removed his fingers. Ignoring the frantic ache in his cock that demanded completion, he went to the bathroom to wash up and then returned to the bed.

Lauren rolled onto her side and watched him return. He fitted her body against his and slid back inside her. She was so wet his cock almost slipped out of her with every stroke. He kissed her and deepened his thrusts until she moaned into his mouth and dug her nails into his back. He felt his come travel up his shaft and a heaviness in his balls.

As he released into her, his sexual glow was enhanced by the thought that there was no way Lauren's parents would be able to ignore her 'I've just been fucked by a cowboy' smile.

Chapter Twenty

Lauren frantically dabbed concealer over her flushed cheeks as Grayson shaved beside her. He caught her eye in the mirror and winked.

'I bet you wish I'd shaved first now, don't you?'

'How did you guess,' Lauren muttered as she studied her neck. Her fingers connected with a sore spot. She turned and glared at Grayson.

'Did you have to give me a hickey as well? How old are you, thirteen?'

He grinned and slapped on some aftershave. Not hard enough for Lauren – if she'd been in charge of the bottle, his ears would be ringing by now.

'Thirty-five this year but thirteen's close enough for me.' He bent to kiss the small mark on her neck, engulfing Lauren in a wave of citrus fragrance. She poked him in the chest and searched in her make-up drawer for heavy-duty concealer.

Grayson put on charcoal-grey pants and an aqua-blue shirt and tie which contrasted well with his eyes.

Lauren fiddled with mascara and blusher, too aware of him standing behind her. She glanced at her gold watch and screeched, 'Oh my God, it's well past seven. We're supposed to be there by now.' She glanced back at Grayson who was putting on his jacket. 'Did anyone call?'

He shrugged. 'How should I know? I'm not allowed to touch your phone any more am I?'

Lauren stuck out her tongue at him, then walked into her closet and studied the row of dresses. What should she wear? Her father would expect something smart and expensive. He'd bought half the clothes in her closet after complaining that she looked too weird in her business attire and too scruffy in her jeans.

She tried her usual trick of closing her eyes and sticking her hand out. She pulled out a short black dress covered in jet beads. Great. Black suited her mood. It complemented the impending storm she imagined gathering on the horizon of her personal life.

'Don't wear that.'

Lauren turned and bumped up against Grayson. Damn, the man looked great in a suit and even better out of one. Her body leant into his as if seeking the source of the sexual explosion he'd put her through earlier.

'What's wrong with it?'

Grayson took the hanger out of her hand and slotted it back on the rail. 'Black's not the best colour on you.' He smiled at her, his left hand caressing her butt. 'I wish I'd brought your cowgirl outfit along with me.'

With the air of a man with a purpose, Grayson flicked through the row of dresses. He continued talking as he looked. 'I bet you didn't buy any of these. They just don't seem to be your style.' He stopped and studied her expression. 'Daddy bought them, right?'

She nodded. 'But I need to wear one tonight, Grayson. I don't want to ... disappoint him.' She hated the way his expression changed when she said that. He obviously thought she was a weak-minded idiot. Of course, he had no idea what her father was capable of. And perhaps he was right. She tried to make a joke of it. 'Look, we're already going to be late and Dad's pre-programmed to hate you on sight. If I wear something he approves of at least I'll get brownie points for that.'

Grayson turned back to the rail. 'OK, but let me pick the dress, please?' Within seconds, he handed her a sage-green chiffon dress with subtle gold embroidery on the bodice and hem. 'Try this one.'

He helped her into the dress, zipping up the back, kissing her shoulder as he connected the last hook and eye.

Lauren studied her reflection in the mirror. She'd never worn this particular dress before. On the hanger, it looked flowery and insubstantial. To her surprise, it brought out the unusual colour of her hazel eyes and the A-line skirt emphasised her narrow waist. She smiled into Grayson's eyes. 'It's all right. I look OK.'

He wrapped his arms around her waist and put his chin on her shoulder. 'No, you look beautiful.' He kissed her throat. 'The trouble is now I want to tear it off you and take you back to bed.' He hesitated. 'Hell, I'm not your father. I'm not supposed to dictate what you wear. If you hate it, take it off and wear the black.'

Lauren elbowed him in the ribs and he stepped back. She found some gold sandals and a small matching evening purse, and then went to put on her lipstick.

Grayson leant against the wall and watched her. 'The dress you wore last night, was that one of your father's presents?'

'No, that was from Ella. She found it for me in a thrift store in Berkeley. It's one of my favourites.'

Grayson looked pleased. 'I'll have to thank Ella. I liked that dress. It had distinct advantages.'

She darted him a reproving glance. 'For you, maybe. I felt half-naked.'

Grayson closed his eyes and smiled as if remembering something good. When he opened them again, Lauren had to force herself to stop looking at him. She dabbed face powder across her cheeks and picked up her purse.

'Are you ready?' Grayson asked. 'I've called a cab. It's going to be OK, Lauren.' He strolled towards her carrying her long black coat. He helped her into it, his fingers warm on her bare arms. 'Trust me, I can be very charming when I want to be.'

Grayson studied the brightly lit hall as Lauren took off her coat and handed it to her father's butler. The butler, of course, had an English accent and referred to Lauren as 'Miss Laurie' as though she were still ten years old.

The circular hallway was paved with cream limestone tiles. A crystal chandelier hung from the fifteen-foot high ceiling illuminating the genuine French antiques positioned in the enormous space. Grayson studied a portrait hung in between the double staircase. Paul Redstone stood behind a chair, which contained his wife and a little blonde-haired girl. Mr Redstone's aggressive stance dominated the picture as he appeared to dominate his family in real time.

Grayson touched Lauren's elbow and pointed at the portrait. 'Is that you?'

'Yes, although the artist made me look more angelic than I ever was. My mother had to bribe me with candy to make me sit still for more than five minutes.'

Grayson tightened his grip on Lauren's arm. If he had a daughter wouldn't he want to protect her from any man who even dared to look at her? He suddenly felt some sympathy for Lauren's father.

'Shall we go up?' Lauren said. 'My parents are waiting for us.'

Lauren took his hand and Grayson allowed her to lead him up the white-carpeted stairs. A couple stood framed in the double glass doors leading to a drawing room. Grayson deliberately focused his attention on Lauren's mother. She was slender for her age, her body shape reminiscent of Lauren's. The only things that jarred were her features, which had obviously been improved upon by a plastic surgeon.

She wore a short green suit and several gold neck-laces. When she held out her hand to Grayson, it seemed weighed down by the huge rings and chunky bracelets which adorned it. He smiled reassuringly into her wary eyes as her hand trembled in his.

'I'm Grayson Turner. Thank you for inviting us here this evening.'

He turned to greet Lauren's father. They were much of a height, although Paul Redstone was heavier in build. His hair was silver, his eyes the same volatile hazel as Lauren's. His handshake bore none of the timidity of his wife's. It was a true politician's hand-shake – just enough pressure to command respect and not enough to overwhelm. It reminded Grayson of his father.

'Grayson Turner, sir. It's a pleasure to meet you.'

He met Mr Redstone's aggressive stare straight on. He'd learnt long ago how to judge an opponent. From his belligerent expression, Grayson knew that Lauren's father considered himself one of the big sharks. In his world, Grayson probably figured as a bottom feeder.

'Mr Turner. I've heard so little about you.'

'Please call me Grayson, sir.'

Grayson stepped back as Mr Redstone allowed Lauren to kiss his cheek. He frowned as he looked at her dress.

'Why did you wear that old thing? It's two seasons out of date.'

Lauren smoothed down her skirt and gave her father a bright smile. 'Then it's a classic. I like it. You know I never wear anything new. Who cares?' She gave Grayson a sidelong glance. 'At least it's not black and boring.'

Mr Redstone ushered them into the drawing room. Again Grayson was assailed by the unobtrusive smell of too much money. Everything in the room had been chosen with exquisite care to display quiet wealth and opulence. His gaze settled with deep appreciation on an original Picasso hung over the fireplace.

At least Lauren's father had taste. His own father, Beau, tended more towards the Hugh Heffner style of décor. Bordello-type furniture covered in scantily clad women.

Lauren sat down on the spindly legged couch and Grayson went to join her. She hadn't folded when her father criticised her dress. She'd stood up to him, using humour and good manners to deflect the sting of his remarks.

'Would you like something to drink?' Mrs Redstone gestured to the butler.

Grayson accepted a glass of excellent white wine and so did Lauren. Mrs Redstone sat opposite them, a glass of mineral water clutched in her hand. Lauren smiled at her mother.

'Is that emerald ring new, Mom?'

Mrs Redstone extended her right hand. 'Yes, your father bought it for me to celebrate our wedding anniversary.'

Grayson pretended to admire the ring. 'And how many years have you been married?'

A peculiar expression crossed Mrs Redstone's face. 'Too many,' she whispered in an aside. Then she said loudly, 'Thirty-two glorious years. I consider myself a lucky woman.'

Grayson glanced at Lauren and wondered if he'd imagined the first comment. Mr Redstone strolled over to stand behind his wife's chair.

'I'm lucky that she puts up with me. She's a saint.' He rested his hand on his wife's shoulder. She seemed to sink into her chair under the weight. Mr Redstone's gaze flicked over Grayson.

'So I understand you're some kind of cowboy, Grayson.'

'I live on a ranch and I keep horses on it, so, yeah, I suppose you could say that.'

Lauren cleared her throat. 'Grayson owns and runs a stud farm and horse-training centre in Oregon. I've been helping him out with some business deals recently.'

Mr Redstone smiled. 'From what I hear, you've been doing a lot more than that.'

Grayson tried not to react. Had Mr Redstone found out about their marriage? He wouldn't put it past him. 'Don't put yourself down, Lauren.' He ignored the apprehension in Lauren's eyes and turned to her parents. 'Lauren's been great. She's kept me company this weekend. I haven't stayed in the city for a couple of years and everything changes so quickly.'

Mrs Redstone got to her feet as the dinner gong sounded. 'That sounds fascinating. Where has Lauren taken you? Be sure to visit the new farmers' market in the Ferry Building tomorrow morning. It's well worth a trip.'

Grayson tucked her arm through his and escorted Mrs Redstone into the dining room. She squeezed his bicep as they approached the table and whispered, 'Don't let Paul intimidate you. Lauren needs someone who can stand up to him.'

'Don't worry, ma'am, I've got it covered,' Grayson murmured back as he pulled out a chair and helped Mrs Redstone sit down.

Lauren smiled encouragingly at Grayson as he put down his napkin. He hadn't seemed bothered by the appetiser which consisted of steamed artichokes and clams. Lauren knew her father had ordered them because they were notoriously difficult to eat. He'd done it to a previous boyfriend of hers. It had been the final nail in their relationship. He'd never called her again.

'What do you think of Lauren's little business then, Grayson? It's a shame she didn't remain a lawyer. She could've helped you with your little –' he pretended to search for the word '– ranch.'

Grayson looked so calm Lauren wanted to kiss him. 'I think Lauren's doing too well to worry about my little ranch.' He leant forwards, food forgotten, the pride in his voice unmistakable. 'Did she tell you that she's producing commercials for the PBR? That's a big opportunity. You must be so proud of her.'

'Oh, we are.' Mrs Redstone spoke and then cast a nervous glance at her silent husband.

Grayson smiled approvingly at her. 'Unofficially, Lauren's also been helping me develop a small business park on the edge of my land. She's already come up with one business interested in renting some of the units and the plans haven't even been processed yet.'

He grinned at Lauren who smiled back. Glad of his support, she loosened her grip on her fork.

'Ah, that's right.' Her father looked pleased, too pleased. 'I had a phone call from the wife of an old buddy of mine who lives out that way.' Lauren tensed as her father turned his attention on her. 'Do you know her, Lauren? She said she'd met you at the town meeting to discuss the business units.'

Lauren's fork slid from her grasp and clattered on the table. 'If you told me her name, I might be able to remember.'

'Her name is Anna, Anna Paulson. She's married to a guy I used to work with, Roger Paulson.' His sideways glance included Grayson in the discussion. 'Said she was a neighbor of Grayson's here. Is that so?'

Grayson sat back in his chair. 'That's right.'

'I gave Anna my old business card with the address of your law firm on it when we met,' Lauren said, 'but I don't understand why she contacted you.'

'Because, my little ignoramus, she hoped I'd use my

influence on you to stop Grayson's plans for the town. Apparently he's upsetting a lot of people down there.'

Lauren met her father's gaze head on. 'Why would she think you'd be able to do that?'

He reached across and patted her hand. 'Because I'm your daddy, and when it comes down to it, blood is thicker than water.'

Lauren got slowly to her feet. 'If you think I'd interfere in Grayson's private affairs just to satisfy the whim of an ageing wannabe actress like Anna Paulson, or her husband because he happens to be a buddy of yours, you're mistaken.'

Grayson leant across the table and took her hand. 'I think you're forgetting something else, sir. The land belongs to me. Any decisions that are made about it are mine. Even if you could convince Lauren to help you out, she'd still have to get through me.'

Lauren sat down again with a bump. She'd never felt so angry in her life, yet part of her was shocked because she'd dared to stand up to her father. Grayson was still talking.

'If you're interested in finding out both sides of the story, sir, I can get Lauren to show you a copy of my business plan.'

'That won't be necessary.' Her father's smile was so patronising that Lauren gritted her teeth. Why was he so interested in Anna Paulson's complaints about Grayson? What did he have to gain? 'I don't have time to dabble in such small concerns. I leave that to Lauren here.'

The butler brought in the next course. Lauren wanted to weep when she saw it was seafood still in the shell. She fought an urge to throw all the platters in the air, grab Grayson's hand and make a quick getaway. Instead she took some crab and concentrated on working the thin strip of white meat out of the narrow leg channel.

Grayson winked at her and then turned back to her father who began to grill him about his business income.

'He's a very nice young man, Lauren.'

Her mother's whisper made Lauren jump. She smiled gratefully. 'Thanks, Mom. I like him too.'

'He looks very familiar. Are you sure he's from Oregon?'

Lauren's mother had a legendary ability to remember faces which was why she was such a successful hostess.

'I think he was born in Texas, but his family moved around a lot. If you find out he's a famous soap star or escaped convict, let me know won't you?'

'I surely will, dear. Now don't forget to bring him to my birthday lunch tomorrow.'

Lauren groaned. 'I thought we agreed I could skip the big formal party this year and just take you out to dinner by myself?'

Her mother glanced across the table. 'Paul told me I must insist you come. He says he has a surprise for you.'

Lauren knew she had no choice. She couldn't risk her mother being blamed for her non-appearance. 'We'll come, Mom, but we'll only stay for a little while. Grayson has to get back to Oregon.'

And out of my life, she thought miserably. And how on earth was she going to deal with that?

Chapter Twenty-One

Grayson stole a glance at Lauren's profile as the cab headed back to her apartment. She'd made no attempt to hide her desire to leave her parent's house as soon as possible. He reached across and took her hand. Her fingers were icy cold.

'I told you we'd survive,' he said softly.

Lauren continued to stare out of the window.

'Your mother is very sweet.'

'Yes, she is.'

Grayson was almost pleased when the cab stopped. He wasn't used to initiating delicate conversation. Call him a sexist pig, but that's what women usually did best.

Inside her apartment, Lauren walked straight through her bedroom and into the bathroom. Grayson heard the door lock. He took off his jacket and tie and returned to the kitchen to make coffee.

When Lauren reappeared he was ensconced on the couch watching a ball game. She'd wrapped herself in an old pink bathrobe and left her damp hair loose. She looked surprised when she saw him as if she'd half-expected him to have left. To his relief, she came to sit next to him.

He kept his gaze on the screen as she leant back against his chest. Her body was as unyielding as a steel post. Grayson tucked a stray lock of hair behind her ear. 'Does your father do that to all your boyfriends?'

'What?'

'Try to intimidate them.'

She shrugged. 'I told you what he was like. You were the one who wanted to meet him.'

'Did you expect me to bail out on you the minute he started on me?'

She moved abruptly out of his arms. 'Why shouldn't you? Everyone else has.'

He stared at her, feeling curiously insulted. 'I told you, I'm not easily scared. I've dealt with a lot of bullies in my life. Your father was nothing new.'

She crossed her arms and stuck her chin in the air. 'The whole evening was designed to intimidate you.' She brushed angrily at her face where a single tear slid down her cheek. 'Even the food. Why aren't you mad?'

Grayson realised she wasn't annoyed at him but at her father. 'Because if I had a daughter like you I'd be protective of her as well. I wouldn't want some asshole walking in and taking her away from me.'

She knelt up on the couch, her fists clenched. 'You don't understand. That's what he likes people to think, but it goes way further than that. He's possessive to the point of obsession.'

She broke off and moved away from the couch. 'Dammit, I should've checked for bugs before we even started this conversation. Whenever I go away for the weekend, he gets in here and plants the darned things.'

Grayson followed her into the kitchen feeling as if he'd stumbled into a bizarre spy movie. She rummaged in her purse and produced her cellphone. She punched in a short number.

'Kevin, did my father or any maintenance guys come up to my apartment last weekend?'

Her shoulders sagged as the guy on the other end of the conversation obviously returned a negative.

'Great. Thanks, no everything's fine. I'll call you tomorrow.'

Grayson waited until she returned the phone to her purse. 'Will you please tell me what's going on?'

Lauren walked back into the family room and sat on the couch. 'I found out a few months ago that my father was "listening in" on my conversations. He let something slip that I knew I hadn't discussed with anyone but Ella.'

She drew her feet up under her. 'I confronted him about it. He promised not to do it again, but you never know with my father. Now I've asked the building supervisor to deny entrance to anyone except the emergency services when I'm not here.'

Grayson remained leaning against the wall. He had the strangest feeling that if he attempted to reason with her, Lauren would show him the door. He studied her resolute face. Why would she even bother to lie about something like that? It might explain her reluctance to get involved with him.

'When did you first begin to believe your father was interfering in your life too much?'

Lauren half-smiled. 'When he sent two of his bodyguards to threaten the guy who asked me to my junior prom. I was all dressed up and ready to go when my date called and said he was sick. Daddy stepped in and took me himself. God, I was so grateful.'

Grayson nodded. 'So what happened to the guy who took you to the senior prom? Did he get sick too?'

'Oh no, he broke his leg on the day of the prom. Someone pushed him down a flight of steps at the mall.'

Grayson straightened up. 'And you think your father had something to do with that as well?'

'You don't believe me, do you?' Lauren got up, wrapped her arms around her waist and walked across to the window.

'Honey, I'm not judging you. But you must admit it does sound ...'

'Far-fetched, impossible, fantastic?' She shrugged. 'He's scared off every single boyfriend I've ever had. It's amazing I ever managed to lose my virginity. Why should anyone believe that a fine upstanding citizen like my father could really be a monster? I've spent years denying it to myself.'

Grayson sat on the couch she'd vacated and stared at her averted profile. 'If you think he's got a serious problem, why haven't you talked to your mom about it?'

'I have. Why do you think she's had all that plastic surgery, Grayson? Is that what you expect bored rich woman to do?' She swung around, her hands on her hips. Tears glinted in her eyes.

'I asked my mom to talk to him after he threatened yet another boyfriend of mine and guess what he did?'

Grayson shook his head, a bad feeling in his gut.

'He called me and said that Mom had had a terrible accident and was in the hospital. When I got there, I overheard Mom's doctor telling her that he didn't believe she'd fallen against the glass mirror, that she'd been deliberately pushed into it. She refused to change her story but I know who did it. The same man who paid for all the surgery to remove the thousands of splinters of glass embedded in her face.'

Grayson fought an urge to throw up.

'I never asked Mom to help me again.'

Grayson got to his feet and closed the distance between them. He pulled Lauren into his arms. She was crying hard now, her tears soaked his shirt. 'It's all right, baby,' he whispered, knowing that at this moment she needed to be held and comforted more than anything else.

When her sobs subsided, he picked her up and took her to bed. She kept her face buried against his chest as he wrestled with her dressing gown and under-clothes. When she was naked, he settled her against the pillows and stripped off his own clothes. He slid his arm beneath her shoulders and eased her against his chest.

She sniffed and burrowed closer into his warmth. Grayson stared up at the frilly bed curtains. Damn, what could he say to her? He doubted she'd ever told anyone apart from Ella about what had happened to her mother.

It sure explained her reluctance to get involved with him. From her perspective, relationships caused pain to the people she loved. And marriage? Christ, that must seem like the ultimate trap. He smoothed her hair away from her flushed cheek. She looked up at him, her hazel eyes wary and defeated. A wave of tenderness engulfed him.

'Do you want to settle with your father once and for all?'

Lauren nodded.

'Will you let me help you?'

Her beautiful eyes brimmed with tears again. 'I don't want you to get hurt.'

He rolled her over onto her back and smiled. 'Honey, I'm a grown man. I can take care of myself. All we have to do is stick together. He can't defeat us if we do that.'

He kissed her mouth, tasted the salt of her tears. 'You're a strong woman, Lauren Redstone. You've fought hard to live a decent, successful life despite your father. Do you want to give that up?'

Lauren stopped crying. 'No, I don't. I want him to understand that there are other more important things in my life now.'

She hadn't mentioned him, but Grayson felt a surge of hope. She wiped her hand across her reddened nose.

'After he hurt Mom, I tried to do everything he said. I was so scared he'd harm her again. It's taken me years to find the courage to leave my job at his company and set up on my own. He doesn't like it, but so far I've managed to keep things going without running back home to him.'

Grayson wondered anew at the courage it had taken her to live out her fantasies with him in Las Vegas. Perhaps her decision to marry him had really been a cry for help or an unconscious decision to do something that put her beyond her father's reach. If that was the case, she'd chosen the right man. He would do anything to prevent her from getting hurt.

Grayson kissed her forehead. Was it a good time to remind Lauren that they were of age and legally married and that her father couldn't do anything about it? He studied her miserable, swollen face and decided not to push his luck. In her volatile state she might take his words the wrong way. The last thing she needed was to feel he was becoming possessive or staking some kind of claim over her.

'We'll get through this,' Grayson said. 'If you're worried about your mother, we can help her too. I have some connections that might be able to prevent your father from harming either of you ever again.'

Lauren gave an odd sigh and closed her eyes. Grayson tried to relax as her body slipped into slumber. When she'd settled completely he wanted to take a shower and make some phone calls. He needed help. Unfortunately that kind of help didn't come cheap. Dammit, he might just have to contact his father.

Chapter Twenty-Two

Grayson winced as the alarm clock went off right by his left ear. It was Sunday. Why had Lauren put the blasted thing on? He groaned as he felt her stir beside him. While she disappeared into the bathroom, Grayson picked up the pink clock and studied the illuminated dial.

He wasn't sure why he felt so tired. It was three hours later than he normally got up, but then he wasn't used to staying up all night any more. He used to find the pace of the city exhilarating; now it made him think of home.

Dammit, when had he got so boring? Lauren thought he was crazy wanting to live out in the middle of nowhere all year round. Perhaps it was time for him to make a compromise as well. He was only 35. If Lauren could adapt to Oregon, it was only fair that he should resign himself to spending more time in the city.

His thoughts turned to his conversation with his father. It hadn't been easy, asking his father to use his fame to help smooth his path with Lauren's dad. He'd also agreed to provide Grayson with information about Paul Redstone's more shady business activities in case being nice didn't work.

A fist knotted low in his gut. He was leaving today and, despite his best efforts, he still wasn't sure whether he'd convinced Lauren to stay married to him.

With all the problems with her father, he'd got distracted from his main aim to stop her filing for divorce. Didn't she understand that if she lived at the ranch, she could pick and choose who came to visit and who she visited in return?

He grinned as he pictured Ella strutting her stuff in Springtown's only sports bar. The clientele would never know what hit them.

'What's so funny, Grayson?'

Lauren leant over him. She smelt of roses and looked drained but her smile was full of tenderness.

'You are.' He grabbed her elbows and toppled her over onto the bed. She squeaked when he slid his hands down from her waist and cupped her butt. 'I'm beginning to think you've lost interest in me as a stud.'

It was morning. He was a man. He was alive. He dragged the covers out from between them and glanced down at his erection. 'This guy's going to get a complex soon if you don't give him some attention.'

Lauren straddled him and slid down over his shaft. She closed her eyes as he circled his hips. He slid his fingers from her waist to her pussy and stroked in time to her languid movements. Slow and steady, like her soft even breaths, like gentling a young horse. He didn't want to rush her or destroy the sweetness of making love in the soft morning light.

With an urge to taste more of her, Gray planted his feet on the bed and pushed himself up into a sitting position bringing Lauren with him. His face disappeared into the softness of her breasts and he reached eagerly for her nipples. He felt her tense and began to move faster, compelled by her sheath squeezing his cock like a fist.

He brought his mouth up to cover hers as she came and moaned her pleasure into his kiss. He followed her lead and allowed himself to go over with her. She fell forwards, her face resting on the curve of his shoulder, her hair tickling his chest. Reluctant to move, he smoothed his hands over the graceful curve of her spine. He could stay that way forever.

Slowly, Lauren lifted her head and stared at him. He frowned when he realised there were tears in her eyes. Was she crying for him or in fear of her father? His sense of well-being fizzled and died.

She gave him a weak smile and moved off him. 'I'll go and shower if that's OK. You can go after me.'

Grayson didn't reply. He rolled onto his front and buried his face in the pillows. Lauren's elusive scent invaded his senses. He'd know her blindfold. He glanced at the bathroom door, which was firmly shut. She'd offered him no invitation to share her shower. Maybe it was just too small but somehow he didn't think so.

Lauren inhaled the mixture of scents from the pot of aromatic herbs Grayson had bought her at the Ferry Building farmers' market. They'd stopped for coffee at one of the shops overlooking the bay. Grayson sat opposite her, the tip of his cowboy boot touched her shoe. His checked blue shirt was open at the neck. She wanted to kiss the soft place where his collarbone met his shoulder.

She put down the clay pot and picked up her tea. They had a couple of hours before they needed to get ready for her mother's birthday lunch. After that, Grayson would have to make his way straight to the airport. Lauren let out a sigh.

'Penny for your thoughts?' Grayson asked, his smile as guarded as her own.

'I was just thinking about you leaving. What time is your flight?'

'About seven. But it's no big deal. If I miss it there are others.'

'Why should you miss it?' Lauren held his gaze over the rim of her cup. 'As long as we make sure you leave the party early enough, you'll be fine.'

Grayson put his coffee down with a thump. 'If it's

too much of a hassle for you I can always catch a cab. Don't worry about spoiling your day.'

Lauren concentrated on mopping up the spilt coffee before it reached her side of the small table. 'What's the matter with you? You've been in a foul mood since we got here.'

He gave her one of the long measuring glances she hated. 'In case you haven't noticed, I have to go back to Oregon tonight. We had a deal about discussing the ongoing nature of our relationship and you don't seem to give a damn about it.'

'Of course I do! But how can I worry about that when we have to deal with my father?'

Grayson took off his hat and ran a hand through his hair. 'I know he's a major problem, but he's not the be all and end all. What about us? What about how we feel about each other?'

Lauren squeezed the soggy wad of napkins in her hand until the coffee ran back out again. Sometimes Grayson was too single minded for her peace of mind. 'I'm not saying we have to break it off,' she said carefully, 'I'm just saying that we need to prioritise...'

Grayson shot to his feet, grabbed his cup and headed for the nearest trash can. Lauren tried to breathe deeply as he strode back to the table. He didn't sit down again.

'One thing I've learnt, Lauren, is that love isn't something you prioritise. I tried that with my mom, and she died of cancer before I got to her on my "To Do" list. I'm not prepared to neglect the people I care about any more.'

Lauren stood up, aware of the interested glances around them and of Grayson's scathing magnificence as he stood over her, daring her to contradict him. Was he saying he loved her?

Without replying, she turned and headed outside. Grayson followed slamming the door behind him. Seagulls stalked the wooden walkways, ready to snap up any scrap of food. The smell of decaying fish and stagnant water hung in the air. Wisps of fog like long bony fingers stretched out from across the bay to caress the tops of the buildings.

Grayson took hold of her arm and turned her to face him. 'What's wrong with me? I'm not being conceited here, but I'm generally considered to be a decent guy. I pay my bills, I don't live with my parents and I haven't got any dark secrets that I won't happily reveal to you if you ask.'

What could she say? Yes, he was her perfect man? Yes, she loved him with all her heart? All true, but could she really open up to him before she cast the shadow of her father and her fear of family ties out?

'You don't understand. Everything I feel for you is so new. I care for you, Grayson, but –'

He put his finger against her lips. 'I'm not sure I want to hear it. Listen to me.' The intensity in his voice was matched by his expression. 'We can make this work. You can keep an office in the city and at the ranch in Oregon. You can commute between the two. Hell, I'll even share office space here with you as well. I'll have every high-tech gadget you need to stay connected installed at the ranch so you'll never have to worry.'

Lauren fought a ridiculous urge to stamp her foot. Why was he being so nice? It would be so easy just to say yes. Didn't he understand that she wanted to come to him free and clear? She'd fought so hard to become an independent woman. If she gave in and allowed him to take over the job of protecting her, providing for her, she'd never feel like an adult.

She reached out to stroke his cheek. 'I need to get through this lunch with my parents first. Can we talk about this later?'

His frustration was obvious. She watched him

struggle with it and then take a deep breath. 'OK, if you promise you'll think about what I've said.'

She managed a tremulous smile. 'Of course I will.'

His face relaxed and he bent to kiss her, leaving the taste of coffee on her lips. By mutual consent they turned back into the Ferry Building.

Lauren slid her hand into Grayson's. Was she being too cautious? Her experience had taught her not to trust anyone, particularly a charming man. She'd just escaped the machinations of her father and established her own business. In a few more years she hoped to be free and independent enough to trust her own judgment. Why couldn't Grayson understand that? Why couldn't he just disappear and turn up again in five years when she would be ready to deal with him?

She glanced up at Grayson who had stopped to sample some goat's cheese from an organic farm. He was deep in conversation with the shop owner about how goats were fed as compared to horses.

Grayson was right. It would be hard to find anyone who suited her better, even if she looked for the rest of her life. He was phenomenal in bed, he made her laugh and he could cook. Why was it so difficult to fall in with his plans? How would she feel if he walked away and never came back?

The thought of never seeing him again made her grip his hand hard. He broke off his conversation to look down at her, his expression full of concern. She stared into his blue eyes searching for answers. But she knew that the only place she'd find them would be in her own heart.

Chapter Twenty-Three

Lauren steered Grayson into her closet. 'You might as well pick me another outfit. You did such a good job last time.'

To her relief, Grayson smiled. He'd remained quiet since their return, his expression distant, his eyes impossible to read.

'I'd be glad to. Where are we going?'

'Half Moon Bay. My parents have another house there near the beach. It can get quite foggy, so don't pick anything too flimsy.'

Hangers clattered as Grayson moved them aside. He pulled out a navy silk dress with white spots. It was cut demurely at the front but swooped down low at the back. 'How about this? You can take a jacket or a shawl for cover up.'

Lauren examined the dress. 'I bought this one a while back, but I don't think I've ever worn it. I always associate navy blue with my school uniform.' She stepped into the dress and Grayson zipped her up. He kissed her shoulder and ran one long finger down her spine.

'It looks great from this angle,' Grayson murmured. 'Are you going to wear it?'

'Definitely.' Lauren searched for a pair of sandals and a shawl. 'I'll need to put my hair up. It'll just take a minute.'

She sat at her dressing table and brushed out her hair. Her thoughts centred on the luncheon to come and whether or not she and Grayson would get through it. Why had her father insisted they attend?

She doubted he'd be inviting them over for lunch if he'd learnt of her marriage. He'd be far too busy arranging her divorce or Grayson's demise.

Grayson waited for her in the kitchen. He'd decided to wear his own clothes and looked far more comfortable than she did. She picked up her car keys and stuffed them in her purse.

'Are you ready to go?'

Grayson shook his head. Her hand tightened on her purse. 'I'd much rather stay here and make love to you,' he said.

Lauren stared at his belt buckle, unable to risk glancing up at his face. He sighed and bent to pick up his bag. 'I guess that's a no, then. I'll take my stuff in the car in case I have to run to get to the airport.'

Lauren locked up behind him, her fingers unsteady. Grayson headed for the elevator, his bag slung over his shoulder. Was this really it? She swallowed hard. If she survived lunch, would he still be prepared to listen to her, or had he reached the end of his patience?

Lauren gave her car keys to the valet and waited for Grayson to come around the car. He stopped on the pink marbled step below her to admire the view. For once, it wasn't foggy. The arc of Half Moon Bay spread in front of them, the silver sand glittered in the sunlight.

Grayson whistled. 'It's a great spot for a house. I nearly bought into a housing development down here a few years ago. The day I came to visit it was so cold and foggy I gave up the idea. God knows how anyone plays golf around here. You'd never find the next hole let alone your ball.'

Lauren continued to walk up the steps, pausing every so often to murmur a polite greeting to other guests. She wasn't surprised by the number of people in attendance. Her father always enjoyed entertaining people he considered important. The lower floor of the house had been opened up. The kitchen and family room housed the bar, and the ornate dining room was already being prepared for a buffet.

Outside, the back yard was shielded from the winds and glare of the sun by canvas sail panels strung overhead. Lauren saw her mother in the middle of the garden. Lauren waved but her mother's attention was focused on the tall man she was talking to.

Lauren paused to look back for Grayson. She spied him in the kitchen with a familiar face.

'Hi, Ella.' Lauren kissed Ella's cheek. 'I see you've found Grayson.' She smiled at her two favourite people in the world.

Ella flipped her long hair back over her shoulder. 'Hi, sweetie, I was just congratulating Grayson on making it through the weekend.' She nudged him in the ribs and winked at Lauren. 'I was also apologising for my behaviour. I think he's a keeper, don't you?'

Lauren tried to smile but found it hard. She wasn't ready to admit how much she'd come to care for Grayson in front of Ella.

Grayson's dry voice interrupted her thoughts. 'I'm not sure that Lauren agrees with you. She's definitely playing hard to get.'

Lauren's gaze flew to his face. Although he smiled, his eyes conveyed the stark truth behind his words. Before she could attempt a reply, someone else joined their group.

'Grayson, fancy meeting you here!'

Lauren turned around to find Anna Paulson easing forwards to kiss Grayson's cheek. Anna wore a simple white sheath dress which showed off her spectacular figure and smooth tan.

'Oh, Lauren, dear,' she cooed. 'You're here. Wasn't it kind of your father to invite me to his party when he found out I was all alone in the city?'

Grayson removed Anna's hand from his arm with his fingertips. 'I hear you've been meddling, Anna. Where's your husband?'

'He's back at home, as well you know, Grayson. I'm dealing with this business without him.'

Ella hadn't taken her eyes off Anna since she'd started speaking. Suddenly she scrabbled in her purse and brought out a pen and piece of paper. 'I've just realised who you are!'

Anna preened slightly, a gracious smile on her lips.

'You were in that porn vampire movie, *The Stiffies and the Dead*!'

Anna's perfect mouth tightened. 'I don't recall that movie. Perhaps you're mixing me up with someone else.'

Lauren pressed her lips together in a desperate attempt not to laugh as Ella shook her head. 'No, it was definitely you. How could you forget? That movie is so bad it's good. It's a classic.'

A blush rose on Anna's tanned skin. She raised her voice in an attempt to out-shout Ella's enthusiasm. 'It's very sweet of you, dear, but I'm certain I wasn't in that movie. Perhaps you're thinking of my work on the daytime soaps? I've played several characters over the years.'

'Nope, I'm sure. If you have a heart tattooed on your left butt cheek, you're definitely Tara Titnipple.' Ella went for the hem of Anna's dress. 'Shall we check?'

Grayson grabbed Ella's hand. He was grinning. 'There's no need. I can confirm she has a tattoo right where you said.'

Anna straightened and glared at Ella. 'You should obviously be in a mental asylum.' She turned to Lauren. 'I assume she's a friend of yours? Perhaps you'll keep her away from me in future.'

Lauren shook her head. 'Sorry, I can't control her

either. Haven't you seen *Pocahontas*? She's a free spirit.'

Anna stepped closer and brought her face right into Lauren's. 'If you don't tell her to back off, I'll be forced to let you in on a little secret.'

Lauren raised her eyebrows. 'What's that?'

'Grayson's trying to screw you. Not just in the sack but in the real world. Ask him about his association with Turner Enterprises. Ask him what he really stands to gain from that piss poor little town he claims to love.'

Anna turned on her heel and walked off, a triumphant smile on her face. Lauren shivered and Grayson put his arm around her.

'Whatever she said, Lauren,' Ella said, 'don't take it to heart. She's obviously a complete bitch.'

Lauren stared after Anna. 'I know that but . . .'

'Let's go and find your mother.' Grayson pulled her along with him towards the back yard. 'The sooner we get this over with, the sooner we can get out of here.'

Lauren looked up at him to try to gauge his reaction. Was Grayson's sudden desire to leave related to Anna's presence? She composed her features into a smile as they approached her mother.

'Lauren, darling!' Her mother's face lit up as she drew Lauren into a hug. 'I'm so glad you came.'

'Happy birthday, Mom.'

Grayson stepped forwards and kissed her mother's cheek.

'Grayson, it's nice to see you again. I've just been talking to your father. I knew your name was familiar. You're very like him.'

Lauren pinched Grayson's hand. The day was getting better and better. 'Your father's here?'

Grayson looked grim. 'I wasn't expecting him to turn up.' He studied the other guests in the yard and then stopped, his attention riveted on the barbecue area. 'He's over there. Hell, I suppose you'd better come and meet him.'

He took Lauren's hand and led her across to the brick-lined patio. The sickly sweet scent of half-cooked sausages, pork ribs and chicken wafted over her. Seated at one of the tables, with his back to them was a man in a cowboy hat. Grayson's fingers tightened over hers.

'Dad?'

The man turned and slowly got to his feet. He had the same lazy grace and height that Grayson did. Lauren gulped as she recognised a face she'd seen on a million magazine covers.

'Grayson.'

Lauren held out her hand. 'It's a pleasure to meet you, sir. I'm Lauren Redstone.'

'Beau Turner.' As if she needed introducing to the infamous ex-Dallas Cowboys quarterback and oil magnate. He gestured at the house. 'Is this your parents' party then? It was kind of them to invite me.'

'Yeah, very kind,' Grayson said. 'How exactly did you manage that, Dad?'

'I was invited by a mutual friend of ours.'

'The only person I know who fits that description is Anna, and she's no friend of mine.'

Beau Turner patted Grayson's arm. 'Son, you've got to let go of the past.' He winked at Lauren. 'I have to all the time or I'd never get any business done.'

Grayson stepped back and brushed at his sleeve. 'Perhaps if you didn't sleep with all your business associates' wives, you'd be more successful. It must be hard constantly looking for new companies to dupe.'

Beau's eyes narrowed. 'Well now, look who's talking. Lauren's father ain't exactly a nobody now is he?'

'Yeah, but I'm not doing any business deals with Mr Redstone. I don't do that kind of negotiation any more.'

Lauren put her hand on Grayson's arm and squeezed hard. 'Are you enjoying your visit to San Francisco, Mr Turner? Grayson says you normally live in Texas.'

Beau's shrewd gaze slid away from Grayson and fastened on Lauren. 'That's true, I do, but when I received information that my eldest son was in the city, I decided to come and see if he'd changed his mind.'

'I'm not coming back to work for you, Dad.'

Grayson's quiet voice held a note of steel. Lauren stole a glance at his face.

'Not even if I offered to retire and leave you as president?'

Grayson swallowed and shook his head. 'No, thanks. I'm happy with what I've got.'

'A piddling horse ranch in the middle of nowhere?' Beau smiled. 'How can a man of your talents be happy there?'

'Because I can.'

Lauren tightened her grip on Grayson's arm. 'He *is* happy there, Mr Turner. It's a wonderful place.'

To her surprise, Beau Turner started to laugh. He poked Grayson in the chest. 'Hey, son, she really believes you're just a simple cowboy. Haven't you told her about all the money you've got stashed away in the bank?' He took a handkerchief out of his pocket and wiped his eyes. 'You're obviously a sweetheart, Lauren, but don't make the mistake of underestimating Grayson. He's been playing this game with me for years and he knows that the winner definitely gets to take it all.'

Lauren let go of Grayson's hand and walked back towards the kitchen. What the hell was going on? That was the second time someone had suggested that Grayson wasn't being straight with her. Granted, neither person had a vested interest in seeing Grayson succeed, but where did the truth lie?

A waiter passed by and Lauren took a glass of white wine from his tray. Grayson strode towards her, a determined look on his face. She swallowed most of the wine and walked away from him. Luckily she knew the layout of the house. He didn't.

The master suite was empty and unoccupied, indicating that her parents didn't intend to stay at the house overnight. The décor at the beach house was subtle and soothing, shades of white and eggshell blue dominated, bringing the feel of the sea inside. Lauren went into the bathroom and repaired her make-up.

What other interests did Grayson have? Was Beau Turner insinuating that everything Grayson had told Lauren was a lie? She couldn't believe it. His ranch did matter to him; she'd shared that with him. She knew it was real.

She carefully outlined her lips and blocked in more colour. Did it matter what Grayson had done before she'd met him? Just because he didn't want to follow his father's footsteps didn't make him a failure or a liar. Lauren smiled at her reflection as she applied the gloss coat to her lips. How ironic that Grayson's father wanted him in the family business when Lauren's father wouldn't consider her capable of running a tea party at his.

The least she could do was give Grayson the opportunity to explain what his father meant. Glad to have made a decision, Lauren dropped her lip gloss into her purse and stood up.

She walked back along the corridor which connected the main suite to the centre of the house. On her right, the caterer had just finished laying out a sumptuous buffet in the dining room. To her surprise she heard Grayson's low voice.

He stood by the buffet table talking to one of her father's most annoying employees. Simon Tilney was an expert at ingratiating himself with his bosses. He'd decided Lauren would make the perfect wife for him and insisted on telling everyone that they were a couple.

To her dismay, the more Lauren denied Simon's insinuations, the bigger they seemed to grow. She paused in the doorway and focused her attention on the conversation.

Grayson's hand tightened on his glass. From his superior height, he studied the top of Simon Tilney's balding head. 'I hear you think you're engaged to Lauren Redstone.'

Simon smiled, his perfectly aligned, bleached teeth seemed too white against his yellowish tan.

'Well, not exactly engaged.' He leant closer to Grayson, dousing him in a combination of alcohol fumes and too much cheap aftershave. 'We have an understanding.'

Grayson sipped his beer and tried to look interested.

Simon winked. 'Let's just say, that I wouldn't normally tell on a lady, but that this particular lady has the hots for me.'

'Really.'

Simon pressed so close that Grayson resisted an urge to step back. 'It's a bit complicated as she's the boss's daughter. She doesn't want everyone to know that we're involved.'

'I can't say that surprises me,' Grayson said. 'She strikes me as a very discerning woman.' He scanned the buffet table and realised he and Simon were alone.

'You'd think so, wouldn't you?' Simon picked up a plate and helped himself to some poached salmon. 'Who told you we were engaged?'

Grayson put down his glass with a decisive thump. 'A little bird.'

'You escorted Lauren to the party didn't you?' Simon made a sympathetic face. 'Didn't she tell you she was involved with me? That was very naughty of her.' He licked his lips and left a splodge of salmon stuck between his two front teeth. 'To be honest, you're not missing much. She's known as the Frigidaire Queen around here.' Simon elbowed Grayson in the ribs. 'You know, if you tried to insert anything it would come back out frozen like a Popsicle.'

Grayson's fist came up and caught Simon right on his chin. With hardly a whimper, Simon arched backwards with all the grace of an Olympic high-board diver. His left hand flew out and his plate disappeared.

With savage satisfaction, Grayson watched the back of Simon's head slice through a cake piled high with strawberries. Frosting went everywhere but the thick sponge slowed his descent until he reached the cake plate and stopped moving. An avalanche of strawberries slid down his unconscious face. With his eyes closed, he looked remarkably peaceful. The cake remaining around his ears supported his neck like an airline pillow.

Grayson flexed his hand. Damn, that felt good. After dealing with his father and Anna, he'd needed to hit something. His triumphant smile faded as he caught sight of Lauren standing two feet away from him. Her blue silk dress was splattered with white frosting. Her face and hair looked like she'd been hit by a plate of salmon.

'Grayson, what on earth have you done?'

He stepped over Simon's outstretched legs and propelled Lauren down the corridor. He found himself in the master suite.

'Let's just say, I cleared up a few misunderstandings.'

'You knocked Simon out, didn't you?'

He ushered her into the bathroom and locked the door. She gasped when she saw herself in the mirror and spun around.

'You enjoyed that?'

'So what if I did? I'm a guy – that's what we do.'

'We're in the twenty-first century now – don't you think it's time to stop grunting and start talking?'

'I talked.'

Grayson closed the space between them and started picking flakes of salmon out of her hair. She smelt weird. Sweet and fishy at the same time. He was glad Simon hadn't slathered the salmon in mayonnaise. He hated mayonnaise.

Lauren grabbed his wrist. 'Stop doing that! I'm waiting for an explanation.'

Grayson looked down at her. A huge dollop of white frosting was wedged between her breasts. He loved frosting. His mom had always let him lick out the bowl. He reluctantly returned his gaze back up to Lauren's.

'Let's just say that I was defending your honour.'

Lauren let out a breath. 'You were? I wish I'd heard the whole conversation.' Grayson was glad she hadn't. She stood on tiptoe to kiss his mouth. 'I'm all for equality, but somehow that makes me feel very ... female. If anyone deserves to be knocked out, it's Simon Tilney. He's been making my life hell for the past year.'

Grayson resisted an urge to thump his chest and make Tarzan noises. He kissed her back and decided he could ignore the scent of salmon. By the time he'd licked all the frosting off Lauren's breasts, everything would taste as sweet as candy.

She caught his chin in her hand before he could get close to her. 'We need to talk, Grayson.'

He fought a groan. 'Dammit, woman, weren't you the one who wanted to leave all the talking till later?'

She stepped back from him and fussed around at the sink until every trace of salmon had disappeared from her hair and face. 'Don't you think it's strange that both your father and Anna Paulson just happen to turn up at my mother's birthday party?'

Grayson studied her resolute expression. 'I have no idea why Anna is here,' he said. 'I did contact my father but I didn't expect him to wangle an invitation here.'

'What did you want to talk to him about?' Lauren asked. 'I thought you hated his guts.'

'I wanted his advice about someone, I mean, something.'

Lauren crossed her arms over her chest. 'And by the way, how come you didn't mention that your father is Beau Turner, the legendary football player?'

Grayson shrugged. 'Because I hate his guts.'

The silence lengthened between them. Grayson held her gaze for as long as he could and then turned away. What was it with women that they expected you to spill your emotions whenever it suited them? He hated talking about his father. He hated the mess his father had made of so many innocent people's lives.

Lauren's quiet voice halted him at the door. 'You're always telling me that I should face my problems with my father. You don't seem to be doing such a great job of it yourself.'

Grayson wrenched the door open and marched down the corridor. How dare Lauren compare her weird relationship with her father to his perfectly understandable relationship with his? Dammit, he'd only contacted Beau to help him make a good impression on Lauren's father anyway. His footsteps slowed as he reached the dining room. Someone had cleared away both Simon Tilney and the ruined cake. Lauren's father stood by the door, his arm around his wife. He smiled.

'Hey, Grayson, is that Lauren behind you? Come on out here with us. We need to cut the birthday cake.'

Chapter Twenty-Four

Lauren blinked as she stepped out into the sunlit back yard. Guests stood in an obedient circle around a table on which sat a yellow-frosted cake complete with candles. Lauren's father clamped his hand on her elbow and manoeuvred her and Grayson into position beside him.

'Let's sing "Happy Birthday" to my beautiful wife!'

Lauren mouthed the words of the familiar song as her mother carefully blew out the candles. Grayson sang loudly beside her, his mellow voice a pleasant surprise. Then the cake was cut and waiters began to distribute slices on yellow china plates, which matched the cake. Lauren tried to step back. To her annoyance, her father wouldn't release her arm. She looked at Grayson but his attention was fixed on Beau and Anna who stood together at the front of the crowd.

'Before you all go off to get some of this great barbecue, I have another announcement to make.'

What had her father triumphed over now? Lauren tried to look interested. She flinched when he slid an arm around her shoulders.

'My daughter Lauren is a very naughty young lady.' He squeezed hard. 'Earlier this year, in order to escape a big wedding, she skipped off to Las Vegas to get married to Mr Grayson Turner, here.'

A few of the crowd began to clap as waiters circulated with champagne. Lauren watched in disbelief as her father shook Grayson's hand.

'Welcome to the family, son. We're lucky enough to

have the groom's father with us today as well.' He gestured at Beau. 'Come on up and join us.'

Flashbulbs exploded as Beau and her father exchanged handshakes. Lauren felt sick. The only good thing was the appalled expression on Anna Paulson's face. Why was her father doing this? She'd expected the complete opposite.

'Mrs Redstone and I are in the process of persuading Lauren and Grayson to have a proper wedding here in San Francisco to celebrate their marriage. When we've sorted out the details, you'll all be invited.'

More clapping followed as her father proposed a toast to the bride and groom. Lauren held her champagne glass so tightly she feared it would shatter. Someone took it out of her hand.

Grayson bent low to whisper in her ear. 'That didn't go as badly as I thought. I'm glad you told him the truth. We'll sort this out.'

Lauren could only stare at him. He probably thought she'd been lying about her father's potential reaction to the news of her wedding. He probably thought she was delusional.

She pulled away. 'I didn't tell him,' she said and Grayson's relieved expression disappeared. 'Excuse me, I've got to ...'

She didn't bother to complete her sentence. Grayson was unlikely to come after her now that she'd spoiled his party.

Lauren sat in front of the mirror in the master bathroom suite and stared at her pale reflection. The way things were going she might as well lock the door and stay in here all day. Perhaps she could crawl into the bed, pull the covers over her head and pretend everything would be all right in the morning.

She should've known her father would find out about the wedding. The question was, why had he decided to publicly acknowledge it? What was it about Grayson that made him acceptable when all her other boyfriends had failed?

'I thought I'd find you hiding in here.'

Lauren straightened as Anna Paulson appeared in the doorway. She knew she should've locked the door.

'What do you want?'

Anna shut the door and sauntered over to Lauren. 'You know why Grayson married you, don't you?'

Lauren pretended to straighten the items on the vanity. 'Because he fell in love with me? That's the usual reason.'

'Don't be so naïve. Even *you* can't believe that. Grayson's first and foremost a business man. And now, with your stupid help, he's trying to screw me and his father again.'

Lauren zipped up her make-up bag. 'I don't know what you're talking about. And frankly, I couldn't care less.'

Anna put her hands on her narrow hips. 'You should care. Grayson's using you. I tried to warn you off when you were at the ranch, but you didn't get it.'

Lauren chucked her bag into her purse and got to her feet. Suddenly things were becoming clear. 'I got it. You used Marcie's jealousy over Grayson to get her to trash the ranch. How very mature of you.'

Anna blocked Lauren's exit line to the door. 'Marcie will get over it. She's just a kid.'

Lauren shook her head. 'She's not a tool to serve your petty disputes, Anna. Perhaps in the future you should fight your own battles and not involve vulnerable kids.'

Anna backed off until she was directly in front of the door. 'You don't understand what's at stake here.'

'I'm a grown woman, explain it to me.'

Anna smiled. 'OK, my husband and I have been buying up land around Springtown for quite a while now.' She gave Lauren an innocent smile. 'Grayson's daddy is a partner in our business venture as well.'

'So?' Lauren tried to look calm.

'So, when Grayson put forward his stupid scheme to build a measly business park at the edge of his ranch, we knew what he really wanted.'

'You think?' Lauren tried sarcasm. It didn't seem to dent Anna's enthusiasm.

'Grayson must have realised we were planning to develop the area into a massive mining and industrial complex.' Anna shrugged her elegant shoulders. 'He obviously wanted in on the project and was just negotiating to get our attention and demand a bigger piece of the pie.'

Lauren began to shake her head.

Anna held up her hand. 'Why do you think Grayson contacted Beau? He hasn't spoken to him for three years. It must be about the industrial project.'

Lauren swallowed hard. Grayson had told her he'd spoken to his father about something. Had he been specific about what? Dammit, she knew he hadn't.

'OK, Anna, you've had your moment of glory.' Lauren reached for the door handle. 'I'll talk to Grayson and see what he has to say about all this.' She gazed right into Anna's eyes. 'In the meantime, keep away from my husband. He doesn't like you and I have to agree with him about that. You're a spoilt selfish bitch.'

Anna refused to budge. 'I haven't finished yet. By marrying you, Grayson's obviously decided to move things in a different direction.' Anna pouted. 'It seems he still bears a grudge about what happened before our wedding.'

Lauren tugged on the handle. 'When you slept with another guy and let Grayson walk in on you? Hmmm, I wonder why that would still upset him?'

Anna grabbed Lauren's wrist. 'It wasn't just another guy. It was Beau. Grayson's decided to get his revenge on us by replacing us in the business deal with you and your wealthy father.'

'You slept with Grayson's father?' Lauren wrenched Anna's hand from her wrist. She felt sick. How come Grayson had omitted that part of the story?

Anna seemed too intent on her own grievances to register Lauren's distaste. 'Grayson's obviously going to ask your father to co-finance the whole business venture now that he's got all the information from Beau. I should've known he was up to something.' She flicked Lauren a glance of disdain. 'Otherwise, why on earth would he have taken up with you?'

Lauren wasn't sure which scenario she preferred least. Either Grayson was lying to her purely on a business level or he was lying to her, period. Even worse, it might explain why her father was so keen to welcome Grayson into the family.

Lauren closed her fingers around the door handle and pulled hard, sending Anna staggering back into the wall. She gave Anna her coolest smile, the one she used on her father.

'Thanks, Anna, you've given me a lot to think about.'

Lauren kept her expression pleasant as she walked along the corridor. Her next step was to corner Grayson and find out the truth. It had to lie somewhere in Anna's dramatic self-centred lies.

'Lauren? Is that you, darling?'

The last person she wanted to see approached her from the dining room.

'Dad.'

He linked his arm through hers and walked towards his study. Inside, the pale coastal colours were banished in favour of strong reds and heavy dark furniture. Cigar smoke lingered along with the scent of barbecue from outside. The walls were covered with photographs of her father with the rich and famous.

Lauren waited until her father took up his usual

position seated behind his desk. For the first time in her life she refused to allow the setting to intimidate her.

'What's going on, Dad? Why didn't you tell me you knew I'd got married?'

She was amazed at how calm and detached she sounded. Long-held slow-burning anger tried to push its way out of her chest. It almost choked her to hold it back.

'I suppose like most fathers, I was waiting for you to tell me yourself.'

Lauren studied his self-satisfied face. 'You know why I didn't tell you. You have a track record of interfering in my love life.'

He looked hurt. 'I've only tried to protect you as any man would protect a beautiful daughter. I've always had your best interests at heart.'

Lauren rested her palms on the front of his leather-topped desk. 'That's the bit I don't understand. You've always had *your* best interests at heart. Why are you willing to accept Grayson?'

He sat back, his expression thoughtful. 'Because for once in your life you've made me proud. You've done what any woman worth her salt should do – found a rich and well-connected husband.'

Lauren laughed. 'Yesterday you were calling Grayson names and trying to make him look stupid. What changed?'

'His father contacted me. I've worked with Beau a few times in the past. I never knew his son was slated to succeed him as president of Turner Enterprises.'

'That's not going to happen. Grayson hardly speaks to his father any more. In fact, I heard him turn down that very offer today.'

Her father chuckled and unwrapped a cigar. 'Well then, the boy displays good horse sense. Why would he want to worry your pretty little head with all these business details? I'm sure he'll let you know when he's decided what he's going to do. That's what I always do with your mother.'

Lauren clenched her teeth so hard that her jaw hurt. It was always the same. He refused to admit she was capable of using her brain. She fought down a desire to argue. She wanted the facts.

'I think you're mistaken about Grayson. But if you don't want to believe me, ask him yourself. All he wants is to live out his life on his ranch and deal with the horse stud and training enterprises.'

Her father scooped up a handful of papers from his desk. 'Nice try, Lauren. Here's a list of the companies Grayson owns and his investment portfolio. If that man's a simple cowboy, I'm the queen of England.'

Lauren bunched the papers in her fist without looking at them. 'Just because business is the most important thing in your life, Dad, don't assume it's the same for others. I'm more interested in running a profitable business than Grayson is.'

He smiled and something fisted in Lauren's stomach. 'Sweetie, it's OK, you can admit it now. You've just been playing at being a businesswoman while you waited for the right man to come along and marry you.' Lauren opened her mouth but her father kept talking. 'You had me fooled for a while there. I was even willing to go along with your plans. Heck, I made sure you won four of your first deals, didn't I?'

His satisfaction rolled over her like a wave. 'What did you say?'

He lit his cigar and took a long pull, then released the smoke through his mouth in a series of rings. 'Did you really think you got all those deals by yourself? I made damn sure that every one of those guys knew you were my daughter and that a favour to you was a favour to me.'

Lauren took a step back and knocked against a chair.

In an effort to steady herself, she dug her fingernails into the polished wood. 'I won those contracts through hard work and dedication. You don't have that much power.'

Her father tapped out the ash from his cigar. His shrewd gaze came up to meet hers. 'You underestimate me.'

He glanced down at another piece of paper on his desk. 'And, of course, the last company you signed, Prairie Dawg Boots, is owned by Grayson Turner. What a coincidence. He obviously thought it was a good way to gain your trust and control you, just like I did.' Smoke swirled around his nostrils as he exhaled. 'It's another reason why I think Grayson and I will work well together.'

Lauren shook her head. 'You're wrong, Dad, but at least I've finally learnt my lesson. In future, you can keep right out of my life. Pretend I'm dead, pretend I never existed, for as far as I'm concerned, you never did.'

She turned to leave, the papers still clutched in her hand. Her father's parting words sounded loud and overconfident as she opened the door.

'When you've calmed down, come back and see me. Your mother and I have a wedding to organise.'

Chapter Twenty-Five

From the top of the cliff, Grayson spotted Lauren sitting on the beach. If it wasn't for a worried Mrs Turner, he would never have known where to find her. He made his way down through the rocks until he stood on the gritty sand.

She didn't turn her head even though she must have heard his approach. In one hand she held a sheaf of papers which were twisted into shreds. Heedless of her silk dress, her knees were drawn up to her chin, her arms wrapped around them. He studied her profile. What the hell had happened to make her look as if someone had run over her puppy?

'Lauren, honey?' His softly spoken words were carried away by the gusting wind. 'Are you OK?'

She wouldn't look at him, her voice was barely audible. 'Why did you lie to me?'

He slid his hands into his pockets. 'About my father? I asked him here to help me out with your father. I thought we'd already discussed that.'

She shook her head, her soft hair, released from its band, fluttered around her face, concealing her expression. 'Not just about your father, about everything.'

Grayson crouched down beside her. 'What the hell is that supposed to mean?'

'Where would you like me to start? With the compli-cated relationship between you, Anna and your father or the fact that you are a multi-millionaire?'

'Tell me which bothers you most.'

As he studied Lauren's hostile body language, Gray

realised he wasn't prepared to roll over and play dead yet. Hadn't Lauren got to know him at all? Wasn't she even capable of giving him the benefit of the doubt? He sucked in a lungful of sea air. It didn't help calm him down.

'I never realised my being a millionaire would be a problem for you.' He tried to inject some humour. 'Hell, most women would do anything to marry a guy like me.'

She shot him a glance full of loathing. 'Now you sound just like my father.'

He held her gaze. 'I hate to keep saying this, but I'm not your father. I'm just the guy who married you and wants to live the rest of his life with you. What's wrong with that?'

'Because you lied to me.' She swiped the hair out of her eyes. 'I thought you were just a cowboy. I thought you were a nice, straightforward, simple guy.'

Grayson refused to drop his gaze. 'I am. Having money doesn't make me a different person.'

Lauren knelt up and threw the papers she held clenched in her fist at him. 'You never told me about your internet companies, your corporate lifestyle and your succession of movie-star girlfriends, either, did you?'

Papers flew around him. He snatched a couple out of the air. 'So who did?'

Lauren looked puzzled.

'Who told you?' He got to his feet. She opened her mouth and shut it again. 'Let me guess. Was it my father or yours?'

He glanced at the papers in his hand, saw his own smiling face ripped from the pages of *Fortune* magazine. A slow knot of anger uncoiled low in his gut. 'I'm judged and condemned, am I? It's OK if I'm a cowboy without two cents to call his own, but it's not OK if I happen to be a rich cowboy?'

Lauren stood up, her eyes a desperate blur in her pale features. 'You're going to be even richer still if your deal to buy up Springtown and turn it into an open-cast mine works out. So much for honesty. That'll bring jobs back to the area for sure.'

Grayson held her gaze. 'I don't know what the hell you're talking about. I haven't made a deal with anyone, but I'm going to find out.' He ripped the papers in his hands in half again and again. 'Perhaps when you've decided who you're really mad at, you'll let me know. I refuse to take the crap from your relationship with your father.'

Lauren poked him in the chest. 'And you think you've behaved much better? After telling me you loathe your father you go into business with him? When are you going to accept his offer and become president of Turner Enterprises?'

Grayson stepped back as the urge to shake some sense into her threatened to overcome him. 'As I said, deal with your own father, I'll worry about mine.'

Almost too angry to speak, he turned on his heel and looked back up the beach. 'I'm going to catch an early flight back to Oregon. There's no point in staying around here when you won't even give me a fair hearing.' He swung around and looked her right in the eye. 'Hey, you should be celebrating. You've finally found your out. As you said, Lauren, it was all about the sex for you, wasn't it? Stupid of me to believe I'd found a woman who could love me and like me for myself.'

He uncurled her fingers, dumped the shredded paper in her outstretched hand and headed back up the beach. It took all his concentration not to look back. When he reached the house, he couldn't resist any longer. Lauren hadn't moved. She stood on the beach, her back to him, facing the sun.

Grayson rounded up his father and Anna Paulson

who were eating barbecue in the back yard and cor-
ralled them in Paul Redstone's office. He locked the
door and stood with his back to it, oblivious to the
storm brewing on his father's face. He glanced at his
watch.

'I have half an hour before my cab gets here. If you
two want me to let you out of here alive, tell me what
the fuck is going on.'

Chapter Twenty-Six

Lauren sank down onto her hotel bed and stared at the grimy drapes. New York in the summer wasn't just hot, it was humid too. After being jostled and pushed on the sidewalk, she was in dire need of a shower.

She kicked off her high-heeled sandals and contemplated the chipped pink nail polish on her toes. She couldn't be bothered to fix the damage. Her fingernails were ruined too. Biting her lip, she shuffled into the bathroom and put the shower on.

She sighed as the water pummelled her skin. She had one more meeting in New York and then she was headed for Pueblo, Colorado to meet with the executives of the PBR and show them her set-design proposal for the first commercial. Hot water streamed down her back. Why wasn't she excited? After all, it was a dream come true.

Every time she tried to enjoy the moment, her father's insinuations came back to haunt her. Had he truly influenced all her business deals? Or even worse, had Grayson manipulated the PBR one himself? She couldn't forget that she'd first met him in Vegas at the PBR finals weekend.

Lauren washed her hair and rinsed away the shampoo. Reluctant to step out of the shower and face the inadequate air conditioning, she allowed the water to cascade over her head. In the week since her mother's birthday party, she'd concentrated on her business and ignored any attempts to contact her. She needed time to come to terms with all the crap that'd been heaped on her.

She pictured Grayson's furious face before he'd abandoned her on the beach. Hadn't he understood that she needed time to sort through everything she'd heard? Like most men, he hadn't been prepared to give her any. To his mind, her decision must've seemed clear cut.

Steam poured from the shower as she opened the plastic curtain and stepped out onto the mat. She would have to face Grayson soon. She owed him that. Her father was a different matter. She walked to the window and looked down on Fifth Avenue. Could she move herself and her business here? Would she be far enough away from her father's reach?

She put on a straight black shift dress, black boots and white lipstick. Black sunglasses completed her look. It suited her mood. New York always brought out her darker side.

The cab dropped her at a new high-rise office building just off Wall Street. She checked the details on the business card the PBR public relations guy had sent her and made her way up to the fourteenth floor. To her surprise, the offices of GAT Industries were almost empty.

She was led to one of the corner offices by an enthusiastic male intern named Dave, who looked barely old enough to drive, let alone work. After knocking loudly on the door, Dave stepped aside leaving her face to face with a familiar figure behind a chrome and steel desk.

'Good afternoon, Lauren.'

Grayson got to his feet but he didn't come around his desk. He wore a dark-grey business suit, blue shirt and silver tie. Lauren clutched her purse to her chest and sank into the nearest chair. Grayson looked as if he hadn't slept much since she'd last seen him. Dark shadows under his eyes made him look older and harder.

She waited until he resumed his seat before dropping her sunglasses into her purse and fishing out her Palm Pilot. The faint rumble of traffic below filtered through the thrum of the air conditioning as he settled back in his leather chair.

'Great office space, Grayson.'

A muscle jumped in his cheek. 'Yeah, it is. I heard you've been looking at rental space. If you were thinking about relocating your company here, I'd offer it to you at a reduced rate. But then, you'd probably think I was trying to bribe you.'

Lauren gestured at the business card she still held in her hand. 'GAT Industries. I should've realised this had something to do with you. What does the "A" stand for?'

'Adam. It's my middle name. I apologise for the deception. I figured the only way I'd get your attention was if I put myself into your world.' His expression became hard to read. 'I appreciate you seeing me. I won't keep you long.'

'What can I do for you?' She was amazed that she sounded so calm.

He met her gaze straight on. 'I wanted to get some things straight.'

'You don't have to do that, I've been thinking . . .'

Grayson drew a leather briefcase onto his desk and opened it with a click. 'Let me finish. It'll be easier that way.'

Lauren sat opposite him, hands folded in her lap. She wondered how she could ever have doubted his business acumen. Like all successful executives, Grayson emanated a sense of calm assurance and power. She struggled to readjust to his unnerving and unexpected presence. Dammit. If he wanted to treat this mess like a business meeting, she would gladly go along with him.

Grayson took out a pile of papers. 'First off, I have

signed letters from my father and the Paulsons confirming that I have no interest, financial or otherwise, in joining their bid to ruin Springtown Valley.' He pushed the letters across the desk towards her. 'When I told you about my plans for the small business units on my ranch, I had no idea what the Paulsons were up to.'

Lauren thought about Anna Paulson's smug assurance that Grayson wanted to be involved in their project. She would love to have been a fly on the wall during that meeting. What exactly had Grayson done to get the letters written?

He ran his hand through his hair. 'I was conceited enough to believe that Anna moved to Springtown because she wanted to resume a relationship with me. I should've known she had other reasons, but that's my problem, not yours.'

When Lauren made no move to get up and take the letters, Grayson paused, then he said, 'I'll leave all this information for you to look over. If you still doubt my word, call my father. He'll tell you exactly what an ungrateful son of a bitch I am.'

'Will he also tell me you're not going to succeed him at Turner Enterprises?'

Grayson looked pained. 'That was a cheap shot. I never intended to take up that position.'

Lauren glanced around the plush office suite and then studied Grayson's expensive suit. 'I can see that now. You really don't need your father's money do you?'

She tensed. Would he pick up her verbal peace offering?

To her disappointment, he gave her a bland noncommittal smile. 'Whether you choose to believe him or not is up to you.'

He picked up another sheaf of papers. 'I also talked to your father.' His smile this time was more definite.

'I had to mislead him into thinking I agreed with his methods of controlling you to get this information. If you call him, I'm sure he'll be delighted to tell you that I deceived him. For the record, I have no intention of doing any business with him either.'

Lauren watched his long fingers sift through the papers on the desk. 'I checked out his claims to have influenced your business deals. Unfortunately, he did initiate some of the original contacts. But all the companies I contacted insisted that they kept you on because of your superior business skills and talent, not your father's.'

Lauren felt a glut of emotion build in her chest. Despite his anger, Grayson had done all this for her?

'As for the PBR commercials, I can only swear that I had nothing to do with them.' He added another set of documents to the pile. 'I've taken myself off the board of Prairie Dawg Boots so that you can deal with Jay and Barry with a clear conscience. And I promise you that, if you contact me in the future, I will always disclose any interest I have in any company you are considering dealing with.'

Lauren studied the papers on the desk. Grayson had just shown her how a real businessman acted. He'd pushed emotion aside and dealt with the issues, treating her like an equal who was capable of understanding them. Then why did she feel like crying?

'Thank you for doing this.'

Grayson sat back, an odd smile on his face. 'Hell, it's the only way I know how to deal with a problem. Run at it head on.'

Lauren gathered her courage. 'I'm sorry about how I treated you at my mother's party.'

Grayson waved a dismissive hand. 'After I talked to everyone concerned, I realised you'd had to deal with a whole series of blows. I'm not surprised you cut up rough at me.'

Lauren studied his face. Despite his words, she knew he must have felt angry with her refusal to listen to him. He'd shown his vulnerable side to her before. Did this 'purely business' meeting mean he'd decided she no longer had a right to share his feelings? Had he decided to move on?

Grayson stood up and shut his briefcase. 'Thanks for listening. When you've read through the documents, let me know if I can help you further. I'll be here for a few more days.'

Lauren stood too, tears close to the surface. He was going? Not even an attempt to kiss her and tell her that he didn't want to lose her?

'What about our marriage?' Lauren said. 'Where does this leave us?'

Grayson patted his jacket pocket and produced a brown envelope. 'I almost forgot. I got my lawyer to draw up the divorce papers. You just need to sign them and send them back.' He placed the envelope carefully on the table. 'I never wanted to trap you, I want you to be free.'

As Lauren reached for him, he headed for the door. His voice sounded husky when he finally spoke without turning around. 'I wish you all the best. Let me know if I can help you out in any business capacity in the future.'

Before she could speak, he wrenched open the door and walked out. Lauren stood frozen in panicked indecision. Then she ran after him. He was stepping into the elevator. She managed to jam the door open with the toe of her boot. He slumped against the back wall of the elevator as if he was exhausted.

'Grayson?'

He straightened up and his intense blue eyes met hers. 'Stay the hell away from me, Lauren. I've played it your way. If you're going to offer to have sex with me whenever I turn up in San Francisco, I'm not interested. I can't do this any more.'

She retreated, shocked by the distress in his gaze, and let the elevator descend without her.

Lauren walked back to Grayson's office and gathered up the papers he'd left on the desk. She noticed two glowing references from her first two clients. Grayson had walked away from her and left her free to pursue her business dreams and her life. The opulent office surroundings blurred as her eyes filled with tears. She'd won. She'd asserted her independence. So why did she feel like shit?

Chapter Twenty-Seven

Grayson got out of his truck and stretched his tired muscles. After the last two weeks travelling the length and breadth of the country, it was good to be back on the ranch. He thought of his last stop at Jay's house and his brother's acceptance of his invitation to visit the ranch and check out the industrial site.

His smile died. At least he'd have some company to look forward to. He whistled for Petty, heard his high shrill puppy barks from inside the house. Grayson frowned. How had Petty got in there?

He tried to relax. It was possible Petty had sneaked in while his housekeeper did her daily check and got locked inside. Gray could only hope that the puppy had access to the litter box in the mud room or it was going to be a real stinking welcome home.

He glanced up at the oak tree that shaded the western side of the ranch. The leaves were starting to turn. Summer was almost over.

Grayson fumbled for his key as Petty's barks reached a crescendo. The screen door of the mud room swung open and Petty leapt straight into his arms. Grayson buried his face in Petty's soft fur and carried him through to the kitchen. The scent of coffee tugged at his senses and he looked up.

Lauren sat at the kitchen table. She wore jeans and one of his old shirts. Scarcely daring to breathe, Grayson set the excited dog down and helped himself to a mug of coffee. He pulled out a chair, the scraping noise loud in the silence, and sat opposite her.

Lauren put down her mug. 'I was hoping you'd be back today.'

Grayson sipped cautiously at his coffee. It tasted good. 'What can I do for you?'

She took a deep breath and locked her gaze with his. 'I've been thinking about what you've told me.'

'And?'

Lauren frowned. 'Just let me say my piece without interrupting, will you?'

Grayson sat back and gestured for her to continue.

'I realised that you are nothing like your father and nothing like mine.' Lauren swallowed hard. 'I almost let my own fears destroy any chance we had to build a relationship.'

He liked the sound of that. A cautious spark of hope kindled in his gut.

'I've always been afraid of making a mistake like my mother did and being stuck in a marriage because of duty or guilt. I shouldn't have assumed all marriages are like that.' She dropped her gaze, stared at his coffee mug. 'Can we start again? Can you give me enough space to find out who I am and what we can be together?'

Grayson reached out and took her hand. His fingers shook. 'We can do whatever we want. It's our marriage, nobody else's. If you want to live in San Francisco during the week, go ahead. If you want to relocate your business to Oregon, we can do that too.' He squeezed her hand. 'You were right too. In my attempts to get back at my father, I've neglected my business opportunities in the last three years. It's time I balanced my life more evenly as well.' She finally looked at him. 'We can make it work, honey, I promise you.'

Lauren stood up, her chair crashed to the floor as she reached for him. He dragged her over the table and into his arms and held her tight. Her hair smelt of his shampoo and her uniquely sensual self.

'I love you, Lauren. I know this isn't what you wanted to happen right now in your life, but we can deal with it. If you're worried about your mother, we can have her live down here with us. I can protect her from your father.'

Lauren stroked his cheek. 'I've already spoken to my mom. She understands what I have to do. She told me to live my own life and not worry about hers.'

'She's a nice lady. Make sure she knows she's always welcome here should anything bad happen.'

Lauren smiled through her tears. 'I already told her that. I knew you'd agree.'

Grayson kissed her fingers. 'We'll sit down together and work out a business plan that allows both of us to work and still take care of the ranch business.' He grinned as Lauren began to unbutton his shirt. 'After we've celebrated our marriage in a more traditional fashion.' He caught her chin in his fingers. 'Do you want a big wedding? We can have one if you want.'

Lauren finished on the buttons and rubbed her palms over his muscular chest and aching nipples. She started on his jeans. 'No way. I'm happy with the ceremony we had in Vegas. It's our marriage and it's about us. We're the only people who know how we want it to work. We don't need anyone else's approval.' She slid his zipper down and put her hand inside to stroke his cock. 'And you're so rich, we don't need any wedding gifts, do we?'

Grayson caught his breath as she tightened her grip. 'That's one way of looking at it, Mrs Turner.'

He gulped as Lauren squeezed hard and said, 'It's Ms Redstone to you. I'll consider hyphenating if we ever have kids.'

'It's a deal.' Grayson picked her up and swung her into his arms. He kissed her warm mouth until she made a needy sound deep in her throat. 'Now let's go and shake on it.'